RECKONING

RECKONING

Sara Jo Cluff

Paperback ISBN 9781686182228
Hardcover ISBN 978-1-7321832-5-4

Printed in the United States of America
First Printing, August 2019

Awkward Pepper, LLC
awkwardpepperllc@gmail.com

Cover images from pixabay.com
Cover design by Sara Jo Cluff

For Mom
My biggest fan

CHAPTER 1
Maya

When I opened my eyes, scarlet blanketed the snow in front of me. My vision went blurry for a second and an internal force weighed down my head. As I turned my body onto my side, pain shot through my leg reminding me of the slashing it took. My pulse beat at the wound, the sting almost too much to bear.

"Maya," a voice whispered nearby.

I turned my head slowly to the other side, sucking in a sharp breath from the pain. It took my eyes a few seconds to adjust, but then I saw her lying there, helpless. From her wounds, she didn't have much longer to live.

"Maya," my mom said softly. She clenched her teeth and closed her eyes, holding back the screams from her pain. A long gash trailed her leg, another slicing the back of her head. She pressed her left hand down on her stomach, but it didn't stop the blood flow.

Suddenly the vision of a sword going through her entered

my mind. It had happened before I passed out.

"Mom." I wanted to tell her it would be okay, but I knew in my heart it wouldn't.

Mom reached out her hand, placing it gently on my arm. "Sweetie, you need to get out of here."

"I can't leave you," I said.

For the first time since I came to, the sounds around me came into focus. Yelling, screaming, and the clashing of swords vibrated the air, making me shiver.

"We both know I don't have much time," Mom said, her voice weak. "You need to take your brother and leave."

Tears filled my eyes as I stared at Mom. Her short black hair framed her round face well. Even lying there in the condition she was in, she looked beautiful. Her brown eyes stared into mine, all the love she had for me pouring out.

I forced myself to sit up and focused my eyes on the war before me. The cold air stung my face, the fierce wind trying to push me back down.

My fourteen-year-old brother and my dad stood not too far in front of me, wielding their swords against the enemy.

Enemy. The word made me shudder. Not too long ago, we were all on the same side. We were friends, companions, and fellow citizens.

But it had all changed.

"Sweetie, stand up," Mom said. "It's time to go."

I turned to look at her, and the pain in her eyes begged me to leave. My hand brushed my side, wanting the sword where it usually sat in my sheath, fastened to my belt. It wasn't there, causing panic to rise.

I couldn't leave without a weapon. I'd never get out.

My heart pounded through my chest as I looked around for my sword. A few feet behind me, it stuck out of a man's abdomen. He was the one who had slashed me, but I had struck him before he could get me again.

I slowly stood, ignoring the cries of refusal from my body. With every ounce of strength I had left in me, I staggered toward my sword. I pulled it from the man's body—the charms on my bracelets clinking together at the movement—not daring to look into his lifeless eyes.

I hobbled to my brother, who fought with a soldier. He must have heard me coming because he dodged a thrust from the man and drove his sword through his stomach, yelling out a mighty roar that didn't fit his small frame. He immediately turned to me and saw my injury.

He was at my side in no time. "Maya, we need to find a place for you to hide. Once we get you safely hidden, I'll go find someone to treat your wound."

"No," I said. "Bruce, we need to leave."

Bruce shook his head. "The battle's still underway. We can't abandon everyone."

"There's hardly anyone left on our side. If we stay, we'll be dead." I closed my eyes, not wanting to see the look on my little brother's face when I told him. "Mom's dying."

All I heard was silence, so I opened my eyes. Panic filled Bruce's eyes as he looked behind me at Mom. He pulled me along until we were at our mother's side.

"Mom," Bruce whispered, putting his hand on her head. He brushed back her hair.

Mom smiled and brought her hand up to Bruce's cheek. "My baby. My Bruce." She coughed, spitting up blood. Bruce went to wipe the blood away, but Mom grabbed his wrist, sliding her hand down to his. "Honey, you need to leave. Go with your sister. Protect her. You're the leader of this family now."

Even in the final moments of her life, she was still a mom. Trying to make Bruce feel important, even though both mom and I knew that he wasn't mature enough.

Bruce held back his tears. "Dad's still here. We can still fight. I have no injuries."

"Your dad won't last much longer," Mom said. "The moment he's dead, they'll come for both of you. You need to escape. Bruce, do you still have that map I gave you?"

Bruce touched the armor over his heart. "I keep it close."

"Good," Mom said. Her voice grew weaker, her words spaced out. "Follow the map; it will lead you to your destination. It's too late to meet up with Scorpion City, so you'll have to make the entire journey by yourselves."

As the tears flowed, I bent down and rested my forehead on Mom's head. "I love you."

"I love you, too, Maya, and my Bruce." Mom coughed. "Now go. Head straight down the mountain as fast as you can. If you don't get there before they do…"

I nodded slowly. "I know." I kissed her forehead and got up, turning to look at Dad. He was still fighting, holding back soldiers from getting to us. His movements slowed, and I knew Mom was right—he wouldn't last much longer. Taking hold of Bruce's arm, I started pulling him away. "Let's go."

Bruce tried to shake me off. "But Dad and Mom." His voice trembled.

"I'm injured, Bruce, so I'll be slow. We need to get going and get as far ahead as we can." I pulled him again and that time he didn't resist.

"Maya, how can we survive?" Bruce asked as we worked our way down the mountain. "You're too injured. You can barely walk."

I'd never been so thankful for the snow. It helped me slide down, so I didn't have to walk as much. "We have to do everything we can. We're the only hope for Juniper right now. We need to join the other revolutionaries. We need to warn them."

A few minutes later, Bruce stopped me. He put his finger up to his lips, motioning for me to be silent. I looked around, trying to find the source of Bruce's worry.

The next thing I knew, Bruce pushed me to the ground and jumped over me. Swords clashed against one another and I looked up to see Bruce fighting with a soldier. The soldier was a lot bigger than Bruce, towering over him. Bruce slowed. I tried to stand, but I fell back down, my body sinking into the fresh snow. Instead, I crawled toward them, unsheathing my sword as I did.

The soldier didn't see me coming. I got close enough that I could slash his leg, distracting him more than causing any real damage. Bruce took the opportunity to drive his sword through the soldier's abdomen. The soldier stumbled back but started forward again. Bruce pulled his sword free of the soldier and drove it through his chest. Blood poured out of the soldier's mouth as he slowly fell to the ground, saturating the snow in red.

Bruce helped me up and dragged me down the mountain, not stopping at any of my cries. When we got to the bottom, he finally came to a stop, but still held me up. My head spun from the loss of blood.

"Sorry," Bruce said to me. "But we had to get out of there."

I winced. "I understand." My injury finally got the best of me and I slipped through Bruce's arms and onto the ground. My strength had completely gone.

I fingered one of the charms on a bracelet—the violin by the feel of it—letting the motion calm me.

Lying there, I looked up at the mountain above me, taking in the view. Flames burned the wood cabins and apartment buildings of the traitors, as they called us. The smoke rose high into what was otherwise a crystal blue sky, all signs of the snowstorm gone. From down here, you could see how big our city was. It covered the mountainside for miles and miles.

I always knew that our homes and buildings were close together, the dirt paths between narrow and winding. But from here, they looked squished. From the sharp angle of the mountain, the cabins looked piled on top of each other.

Laughter escaped my mouth when I looked at the Capitol. It sat clearly in the middle of the city, untouched and unharmed. The buildings and homes were nicer, more spread out.

Even though I had lived in the Capitol, I loved to be in the other parts of the city. I would sneak out at night and walk the dirt paths, taking in the smell of wood and sap. I found out not too long ago that Bruce would sometimes follow me. He loved it out there, too, but thought I'd tell him he couldn't come with me. I smiled. It was true. I wouldn't have let him come.

Bruce sighed and squatted down next to me. "This is going to be impossible."

"Not completely." The voice came from the left of me.

Bruce instinctively stood, his sword unsheathed, ready for battle. I turned to look at the source, the voice familiar to me. I was surprised to see ten people standing there, tired, dirty, but alive. Bruce lowered his sword. They were part of the revolution. We weren't alone in this.

CHAPTER 2
Emmie

As I sat next to her holding her hand, I brushed back her brown curls and stroked her cheek. Her skin burned, her fever still high. I thought of all the good times we had growing up. We had so many fun memories, ones I would never forget. I leaned down and kissed her on the forehead, my lips startled by the heat.

It had been three months since we arrived in New Haven. Three long, torturous months. It had been a bad winter, the snow thick and heavy.

Building our city had been almost impossible. All of it we were learning how to do as we went along. A few of the previous Kingsland citizens had some wood skills, which helped in the building of homes and buildings. But they were small, and the foundation wasn't firm. I'd always worried they would collapse at any moment.

In the beginning, we slept in the headquarters we had found. Some slept out in the cave. But Eric, Mack, Terrance,

Dante, and President Brown had made two trips to Kingsland and one to River Springs, bringing back more people. We were growing. With that many people, you needed your own space.

So, we started with some small log homes. I wanted to build some for the others, but almost all insisted on one for me, my dad, and my brother Derek first.

Vivica had put up a little fight, wanting one for her family. I didn't know why she huffed and puffed so badly. Her dad was the president and her brother Dante, my fellow revolutionary, which was what our residents had started calling us, so they were next on the list.

Sometimes I think she got jealous. I wasn't sure if it stemmed from her brother, from me, or just the fact that she wasn't getting all the attention.

All the trips that were made went well. No injuries, no captures, and no problems. We were able to secure a few buses from both cities and were also able to get our hands on some off-road vehicles, which came in handy for hunting.

People were hearing about our revolution and wanted to join. We'd set up communication with a member of Kingsland and a member of River Springs—Vice President Oliver's son, Austin.

The thought of Vice President Oliver made my heart sink. We had lost him right before we escaped River Springs. He died at the hands of the President, Whit Randall. VP Oliver was truly missed.

With each trip, they were also bringing back more materials, weapons, supplies, and knowledge. The situation in River Springs was getting worse. Whit had shortened his leash around his citizens. Things were getting stricter and the rules were growing.

I had a feeling our trips wouldn't be easy for much longer. Something bad was coming. I could feel it in my bones. It made me nervous that neither of the other two cities who were to join our revolution had shown up yet. President Brown hadn't been able to contact them, either.

"What are you thinking about?" Her voice took me from my thoughts.

I looked at her lying on the infirmary bed. She'd lost weight, which was noticeable because she was already so tiny to begin with. She lost some color in her skin and dark circles sat under her eyes. She'd had a hard time sleeping.

I smiled. "Remember when we were around seven and we went on that field trip?"

"To the river?" she asked, adjusting her light-blue infirmary gown.

"Yes, to the river," I said, taking hold of her hand.

A smile formed on her lips, reaching her eyes. "You caught that butterfly in your hands. I wanted you to keep it, but you wouldn't. You said you wanted it to fly."

I stroked her hand. "Nothing should be held back from its calling in life. Butterflies were made to fly, not be captured."

"You said that would be us one day; free to fly around without the reins of the world." She stroked my hand back.

"You know I love you, right?"

"Almost as much as I love you."

A month after we got to New Haven, my best friend, Dee, became sick. I knew it was bad by the look on Eric and Dante's face. They'd seen it before. Eric with his mom and Dante with his girlfriend, Whitney.

Marie, our resident nurse, had been running tests and doing everything she could to figure out the disease, but so far, she had no luck. We weren't sure how much time Dee had left, but it wasn't much. I tried to stay positive, though my heart ached.

Dee yawned, her eyes fluttering on the verge of sleep.

I kissed her forehead. "Sleep well, Dee."

As she drifted off, I slowly pulled myself away, releasing my hand from her grasp.

When I got to the door, Eric stood there, leaning on the door frame, his blond hair brushed to the side. He wore his white military uniform, identical to what I was wearing.

Some of the River Springs residents had taken to wearing jeans and tees, typical wear for those from Kingsland. A few, though, still wore their fifties-style wardrobes, consisting of dresses, dress shirts, and ties, which was odd to see in our little wooded town.

Eric smiled at me—showing off his perfect set of teeth—and pulled me into a hug.

"She looks worse today," I said.

"Marie said she may be onto something," Eric said. When I pulled back and he saw the hope in my eyes, he quickly went on. "Nothing to cure Dee now, Emmie. I think she's just starting to figure out the disease. What it does to the body and the path it takes. It all stems from the brain, which they never knew before."

"How did they not know that?" For some reason that

seemed like something simple to figure out.

Eric sighed, his blue eyes exasperated. "President Randall never allowed autopsies. They could only see on the outside what it does to the body. But since Dee allowed Marie to do some biopsies on her, Marie was able to run the appropriate tests. She's also been able to check her blood."

I pulled away from Eric's embrace and walked down the hall, away from Dee's door.

He came up next to me, taking my hand. "I know this isn't easy, Emmie. But what Dee's allowing Marie to do is going to be the start of a change. The start of a cure. She's going to save lots of lives."

"Just not her own," I said as tears came to my eyes.

Eric wiped the tears from my cheeks, his hands warm. "I believe everyone has a destiny here on this earth. A place and calling. Some are going to be shorter than others, but they're all worth it." He smiled. "And who better to help people than Dee?"

I offered a small smile in return. "She has the biggest heart of anyone I know."

"She's also a fighter. Who knows, maybe Marie will figure it out quicker than we think? There still may be a chance to save her. She's not dead yet."

"I know, it's just hard."

His eyes lowered. "I know."

I wish I could've met his mother. The stories that I heard from him and his dad, Alexander, let me know what an amazing woman she was. Eric had always said that Dee reminded him of his mom. A sweet spirit and a big heart.

Eric leaned in and kissed me on the lips. When he pulled back, he looked me in my eyes. "I love you."

I smiled as I put my hand on his cheek. "I love you."

A month ago, Eric had told me he loved me for the first time. We were out under the stars one night. A storm was on its way, so the air had warmed. We climbed up to an alcove in the mountain and sat down on a rock. He put his arm around me and held me close as we stared at the clear sky. The stars were endless, covering the sky with their light.

I could tell he was nervous, but I wasn't sure why. He was so fidgety, it drove me nuts. I turned to him and ran my fingers through his thick hair.

"I have something for you," Eric said, reaching into his pocket. He pulled out a small package and handed it to me. When I just held it in my hands, he laughed. "You have to open it."

"I know," I whispered.

We never received presents back in River Springs. Birthdays weren't celebrated, just acknowledged.

I ripped open the brown wrapping to reveal a necklace made of dark twine. Attached to it was a small wood carving.

I held it in my hand, brushing it with my thumb. "It's a butterfly."

"I hope you like it. Dee told me you like butterflies. Archie showed me how to carve things with wood and a knife." Eric laughed. "You don't even know how many tries it took for me to get it right."

"It's perfect. I can't believe you did this for me."

Eric stroked my cheek with his hand. "I'd do anything for

you, Emmie." He took the necklace from my hand and tied it around my neck.

"How does it look?" I asked, looking down at it lying against my chest.

"Beautiful, just like you. I wanted you to have something that symbolized my love for you."

I looked up at him, startled.

"I love you, Emmie." Eric's bright blue eyes stared into mine as he tucked my hair behind my ear.

My heart raced as I leaned my forehead against his. "I love you, Eric."

He'd pulled me close and kissed me under the stars.

CHAPTER 3

Only a couple of days after we first arrived in New Haven, Dante and I sat down to talk. I had met him and the other Kingsland members after some of my friends, family, and I escaped River Springs. We both had dreams about New Haven before we even arrived. Our dreams were very similar, with only a few differences.

"When I was standing on the alcove, Eric and Vice President Oliver were at my sides," I said to Dante. "Mack, Dee, Tina, and my dad were behind me. The first time I had the dream there were two other faces, but they were blurry. When I had the dream again, the faces came into view revealing Eric's dad Alexander, and my brother Derek." I paused. "And when the vice president blew the blue flower into the wind, he disappeared."

Dante furrowed his black eyebrows, noticing the pain in my eyes. "So, Marie and Steven weren't there?"

Relief washed over me when he didn't bring up the vice president.

"No," I said, shaking my head. "But there's the possibility they weren't there because I'd never considered them to be a part of this."

I leaned back against the wall. We were sitting in one of the conference rooms in Headquarters. Well, our version of Headquarters at least. We still had a lot to do in the building and a lot of equipment and furniture to add. We were both sitting on the floor in the empty room.

Dante sat forward. "Eric told me that Steven has betrayed you before, though."

"Yes, but his family was threatened. I probably would've done the same for my dad."

Whit had forced my Recruitment leader, Steven, to spy on me and my friends. Steven did as he was told, but in the end, it didn't matter. Whit killed his family anyway.

Dante scratched at his smooth chin. "But not your brother or mom?"

I sighed. "My relationship with both of them is complicated." I didn't want to continue, so I changed the subject. "What about you? Who was with you on the alcove?"

"My dad, Vivica, Terrance, Archie, Naomi, James, and Lou."

"Not Charles or Denise?" I hadn't known them long, but they both seemed nice and dedicated to the cause.

Dante shook his head. "No, but like you, I never considered them joining before. They always seemed so prim and proper. They were the perfect citizens."

I smiled, thinking of Dee. "Just because you're a perfect member of your city doesn't mean that deep down inside you long for something else."

"True, but we should still keep a close eye on all of them just in case. We have a lot at risk here."

I nodded in agreement.

On the trip back to River Springs, they brought back the guy Marie had been dating. They had only been on a few dates, but Gideon was smitten with her. When he found out she had left, he wanted to come. I was worried at first, thinking he'd only come because of Marie and that I couldn't trust him completely, but the man was passionate about everything. Marie, life, and anything that came in front of him made him happy.

A couple meetings with President Brown, Dante, and me, and Gideon was willing to do anything for us. He was excited and immediately went to training with Mack and Terrance.

We had appointed both Mack and Terrance as our military leaders since they had the skills and knowledge of combat. I had met Mack back in Recruitment during an underwater challenge. He saved my life, which I would forever be grateful for.

Mack and Terrance went to work right when we arrived, training us all in fighting and how to use weapons. Gideon picked up on everything instantly. He was a tall man, with a strong build and great coordination. He turned out to be a great addition to our city.

I was happy with how everything had come together, but something still nagged at me.

I left the infirmary to find Dante. Eric came with me,

holding my hand as we walked. We knew the trips to the cities were important, but it was still hard to be apart from each other for weeks at a time. They were usually only back a few days before they'd leave on another trip and those days, we spent training and building up our city. We cherished every moment we had together.

The bitter cold stung my cheeks the moment we stepped outside.

"Driver!" I yelled as I ran toward a jeep. I hopped in before Eric could claim the seat.

Chuckling, he climbed into the passenger seat, holding on to the roof of the jeep.

Ever since I'd learned how, I loved to drive. Especially in our off-road jeeps, going over the rocky terrain on the outskirts of town. Adding in the crunch of the hardened snow made it more fun.

We found Dante outside with Mack, Terrance, and Gideon. They all wore our standard issued military pants we created. They had a ton of pockets so we could carry equipment on us, including a small set of binoculars, a knife, a compass, and a flashlight. We had four different colors: green, black, white, and brown.

We were all wearing the white that day, mostly because of the snow. Mack and Terrance were always trying to teach us about blending in with our surroundings.

We also had the same colors of button-down, collared shirts, in short sleeve and long. My favorite, though, were our new jackets. Dee and Denise were our seamstresses and came up with the pattern for them. They were nice and thick with a hood we could pull over our heads in the bitter cold, and plenty of pockets on the inside and out. They were also lined with fur thanks to the animal hunting skills the Kingsland members had brought to our new city. I'd never felt something so soft in my life.

The guys were practicing with their bow and arrows. Targets were spread out in a section of the city we had set up for training. I asked Dante once why Kingsland only had bows and arrows. He said they lived in an area highly populated with trees. They were easy and cheap to make but were still lethal.

Mack smiled when he saw us pull up and hop out of the jeep. His red hair was still cropped close, but his few days growth that he usually kept on his chin and turned into a full-on beard. The guys had a bet going to see how long he could get it before he got sick of it and shaved it all off.

Dante had an arrow drawn and was about to release it. Mack waited until the second before Dante released his arrow to address us. "Emmie, Eric! Good to see you."

Dante didn't even flinch, his arrow hitting his mark dead center. "Nice try, Mack, but you'll never break my concentration."

I laughed. Mack and Gideon had been trying for weeks to startle Dante, trying to get him to miss for once. Terrance had warned them it would never work, but they were determined. Dante had the highest level of concentration of anyone I'd ever met.

Dante turned to me and Eric. He had been growing out his black curly hair to get in on the bet with Mack. A small fro had formed. "So, what brings the two love birds out here?"

"I can't stop thinking about the other cities," I said to Dante. "It's been three months and we've had no news."

"Sometimes no news is good news," Gideon said from behind Dante. I raised my eyebrows at him, and Gideon shrugged. "It was something my mom used to say to me."

Looking at him, I could tell why Marie was so attracted to him. His brown eyes always held a laugh and the dimples on his cheeks showed when he smiled. And Gideon always smiled when he was with Marie.

Dante rested his bow on the ground in front of him, setting his hands on the top. "It worries me, too, but what can we do about it? We can't contact them."

"Does your dad know where they're located?" Eric asked. He stood close by me still holding my hand, stroking it with his thumb.

"He has a vague idea," Dante said. "They never gave exact locations in case they were ever caught. When the cities first separated, all of the presidents thought it was best that they all went their separate ways without letting each other know where they were going."

"Just get a fresh start and leave everything else behind," I said, mostly to myself than anyone else. It was what we'd all done to come to New Haven.

"What if we sent some of us out there?" Eric asked. "Go toward the area where your dad thinks they are and see what we can find."

Mack shook his head. "We've never been on the other side of the mountain. We have no idea what's out there or what we'll come across."

"Could it really be that different than where we lived?" Gideon asked.

I looked at Dante and Terrance. "Our two cities seem pretty similar from what we've talked about."

"It's still a risk," Terrance said. He was just as big and strong as Mack.

It was easy to get the women in the city to train with the two of them leading. I always overheard ladies talking about how dreamy they were, but neither of the guys seemed to notice. Terrance stood tall with his bow strapped to his back like it was a part of his body.

"Maybe we should talk to my dad about it," Dante said. "He should be in Headquarters with Naomi and Derek."

I didn't like the thought of being around my brother and Naomi. He had the biggest crush on her, and it was painfully obvious.

Naomi was the type who kept to herself and barely let anyone in. She was a closed book. We could all tell she wasn't interested in him, but Derek didn't care. So many awkward situations came from it that I couldn't help but cringe when I entered a room where they were together. But they were our two technical junkies, so they worked side by side all the time.

"It looks like we have movement in sector seven," Derek said, reaching over Naomi who was sitting next to her. He pointed to the screen to the right of her and leaned in close, just inches from her face.

Naomi rolled her eyes. "Derek, there's no sector seven and that was a bird that flew in front of a camera outside. Now back away."

"Your soft, caramel eyes are so beautiful," Derek whispered.

"I'm about two seconds away from slapping you," Naomi said, her voice tight. She had her black hair pulled back in a french braid.

"I think we're all two seconds away from slapping him," I said.

Derek whipped around, the back of his chair banging into the desk. He was wearing one of his homemade shirts—a resident of Kingsland had shown him how to heat transfer images to his tees and he'd had way too much fun with it. His current shirt had a computer screen with cat ears, its tail a computer mouse.

Derek's eyes widened at the sight of all of us watching him. "How long have you been standing there?"

Dante smirked. "Long enough to see you make a fool out of yourself."

"Mr. Woodard, do I have to remind you of proper conduct in the workplace?" President Brown asked, his deep voice rumbling across the room. He had stepped in moments after we did, so he witnessed just as much. He wore a green polo shirt and black slacks, Kingsland's version of dressing up.

Derek's face turned red. "No, sir." His voice cracked when he spoke.

I could only see the side of Naomi's face, but I swear I saw a tiny smile.

I turned to President Brown. "We were actually coming here to talk to you."

"Let's take this into the main conference room," President Brown said, eyeing Derek who was still sitting close to Naomi.

Derek scooted his chair a couple of inches away from her. When President Brown raised his eyebrows at him, Derek picked up his chair and moved a couple of feet away, looking at President Brown for approval. President Brown nodded at him and Derek let out a breath that he'd apparently been holding.

"Your brother has some serious issues," Dante said to me as we were walking to the conference room.

"Half-brother," I said.

Ever since I found out that the president of River Springs and Infinity Corp was my father, I tried everything I could to not think about it since he was the vilest man I'd ever met. But it also meant that Derek was only my half-brother, which I took every opportunity to expose seeing as he was so disturbing at times.

When we got into the conference room, we all took a seat around the table. Archie, our resident craftsman and a previous Kingsland member, had made the table and chairs out of wood. They were absolutely stunning. I instinctively fingered my butterfly necklace.

"So, what's on your mind?" President Brown asked. He always carried himself with dignity. He was a naturally tall and strong man. Dante desperately wanted to be as big as his father. He had grown a little since we got to New Haven and had bulked up, but he still had some work to do.

"Dante said you had a vague idea of where the other cities are located," I said.

President Brown nodded. "I do. Why?"

Dante, Eric, Mack, Terrance, and Gideon all eyed me. I guess they didn't want to claim any part of the idea, which I still didn't think was that bad.

I sighed and looked at President Brown. "I thought we could send some of us out there and see if we can find anything. It's been three months and none of them have shown up. What if something happened?"

"There's a high chance something did happen," President Brown said. "But I'm not sending any of us out there. We don't know the area."

"So? Wouldn't you want someone to come for us if we'd been harmed or stranded?"

"We agreed that each city was on its own until we reunited." President Brown stood and walked in circles around the table. He usually did that when his mind was set and didn't want to continue the subject.

But that never stopped me. "We're all coming here for the same purpose. These are members of our new city. We need to look after each other."

"Emmie, I appreciate where you're coming from," President Brown said, "but I'm not risking anyone. We have a small city and are dangerously outnumbered from any enemy. For all we know, they haven't arrived because they've been captured. We could walk into an ambush."

I folded my arms in frustration. I understood what President Brown was trying to say, but I hated not knowing what was going on. Patience was not a strong virtue of mine.

"While we're all here," President Brown said, keeping his

eyes on me, "we should talk about the next trip to River Springs. It's about time we leave. Austin Oliver's ready for us to come. He has a lot more people for us, including his mom and his sister and her family."

Hearing the Oliver name took me away from my frustration. There wasn't a day that went by that I didn't think about Vice President Oliver and the sacrifice he made for all of us to be here. Eric must have noticed my reaction because he reached over and took my hand. I gave him a small smile, but it didn't stop the hurt.

"Who are we sending?" Dante asked. He looked over at me and smiled. He and Eric understood me. They'd both lost someone they loved.

"I was thinking Mack, Gideon, Dante, Eric, and Emmie," President Brown said. I could feel him looking at me, waiting for a reaction.

I hadn't been on any trip to the cities. The first one they wanted me to stay behind in case something happened to them so we would still have one of the key players in New Haven. But then Dee became sick and I didn't want to leave her. I still didn't.

"No," I said.

Eric leaned in close to me. "Emmie, you have to go at some point. Staying here isn't going to change anything."

I shook my head. "I don't care. She's getting worse. If I left and came back and she was ..." I couldn't finish. The thought of losing Dee wasn't something I could deal with. I took a deep breath, holding back a sob. Eric let go of my hand and put his arm around me.

"Should Emmie and I be going on trips together?" Dante asked.

A prophecy revealed that a member from each of the four cities would lead a revolution. Dante and I were the chosen ones from our cities. Some days I wondered if Whit, aka President Randall, got it right. A piece of me thought that Austin Oliver was the true revolutionary from our city.

"Dante brings up a good point," Terrance said. "We agreed to keep them on separate trips. We should have Dante stay back here with me so we can watch over the city."

"Alright," President Brown said. "We'll send Tina in your stead, Dante."

Everyone nodded in agreement. Tina had been my Recruitment partner back in River Springs. She was a strong fighter. She picked up on the weapons training like she was born to do it, not to mention she was a quick thinker. If it wasn't for her, we'd both be dead at the bottom of the lake back in River Springs.

President Brown stood at the head of the table. "You'll leave tomorrow morning at first light."

I didn't wait to be dismissed. I stood and left, not wanting to talk about the trip any further. I couldn't leave Dee.

On the way out, I passed the security room where Derek and Naomi were working. I thought I heard Derek say something about his huge biceps. If I'd been in a better mood, I would've gone in there and pointed out that he didn't have any biceps, but luck was on his side today.

CHAPTER 4

"Back so soon?" Dee asked from her bed. She had a little bit of color back in her cheeks.

I sat down next to her, taking her hand. "I just can't stay away from you. You're contagious." I regretted the words as soon as they left my mouth.

Dee smiled, squeezing my hand. "Not according to Marie." I could tell by her tone that she was being sarcastic, but it still didn't make me feel any better.

I frowned. "I'm sorry, Dee. I was talking about your smile and personality, not your condition."

"I know," Dee said. "My disease isn't contagious, so you could've only meant my sparkling personality."

"It is sparkling, you know."

Dee tapped her finger on my forehead. "What's going on in that head of yours?" She seriously was a mind reader.

I put my head down on our clasped hands. "They want me to go on the next trip to River Springs."

"Good. You need to get out of here. I didn't want to say

anything, but you're starting to smother me."

"That won't work."

"I'm being serious. It's claustrophobic. I mean, I know I'm great and all, but enough already. Geez, give a woman some space."

I looked up at her. "How can you joke about this? I want to be here, by your side."

Dee looked me straight in the eye. "Emmie, I love you, tons and tons, but you're going on this trip."

"But ..."

"This is not open for debate. You're going, you'll have fun, you'll kick some butt, you'll save some River Springs citizens, and you'll report back to me with every juicy detail. Understood?"

"Dee," I said, starting to give in.

"This conversation is closed. Besides, I need some cute guys back here to swoon over me and you know my type."

"Want me to see if Tim is available?"

We had grown up with Tim and he had the hugest crush on Dee, but she didn't return the feelings. She liked him as a person, just not in a romantic way.

Dee rolled her eyes. "I need someone to light my fire and rock my world."

"Oh please," I said, laughing.

"Someone to tickle my fancy."

I held up my hand. "Please stop."

Smiling, she reached out and touched my necklace. "Someone who gives me butterflies."

"Well, if butterflies are what you want, then it will be my

personal mission to find them for you."

"Wonderful." Dee sat up a little more in her bed. "So, when do you leave to find my true love?"

"Tomorrow morning."

It was too soon in my opinion. But I guess the sooner I left, the sooner I got back.

She stretched out her body. "So, a couple of weeks of freedom for me."

"You'll miss me."

"I'll definitely miss this face." She took her hand out of mine and squeezed my cheeks together with her fingers.

I laughed. "Now you're just getting ridiculous. What's Marie giving you?"

"I don't know, but it's some good stuff," Dee said with a wink.

A noise came from my communicator I kept in my pocket. I pulled it out and lifted it to my mouth. "What?"

"There's movement out here." It was Tina. She was on guard duty on the east part of the mountains, which was the side the other cities would come from.

"What kind of movement?" I asked, standing.

"There's been a lot of rustling of trees and I think I may have seen someone," Tina said.

"On my way," I said at the same time as Eric, Dante, Mack, and Terrance. We always kept a communicator on us open to the same channel.

"Come back and let me know if any of them are cute," Dee said as I headed for the door.

I turned to her. "What if it's the enemy trying to attack?"

"I'm open," Dee said with a shrug.

I smiled at her. "I love you."

"Love you, too."

Eric was waiting outside Dee's door.

"Have you been here the whole time?" I asked.

Eric laced his fingers through mine as we walked. "Yes, but don't worry, I wasn't listening to your girl talk."

"How do you know it was girl talk?" I asked him, my eyebrows raised.

He shrugged. "You're both girls and you were talking. Hence, girl talk."

"Sure," I said, bumping his arm.

When we walked out of the infirmary, which was connected to headquarters, we went through the weapons area, each grabbing a gun.

Eric always preferred a rifle, and I took one too, but my weapon of choice was the handgun I always had on me. It wasn't good for long ranges, but I had great accuracy with a handgun, better than anyone else in New Haven. I had a connection to it I couldn't explain.

We ran toward the jeep parked outside Headquarters, the old snow crunching under our feet. Dante, Mack, and Terrance were already waiting for us. Eric and I hopped in the back with Dante. Dark clouds loomed overhead, casting a dreary feeling over the city.

Tina was waiting for us at the foot of her stand post. We'd constructed towers at each entrance to our city so we could keep watch on anything coming in.

"There's something about one hundred yards out on the

south end of the canyon," Tina said to all of us. "Whatever's there hasn't moved from that spot in a few minutes. I'm thinking that maybe they spotted me."

"We should split up," Dante said. "Half of us go on the north side and the other half on the south."

Mack ran his hand over his beard. "We'll have to go quietly and stay as covered as we can."

"What if we're outnumbered?" I buttoned up my coat to protect my body from the wind. The canyon made the wind fiercer.

"Won't make a difference in the end," Terrance said. "We either fight them now or wait until they come to us and fight at that time."

I nodded. "I guess that's true. Eric, Terrance, and I can go to the south. Mack, Tina. and Dante can go to the north."

"Sounds good," Tina said. Her long red hair looked vibrant against her white coat. Pulling the hood up, she tucked her hair inside to conceal it. "We'll try to get farther ahead so we can warn you of what's on your side."

"Let's head out," Dante said, motioning for us to go.

He and Terrance both had their bows in hand and their arrows in a quiver on their backs. Mack had a rifle and Tina had a shotgun, which was her favorite to use. I think she just liked the sound of it when she racked the slide.

Eric, Terrance, and I stayed close to the south end of the canyon, next to the mountain. Terrance led the way, with me and then Eric behind. I had my rifle on a sling around my shoulder and my hands wrapped around the grip of my handgun. I held it to my side, aimed at the snowy ground, my pointer finger extended along the barrel waiting to slide onto the trigger at any moment.

We walked as quickly as we could without making much sound. The canyon wasn't too wide, maybe fifty yards, so we could see Tina, Mack, and Dante walking on the north end, up a little way.

Mack held up a fist, motioning for us to stop, so we all took cover behind a tree, waiting for his next signal. I still couldn't see anything up ahead. The area on the south side was densely thicketed with pine trees, making it easy to conceal yourself, which was nice for us, but meant whoever was out there could conceal themselves just as well.

Mack signaled for us to slowly move forward. As we got closer to where he was looking, he pointed at a tall pine tree, its branches lined with snow.

Terrance motioned for Eric to approach from the left, me from the right, and he would go straight on. When he nodded, we separated, creeping toward the tree, weapons ready. We were only a few feet away from the tree when Terrance motioned for us to stop. He had his arrow drawn as Eric and I held up our guns, all pointed at the tree.

I nodded at Eric and we both went around the tree to see what waited for us.

A guy was leaning up against the tree, his dark brown hair hanging past his ears and covering part of his eyes. He looked about my age, tall and strong, and his skin was light brown. By the widening of his eyes when he saw us, he didn't know we were that close. He looked back and forth between me and Eric, not knowing what to do. He held a shotgun, but he had it pointed down.

"Don't move," Eric said quietly.

The guy's eyes stopped on mine, his expression unreadable.

"Slowly put your gun down," I said, stepping in closer, my gun pointed at his head.

Not moving his eyes from mine, he smirked before slowly lowering his gun to the ground and then raising his hands above his head.

Shotguns racking their slides as one echoed down the canyon, chilling me to the bone.

We were outnumbered.

CHAPTER 5

The guy lowered his hands, his eyes still locked with mine. "I think it's your turn to put the guns down." He finally pried his eyes away so he could look me up and down, raising his eyebrows in the process. A playful smile landed on his lips.

I ignored him, keeping my gun pointed at his face. "Who are you?"

The guy took a step closer to me. "Who are you?"

"I asked you first."

He took another step closer to me, leaning his forehead against the barrel of my gun. "Are you going to shoot me?"

It took me a second to process what he had said. His eyes were a beautiful light green, the glint in them making me lose my train of thought. I cleared my throat.

"If you just tell me who you are, we can end this." I kept my eyes focused on his, willing myself not to pull away.

"Santiago!" Someone to the right of us had yelled out.

"Just a second," Santiago said to the person, still looking me in the eyes. He gave me a wink and lowered his voice.

"How about we put the guns away so you and I can go somewhere more private?"

"I don't think so," Eric said from behind Santiago, pointing his gun at the back of his head. Apparently, Santiago hadn't been quiet enough.

Everyone with Santiago didn't like Eric's movement, all of them yelling at us to lower our guns. I looked behind Santiago and saw Mack, Tina, and Dante standing a few yards out, trying to stay hidden from the intruders, but keeping a close eye on us. It wasn't much if an attack started, but it would at least catch them off guard.

Santiago gave me a pout, ignoring everyone else. "Brother or boyfriend?"

"Boyfriend," Eric and I said at the same time.

Santiago tsked. "That's too bad."

"Santiago, stop playing around!" It was the same man from before that called out.

"Alright, alright, don't get your panties in a bunch, Javier," Santiago said, pulling away from my gun. The next thing I knew, he leaned in close to my ear, his movement so fast I couldn't react. "If it doesn't work out, let me know."

I gaped at him but didn't say anything.

"Maybe we should all lower our weapons and have a chat," Terrance said, stepping around the tree, his bow lowered.

"Hey, what's that?" Santiago asked, looking at Terrance's bow. He walked up close and slid his hand along it.

"It's a bow," Terrance said, each word spaced apart as he eyed Santiago.

His candor caught all of us off guard. If he was another revolutionary, we were in trouble. He was worse than Dante.

"What do you do with it?" Santiago asked.

"You shoot arrows with it," Terrance said.

"Can you show me?" Santiago's eyes lit up with curiosity. He rubbed his hands together as if Terrance would show him how to use it right then and there.

"This isn't the time, Santiago," Javier said. He stepped up next to me, his shotgun slung across his back. He stuck out his hand. "I'm Javier."

After placing my gun back in its holster, I reached out and shook his hand. "Emmie."

Javier was just a couple inches taller than me, but I could tell by the thickness of his neck that he was probably strong. He had on a bulky coat, so I couldn't tell for sure. His hair was cut close to his head and his eyes were a dark brown. He turned his head so he could gesture to everyone behind him. There was a small marking behind his ear, but I couldn't tell what it was.

"This is everyone from Scorpion City that we could round up," Javier said. People moved toward us, coming out from behind the trees. There had to be at least a hundred of them, which surprised me. "It's not much, but we'll get more. There should be another group of about fifty already on their way."

I let out a laugh. "We showed up with ten, so this is amazing to me."

"Only ten?" Santiago asked, stepping to the side of me. I noticed he had the same marking behind his ear, so I leaned in a little closer. It was a cross. Santiago saw me looking at it.

"Most of us who joined the revolution have the sign of the cross behind our ear. It's a reminder of our bond and that with the Lord on our side, we can do anything."

The reference to the Lord caught me by surprise. Religion was not something that was talked about in River Springs. Whit didn't like the idea of residents worshipping anyone but him.

"Neat." It was all I could think of to say.

Santiago laughed. "Yes, neat. So, are you going to keep us out here all day, or can we head in?" He patted his stomach and winked. "I'm starving."

Eric came up right next to me, taking my hand and holding it tight. I looked at him as he glared at Santiago. I'd never seen him like that before. I gave him a small smile and squeezed his hand.

Mack, Tina, and Dante all stepped forward, startling some of our new members. A couple of them brought up their shotguns.

"They're with us," Terrance said. He looked at Javier. "Follow me."

I moved to walk as everyone else did, but Eric held me back, waiting until there was some distance between us and Santiago.

"Jealousy looks good on you," I whispered in Eric's ear.

"I'm not jealous," Eric snapped. He immediately blushed. "Okay, maybe I was a little jealous."

I let go of his hand and wrapped my arms around his neck. "You have nothing to worry about. He doesn't even come close to comparing to you."

Eric raised his eyebrows. "Not even a little?"

I shook my head. "Nope. You are and always will be the one I love." I pulled him in and kissed him on the lips. I tried to back away after a few seconds, but Eric pulled me closer and kissed me with the most passion I think he ever had, his lips moving heatedly on mine. After a couple of minutes, he finally let me go.

"I think I need to get you jealous more often," I said with a smile on my mouth.

Eric shook his head. "No way. I don't need competition."

I rolled my eyes. "You don't have any competition. Santiago seems like the type who would flirt with any female. I'm sure there was nothing serious behind it. He'll move on to someone else the second he gets the chance."

"You have no idea how hot you are, do you?" He leaned in and kissed my neck.

"The only one I care about is you." I hugged him tightly. "I love you."

"I love you, Emmie," Eric said. He pulled away. "I guess we should get going."

I turned around to see everyone already way ahead of us. "I guess so." I took hold of his hand and we started walking back to our city.

I smiled at the thought of adding a hundred and fifty new members to New Haven. We definitely had a lot of work to do to fit them all.

CHAPTER 6

Santiago flirted with Tina on the walk back to the city, which was understandable because she was gorgeous. She flirted right back, but I could tell there wasn't much feeling behind it. She still had feelings for Luke, a resident of River Springs. We had wanted him to come with us to New Haven. Blinded by his father's views, he refused to leave. Or maybe he really did agree with the way Whit ran the place.

President Brown was waiting for us at the entrance to the city. Mack had radioed him to let him know we were coming.

While Steven, my Recruitment leader from River Springs, and James, a previous resident of Kingsland, gave our new residents a tour of our small city, we took a few of them to Headquarters to talk. Santiago was among them, who turned out to be their revolutionary.

Javier, Santiago's older brother, came too. They also had a little sister named Rosie. Santiago, Javier, and Rosie were the vice president's children. Their mom, Carmen, had come with them on the trip. She and Rosie were out on the tour. Their dad, Vice President Oscar Mendes, was on his way with another group, scheduled to arrive within a week.

Fernando also joined us in Headquarters. He was their military leader. The man was tall, extremely bulky, bald and covered in tattoos from head to toe. I tried to keep myself from staring, but I'd never seen anything like it before. He also had a piercing in each ear.

All the girls and women from Scorpion had at least their ears pierced once. A lot had multiples piercings, some in surprising places like their nose and lip. Even some of the guys had piercings, but only in their ears. Santiago had one ear pierced and Javier had both pierced. No one in River Springs had anything pierced. It was frowned upon, like a lot of other things.

We sat down around the table and let them tell us about their journey. They had a lot of rioting in Scorpion, which was why it took them so long to get out. They were trying to round up as many people as they could since they probably wouldn't be able to get back too often.

"When we got to the rendezvous point where we were supposed to meet the last city, we waited for a few days, but they never came," Javier said, leaning back in his chair.

"We couldn't wait any longer," Fernando said. He'd squeezed into a chair at the end of the table. The chair creaked under all the muscle, but somehow it held. "Everyone was getting restless and the food was running low. We thought that maybe we were so late, they'd already moved on themselves and would be here."

I shook my head. "They haven't shown. There's been no

word from them in months."

"When was the last time you were in contact with them?" President Brown asked.

"It's been four weeks," Javier said. "We were both going to leave within a few days, but we got caught up. They must have, too."

"Their city is in a worse state than ours," Fernando said. He folded his arms, his biceps bulging. "There's been a war going on for at least a year."

"I was worried about that," President Brown said with a sigh. "I knew a war had started, but I was hoping they would still have a chance to get out. They were outnumbered, so the chances were slim."

My heart sank at the thought of none of them surviving. I wanted to be optimistic, but since we hadn't heard anything for so long, I could only think the worst had happened.

"How many members do you have?" Santiago asked. He finally tore his eyes away from Tina to tune into the conversation. Tina looked at me and rolled her eyes.

"Well, we originally started with twenty," President Brown said. "With our two trips to Kingsland, we have been able to rescue a hundred and twenty members. The River Springs trip provided us with seventy more. We have another trip scheduled to leave tomorrow. Our contact there has a hundred and thirty people ready to go."

I gasped. "One hundred and thirty?"

President Brown nodded. "That's what Austin said the last time we talked a couple of days ago. Residents are getting fed up with President Randall and his lies. With those one hundred and thirty, our new group of one hundred, and everyone already here, we'll be up to four hundred and forty. That's not too bad for only a few months."

"Don't forget the other fifty on its way from Scorpion," Santiago said, clasping his hands behind his head.

"Yes, that's right," President Brown said. "So almost five hundred."

Mack stroked his beard. "We'll still need a lot more if a war were to break out."

"That's true," President Brown said. "I'm hoping with the number of people we'll have soon, and hopefully with the other city joining us, we'll be able to assign a group of people to be our resident city rescue team. That way we can just have them going back and forth between cities, constantly getting people out."

Santiago dropped his hands. "Can we go with you tomorrow to River Springs?" His eyes bounced in excitement.

"I think that would be a good idea," Terrance said, looking over at Mack. "We only have five going. With the current shape of River Springs and the tighter security, it would be good to have more heads."

"I agree," Mack said. "We should have Santiago, Javier, and Fernando go. Get them acquainted with the area and the way we run missions."

"Sounds good," President Brown said.

"Sorry to interrupt, but I need Emmie for a minute." Marie had leaned her head in the door, looking at me. She'd grown her brown hair out since we'd left New Haven, so it now hung past her shoulders.

"No problem," President Brown said. "We've finished with everything important." He nodded for me to leave.

I hurried out of my seat and out the door. "Is it Dee?"

Marie shook her head, straightening out the shirt of her nurse's uniform. "No, Dee's fine. It's Lou."

Lou was a fourteen-year-old boy from Kingsland. He had come with the original group with his dad, James.

"What's wrong with him?" I asked as we walked toward the infirmary.

"He's sick." Marie took a deep breath. "Same symptoms as Dee."

"Oh, no." My stomach churned. He was so young, and all James had. "Does James know he's with you?"

"No," Marie said. "He knew he was coming down with something, but he thought it was just a cold. Lou brought himself to me. I've been trying to find James, but I couldn't."

"He's out with Steven giving a tour of our city to the new residents," I said, focusing on each step so I wouldn't lose my balance. Two of our members sick with the disease in only three months of being there was not good.

"He seems worse than Dee," Marie said as we stepped into the infirmary. She stopped outside a door. "He's in there."

"Worse?" I asked.

"I still don't know much, Emmie," Marie said, rubbing a finger over her eye like she was tired, "but it may affect some people more than others. Race could have a play in it, too."

I nodded. "Have you told Dee?"

"Not yet," Marie said. "I was waiting to tell James first."

I pulled out my communicator. "James?"

After a few seconds, his voice came from the other end. "Yes?"

"We need you in the infirmary right now," I said. "Just have Steven give the rest of the tour."

"Is everything alright?" James asked.

"Just get here quick," I said. There was no way I was telling him over an open communicator. I looked at Marie. "Maybe you should wait for him at the entrance to the infirmary. I'll go talk with Lou for a moment."

Marie nodded, turned and walked away. I took a deep breath before I entered Lou's room. I was startled by his condition. He looked so thin and fragile. I was trying to remember the last time I'd seen him, but I would've remembered him being that skinny. His breathing was raspy and deep. He turned and looked at me, giving me a small smile.

I smiled back. "Hey, Lou."

"Hi Emmie," Lou said, his voice barely audible. "Marie told you?"

"Yes, I just heard." I sat down on a chair next to his bed. His room was set up just like Dee's, with an infirmary bed, two chairs, and a cabinet for medical equipment.

My favorite, though, were the paintings in the rooms. Vivica was an amazing artist. She had painted a bunch of pictures for each room in the infirmary. I loved looking at them. All the colors made my heart swell. They were nature paintings, some of the snowy mountains, some of flowers blooming in the spring, and some of rivers flowing through the valley. They gave you a feeling of hope.

"I love it, too," Lou said, noticing me staring at the

painting next to his bed. It was a field of wildflowers with butterflies flying about. I stroked my necklace.

"For as hardheaded as Vivica is," I said, "she sure has a soft spot for nature."

Lou let out a small laugh. "I know."

I reached out and held Lou's hand. "How are you holding up?"

Lou shrugged. "As well as I can. Not much I can do."

"Marie's very smart," I said. "She's getting closer and closer to figuring this all out."

"I have faith in her," Lou said.

I heard James' voice in the hall. "Well, I better leave so you can spend some time with your dad. I'll be back later."

"Thanks, Emmie," Lou said. "You've always been so nice to me."

"Well, you're easy to love." I kissed him on the cheek and left the room.

When I stepped out, James and Marie were talking in the hall. The look of despair on James' face tore at my heart. Marie needed to figure it out soon. We couldn't lose Lou.

CHAPTER 7

The next morning, we set off before dawn. We had a lot of ground to cover and wanted to get there as fast as we could. With everything we'd learned in the past few months and the strength we'd gained, our trips were faster. We had more energy, but most importantly, more hope. We had a home to return to.

We made it to the outskirts of River Springs in a week. There was an old highway that ran behind the city. Once we got to it, we followed it down. I hadn't been that way before, but the others had. When we first escaped River Springs, we took a completely different route. They soon found that this way was faster.

Richie and his family were waiting in a bus full of supplies on the edge of the road. When Richie saw us approach, he jumped out of the bus and went to give Eric, his cousin, a hug. He hugged me after Eric.

"Nice to see you again," I said to Richie. I had met him on my first day of Recruitment. Eric had given me a ride on

Richie's motorbike.

Richie smiled. "You too. I'm just glad to get out of this hell hole." He looked over at the bus, where his wife watched us from a window. "Annabelle is nervous. She's afraid of something happening to the baby."

"Did Annabelle already have the baby?" Eric asked.

"Yup, a big sucker at that." Richie whistled. "He weighed eleven pounds two ounces."

My eyes went wide. "Wow. Congratulations."

"Thanks," Richie said.

"Well, things will be fine once we get going and get back to New Haven," Eric said. "We desperately need you there. The couple of buses we have aren't working anymore."

Richie was a mechanic for Infinity Corp. He grinned at Eric. "Did you try putting some gas in them?"

Eric rolled his eyes. "You have to give me some credit, man. Of course, I tried putting more gas in them."

"Just messing with you." Richie laughed. "I'll look at them first thing, I promise." He stole a quick look at the bus. "We just finished loading up the bus and are ready to go. If you don't mind, we're going to take off. Austin already gave me a map."

Eric nodded. "Have a safe trip. We'll see you in a little over a week if everything goes okay."

"Sounds good," Richie said. He ran back to the bus, started it—the engine rumbling to life—and drove off down the highway.

We continued down the road for another five minutes. President Brown had given me the channel to communicate with Austin Oliver, so when we came to a stop, I called for him.

A few minutes later, he spoke. "That was fast."

"We were in a hurry," I said. "The trip home won't be as fast, though."

Austin gave a small laugh. "True. You'll have a lot more people, including children."

In all our trips, we hadn't had a lot of children come with us. Those with kids didn't want to risk it. I think most of them were starting to realize they didn't have a choice. It was either now or never for them.

"That's good," I said. "Dee's anxious to start up a school." I tried not to think about the fact that she may never see one built.

"How's she doing?" Austin asked, his tone laced with concern.

"She's a little worse but still stable. We've had another in our city become sick and he's weakening at a higher rate."

"President Brown told me about him," Austin said. "I have good news, though. I'm sending a doctor with you who'll be able to help. Dr. Stacey's already been researching the disease for years. I have some research notes for Alexander, too."

Alexander was a researcher for Infinity Corp before he was taken and detained by Whit. His son, my boyfriend Eric, thought he'd been dead for years.

"That's wonderful," I said, relieved. "We need all the help we can get. I don't think either of them has much time left."

Austin sighed on the other end. "Where are you right now?"

"About fifty yards out, near the entrance to the cave," I said. "This is where President Brown told us to come."

"Yes, that's good. I've already sent them through the underground tunnel. They've been waiting for my command to enter the cave. Hold tight while I give them the go-ahead."

We waited a few minutes before Austin came back. "Head for the tunnel and try to keep cover. You need to get them out of there quickly. I would suggest running for as long as you can once you get out."

"When will you be coming, Austin?" I asked.

"I hope on the next trip," Austin said. "I need to find someone here I can trust to continue the movement in River Springs to free our people. Until then, I need to stay. Emmie, take good care of my family."

"I will, Austin, I promise." I would do anything to protect the Oliver family. They had already sacrificed their dad.

"I do have one surprise for you, though," Austin said, his voice hesitant. The members who were with me had already started moving toward the cave, so I stood alone.

"What is it?" I asked.

"Joshua Randall is among the residents you'll be taking back with you."

My heart stopped. "What?"

"I know this is shocking news, but I trust him," Austin said. "We've been friends since we were little. He's never agreed with his dad about anything. I even did a lie detector test on him to see if he was lying about anything and he passed."

"Are you positive?" I barely managed to get the question

out. The shock hadn't subsided.

"Positive. Emmie, you can trust him. I would bet my life on it." Austin paused. "You two will have an interesting conversation, I'm sure."

Total understatement. I'd found out a couple of months ago that Whit Randall was my real father, which made Joshua my half-brother. I'd been thinking for the past little while that all my half-siblings were terrible people. But maybe Joshua was going to turn out to be a good guy.

"Well, if you trust him, I guess I'll have to."

"Thanks, Emmie, and good luck. We'll talk again soon. Oh, and send Dee my best."

"I will, Austin. Thanks for everything."

I pulled myself together and went toward the cave. When I got close, I heard some commotion. My heart raced, the thought of them being caught coming to mind. When I entered the cave, it was something completely different.

"Don't move!" Mack yelled. He pointed a gun at Joshua.

"Don't shoot me!" Joshua shouted. His eyes were wide with panic. It was hard for me to look at him. With his suit and tie, plus the blond hair, he reminded me of his dad. *Our* dad.

All the River Springs residents glanced around in confusion and alarm. The Kingsland and Scorpion members looked confused, too, but they all had their weapons trained at Joshua.

"Stop!" I yelled. Everyone turned to look at me. "He's with us. It's okay. We need to go, now."

"What are you talking about?" Mack asked me. "We can't trust him. He's a Randall!"

"Well, last time I checked, so am I," I said, ignoring the shiver that went through my body at the thought of being a Randall. "We need to head out as quickly as we can. Is there anyone injured in any way?"

There were a few murmurs of no and some shaking of heads.

"Good," I said. "We'll have to run the first little bit. Just go as fast as you can. Mack, why don't you take the lead and Eric and I will stay in back. Everyone else who came with us, scatter throughout the River Springs members and make sure they're getting the help they need. Let's head out."

Mack hesitated for a second, but then nodded and took off. All the River Springs members hurried after him, eager to get out. I walked up to Joshua, who was still a little shook up.

"I'm sorry about that," I said to him. "It's hard to trust a Randall."

Joshua gave me a small smile, the warmth showing in his blue eyes. "I understand that." He paused for a second. "So, you and me, we're, uh …"

"Yeah, I know," I said. "Crazy, right? Life is just full of surprises."

Eric came up next to me. "What's going on?" He eyed Joshua.

"Austin told me he was coming and that we could trust him," I said to Eric.

"You can trust me," Joshua said. "I hate my father. I always have."

"You never seemed to hate him before," Eric said, his voice sharp. It would take a while before any of us could fully trust Joshua.

"Do you know how scary it is having that man for a father?" Joshua asked. "I never wanted to cross him or let him know I despised him." His blond hair was the same shade as mine, something I'd never noticed before.

"We don't have time to talk about this," I said, taking Eric's hand and squeezing it.

Eric stepped in close to Joshua, using his height to his advantage. He looked down at Joshua. "We'll be keeping an eye on you. If you even take one step out of line, you're finished. Do you understand?"

Joshua nodded. "Yes. I expected this reaction. I'm on your side, Eric, and I swear I'll prove it to you."

"Good." Eric stepped back and looked at me. "Let's get going."

I grabbed Joshua's arm and squeezed it. "You first."

Joshua nodded and ran after the group.

Eric looked at me. "You sure about this?"

"I trust Austin, so I'm willing to give Joshua a chance. I think I'm living proof that we don't always take after our parents."

"But you didn't grow up in the same house as President Randall."

"I know," I said, "but I was close enough."

"Fine." Eric leaned in and kissed me on the lips. "Let's go."

We only got twenty yards before we were ambushed.

CHAPTER 8

At least twenty men came from behind us, the sounds from their guns ringing in the air. Eric and I dove to the ground and crawled to the nearest tree to take cover. Within a minute, Tina, Santiago, Javier, Fernando, and Gideon were near us, firing at our attackers. We needed Mack, who I had sent away first.

I took my communicator out of my pocket. "Mack! We need you. We're under fire!"

"I'm on my way back," Mack yelled. "Send Gideon to replace me and lead the citizens to safety."

Gideon was only a tree away from me.

I turned to Eric, who stood right behind me. "Cover me!"

"What?" Eric yelled. "Where are you going?"

"To Gideon." I came away from the tree for a split second and saw someone coming out of the corner of my eye. I fired two shots, hitting the guy in the chest.

"Go when I say," Eric said, letting out a few shots at another guy coming toward us. I readied myself for the move.

"Go!" Eric shouted.

I dove toward the ground, rolling until I was at Gideon's tree. I stood, taking cover right next to him.

"Gideon," I said, making sure he could hear me over the gun fire. "Mack's on his way back. You need to lead everyone else back home." Gideon's face pulled tight. "We need Mack, Gideon. He has the best military training of anyone here. We're outnumbered. If we don't hold them here, they'll kill everyone we just rescued."

"Why me?" Gideon asked.

"You're the best one to lead everyone to safety. You're great with navigation and you're a natural leader. They'll trust you." He didn't look too convinced, so I continued. "You have a lot of potential, Gideon. If none of us that stay behind make it, I have the most faith in you to take over in my spot."

Gideon looked as shocked as I felt when I said it. "Do you mean that?"

I nodded. "Yes." I really did. He was willing to do whatever it took to protect our city and had the drive and passion to back it up.

He still seemed sad to be leaving, but he nodded and took off. I tried to shift my focus back on the fight behind me.

I turned to see someone from River Springs. Someone who helped in holding me and everyone I loved as prisoners. A man who helped in the murder of Vice President Oliver. SO Pierce Martin.

His eyes were hungry as he came toward me. He'd wanted me dead and would love to be the one that killed me. He already had his gun pointed at me, his finger on the trigger.

"Well, well, my favorite Recruit," Pierce said, his voice arrogant.

I rolled my eyes. I couldn't stand the guy. "My least favorite, egotistical, murdering tool."

Pierce growled. "I haven't missed that snappy attitude of yours."

I smiled. "I haven't missed that ugly face of yours."

Pierce tightened his grip around his gun and took a step closer to me. "You're pathetic, you know that?"

"Me, pathetic?" I gestured toward his hand. "You're the one pointing a gun at a teenager. How does that make you feel? You're weak and enjoy killing kids. So, no, Pierce, I'm not the pathetic one. You are."

I raised my gun as fast as I could, but the shots went off before I'd even raised it halfway. I closed my eyes, waiting for the pain, but nothing came.

Confused, I opened my eyes and examined my body. No holes or blood. I looked up at Pierce. His eyes were wide open, his hand clutching his stomach where blood poured out. He fell forward, his gun falling from his hand.

My heart felt like it was going a thousand beats per minute. A noise sounded to my left, so I turned and pointed my gun at the source.

"Don't shoot!" It was Joshua. He was the one who had shot Pierce.

Dizziness overcame me, so I leaned against a tree. "Where did you get the gun?"

"Santiago," Joshua said. He'd taken off his blazer, but he still had on his tie and had a bag slung around his shoulders. It looked a little bulky and heavy.

"You should've handed your bag to someone else," I said. "It will be hard to fight with that."

"I didn't want to part with it," Joshua said, his eyes telling me to close the topic.

"Thank you," I said, looking him in the eye. "You saved my life."

"I told you I'm on your side, Emmie."

I was about to say something when Joshua pushed me to the side and fired off a few more shots. Someone else had come toward us and Joshua had once again saved my life.

He turned to me. "I'm going to prove it to you, Emmie, just you wait and see." He turned away, continuing to fire at oncoming enemies, until he was out of sight.

I wanted to trust him. He had just killed two people to save my life. But if he was as evil as his dad, wouldn't he be willing to kill some of his own if it meant infiltrating our new city? Whit would do anything to benefit himself, including sacrificing the life of his child.

"I was hoping I would find you." The voice came from behind me. It was loud, high pitched, and extremely annoying. I would know that voice anywhere. Amber.

I turned around to see her standing there, leaning against a tree. Her black hair was still cropped short and her gray eyes held boredom. She twirled a knife in her hand.

"Please tell me you didn't bring a knife to a gun fight, Amber," I said, pointing my gun at her.

Amber patted her side where a handgun rested in a holster on her hip. "I have a gun, but I thought it would be more fun to actually fight you to your death instead of just shooting you. There would be no fun in that." For someone that had been certified as a psychopath, it made sense she'd want to kill me with her bare hands.

She looked down at Pierce's body on the ground. "I would be sad since he was such an asset to our city," she said, giving him a kick, "but it just means that I'm the one who's going to kill you." She giggled. "It must be my lucky day."

She didn't have one ounce of human decency in her. I wanted to just shoot her right then. This was a war after all. But I still had a hard time wrapping my head around the thought of taking someone's life, even if it was someone as evil and crazy as Amber.

Of course, I had wanted her dead for years, but that didn't mean I wanted to be the one to do it. It was much easier if someone was shooting at you and you had to shoot back to save your own life. But she was just standing there with a knife. If she would lunge at me or something, it would make the decision easier.

Amber tsked. "Oh, come on, be a good girl and put the gun down. Let's fight this out, see who the real winner is."

"If I put my gun down, that leaves me with nothing. You still have a knife. That's hardly fair." I lowered my gun to my side. "Unless you're too chicken to fight me bare handed."

"Please!" Amber laughed. "I could fight you blind folded and I'd still win."

"Lower your knife."

"Lower your gun."

"Same time," I said. She nodded at me and we both

lowered our weapons to the ground, keeping our eyes trained on each other. "The gun, too, Amber."

Amber huffed as she took her gun from its holster and put it on the ground. "You don't know how long I've dreamed about this." She took a step toward me. I did know. She'd wanted to kill me for years.

I raised my eyebrows. "That's kind of creepy that you dream about me so much. I didn't know you were so obsessed."

Amber growled and pounced on me, sending the two of us to the ground. I could already tell she had beefed up since I last saw her, but so had I. Grabbing the sides of her shirt, I twisted her so I was on top, pinning her down. I took two swings at her face, one landing on her jaw, the other on her nose. She took her hands and pushed my face back, then jammed her foot into my stomach, sending me off her.

She was on top of me instantly, pounding away. I tried to get out of her grasp, but she was much stronger than me, which I hated to admit. After at least ten punches from her, she got tired for just a second, but it was long enough to push her off me.

I slowly stood, blood dripping from my nose and mouth. From the pain, my nose had to be broken.

Amber laughed at me. "You're weak, Emelia." She slowly circled around me. "Are you sure you don't want to surrender now? I would love to kill you, but President Randall had specific orders to bring you to him alive."

"Then why did you say you were going to kill me?" I asked, my voice weaker than I wanted it to be.

"You're arrogant, Emelia. Completely full of yourself. I knew it would work you up. Get you to fight me." Amber stopped just inches from my face. "You're too predictable."

I looked her in the eye. "Am I?" I swung my leg around, slamming it into hers, sending her to the ground. Grabbing her knife that was on the ground, I jumped on top of her and held it to her throat. "Am I predictable, Amber?"

She tried to be tough, but fear settled in her eyes. "You wouldn't do it, Emelia. You don't have it in you."

I pressed the tip of the knife deeper into her skin, barely piercing the surface so a little bit of blood came out. She was right, but I wasn't about to divulge that fact. "You have no idea what I'm capable of." In one swift motion, I turned the knife around and jammed the butt of it into her head, knocking her unconscious.

"Emmie!" I recognized Mack's voice and got up to go to him. I was almost to him when something hit me from behind, knocking me to the ground. I tried to keep my eyes focused, but everything went blurry right before my world became black.

When I awoke, I was laying on the ground. I pressed a shaky hand to my nose, wincing from the pain. Someone had cleaned the blood from my face. Though my head felt heavy, I tried to sit up.

"Whoa, there, not so fast." I turned and focused on the person sitting next to me. Mack.

"What happened?" I asked him.

"Someone knocked you out and tried to take you," Mack

said, sharpening his knife on a piece of wood. "But I got there in time to make sure they didn't capture you."

"Thanks." I put my hand on my head, wishing I could control the pounding inside.

Mack sighed and kept his eyes on the ground.

"What's wrong, Mack?" I asked. He wouldn't look at me. "What's wrong?"

When he didn't respond, I sat up and looked around. I counted, making sure everyone was there, but one was missing.

I turned to Mack. "Where's Eric?"

Mack just sat there, sharpening his knife.

"Where's Eric?" I yelled as loud as I could.

"They have him." Santiago came up next to me. "Emmie, they took Eric."

CHAPTER 9

I stood, which was a bad idea. My world spun so fast, I quickly lost my balance and fell back down.

Tina rushed up next to me, sat down, and put her arm around me. "Are you okay?"

I looked at her until she came into focus. "No, Tina, I'm not okay. I got beat up by Amber, of all people, and my boyfriend has been captured by the owners of Infinity Corp. Who knows what they're doing to him right now? That's if he's even alive."

My stomach twisted at the thought of Eric being dead. I wanted to think positive, but Whit was capable of horrendous things, including murder.

"He's alive," Mack said, now cleaning one of his guns.

I balled my hands into fists, resisting the urge to punch him. "How would you know?"

"He's leverage. They won't kill him yet." Mack kept his focus on his gun.

"Yet!" I yelled at Mack. "YET! That means they will. And

we're just sitting here. We should be there, rescuing him!"

"No, we should be right here, on our way back to New Haven," Mack said, his voice calm. "We can work out a game plan then."

"It will be too late!" I tried to stand again, but Tina pulled me down.

Tina stroked my hair, keeping her voice quiet. "Just take some deep breaths, Emmie."

I shook her off me and stood, ignoring the dizziness. "Well, you can all sit here doing nothing, but I'm going back there."

Santiago came right in front of me, not letting me past. Keeping his mouth shut, he folded his arms and stared at me.

"You're not going back there," Mack said.

"Screw you, Mack. You can't stop me." I pushed Santiago out of my way and moved toward River Springs.

Mack suddenly stood right in front of me. He had his face only inches from mine. "That's enough, Emmie. You aren't going back there and that's final."

"You can't tell me what to do," I said to him, my jaw tight. My fists were ready to swing at any moment.

"You put me in charge of our military unit, which makes me the commanding officer, so I *can* tell you what to do." Red covered Mack's face, the veins on his neck popping out. "You're going to take a deep breath and calm down. You're injured. You need to recover, and you need time to think everything through."

My breathing sped, my face probably redder than Mack's. "What's there to think through? They have Eric, Mack! They're going to kill him if we don't go save him! I can't believe you just left in the first place. You should've stayed!"

"I hate Infinity Corp as much as you, Emmie, but they did get one rule in Recruitment right," Mack said. "Not having teenagers date."

I pulled my face away from his, taken aback by his comment. "Excuse me?"

"You're acting like a little schoolgirl and not thinking rationally. If we would've stayed there, we would all be dead right now." Mack took a step closer to me, his toes touching mine. "My duty as the commanding officer is to protect my unit and bring back as many as I can alive, not dead. Staying there would have been suicide. We were outnumbered. With the abduction of Eric, it distracted the enemies for enough time for us to escape. If anything, your boyfriend saved us."

I stared at him, my whole body shaking. I couldn't calm myself.

"Now, we're going back to New Haven and we're going to sit down like adults and think out a plan," Mack said. "We have a leak inside our city. They knew we were coming. We need to focus on trying to figure out who that leak is, and we'll have no more outbursts from you. We need to catch up with Gideon and the others."

I shook my head. "I can't believe you would just leave someone behind like that."

"Enough, Emmie!" Mack roared. "This is war and last time I checked, there are causalities in war. You're going to lose people close to you, people you love, but there's nothing you can do about it. Don't forget, Emmie, you started this all yourself. You started this revolution back in Recruitment. If you thought we would just walk away from River Springs without any consequences or causalities, you were sadly mistaken and extremely naïve. You're the revolutionary leader, Emmie, whether you like it or not. So, suck it up."

Mack stepped back and stormed away from me. I turned to look at him. "What if I'm not?"

He stopped and glanced over his shoulder at me. "What?"

Looking down at the ground, I tucked my hair behind my ear. "What if I'm not the leader? What if Whit was wrong? It could be Austin. Or Joshua."

Out of the corner of my eye, I saw Joshua move. I had completely forgotten about him until I said that. He leaned against a tree, shifting uncomfortably.

"It's you, Emmie," Mack said.

"How do you know?" I asked.

"I just do." Mack calmed, his shoulders starting to relax. "Look, I know this is hard, but it's reality. The Emmie I first met back in Recruitment was a leader. She was strong, confident, and didn't back down."

"I'm trying to not back down right now, but you're not letting me!" I screamed at him.

Mack shut his eyes for a second, trying to compose himself. "She also thought rationally. She was levelheaded. I don't know what has happened to you, but this new you is not working out. We need the old Emmie back. That girl, no, that woman, is our leader. She's who New Haven needs. She's the one I respect. She's the one I followed." Mack came up next to me, but his eyes were softer this time. "You have it in you, Emmie."

I put my hands over my eyes and cried. Mack's hand

rested gently on my arm.

"Emmie, we'll figure this out. But standing around here arguing isn't going to save Eric. We need to get back to New Haven and talk with President Brown and Dante. I promise we'll do everything we can to save Eric, but I need your promise that you won't let your emotions overtake you. It won't do anyone any good if they do."

I just nodded as I continued to cry. Mack walked away, shouting at everyone to grab their things and start walking. I couldn't move. I was in pain and heartbroken.

"Come on," Tina said, wrapping her arms around me. I took my hands off my eyes and threw my arms around her. She stroked my hair. "It's going to be okay, Emmie. We'll get him back."

Tina let me cry for another minute before she told me we had to get going. When I stopped crying and looked up, Mack, Javier, and Fernando were already yards ahead. Santiago and Joshua stood nearby, waiting for us. They both gave me sympathetic smiles, which for some reason made me feel worse.

As much as it pained me, Mack was right. I couldn't lose Eric. I might lose Dee and adding Eric on top of that was something I couldn't stomach.

But this was war.

I intended to fight for everything Whit had stolen from me.

CHAPTER 10

I tried to walk as fast as I could back to New Haven, but the heaviness of my heart was like a strong force, stopping me from going forward.

There were so many moments where I wanted to turn around and run back to River Springs to get Eric, but Mack was right. If I went back, they would kill me and then kill Eric if they hadn't already.

We met back up with Gideon and the others the next day. They had run for long as they could, but eventually, the adrenaline wore off and they got tired. We should've caught up with them sooner, but I slowed everyone down.

"Emmie!" I stopped walking to see who called my name.

Will came toward me, a smile on his face. We went through a challenge together in Recruitment. The worst challenge ever.

I hugged him when he got to me. "How are you doing, Will?" I was glad he wasn't much taller than me because I didn't have the strength to lift my arms that high.

"Much better than you, it looks like," Will said, eying my face. He straightened his square-framed glasses.

"I think everyone's doing much better than me." I continued moving, gently touching my tender nose.

"What do you mean?" Will asked, keeping pace with me.

I shook my head. "Nothing." Apparently, the word about Eric being captured hadn't gotten around. "Are you here by yourself, or did your family come?"

"Both my parents and my little sister are right over there." Will pointed at them. They were walking a little way behind us. He looked exactly like his mom. She had the same round face, dark hair, and glasses. "My mom's brother and his family are here, too."

Seeing all the River Springs residents in their fifties style clothing, including suits and dresses, reminded me how much I didn't miss wearing a dress or skirts.

"That's great," I said. "It's nice to have family out here."

Will looked like he wanted to say something, but he stopped himself.

"What?" I asked him.

Will straightened his glasses again, even though they didn't need to be fixed. "What?"

"What were you going to say?" I asked.

"Uh, I was just thinking about your mom." Will looked at me, waiting for a reaction.

I wasn't even sure what reaction to give. "What about her?"

"I saw her the other day with President Randall," Will said.

"Where?"

"They were doing home inspections," Will said. "They were the ones who came to our home."

"How did she look?" I wasn't sure if I wanted to know the answer.

Will shrugged. "She looked good, I guess. Happy."

Well, that wasn't the answer I wanted. She was happy without us. I had hoped she at least missed us, but that was probably far from the truth. Whit probably gave her everything she wanted.

I wondered how Mrs. Randall fit into the whole equation.

"Oh, I mean," Will stammered. "I shouldn't have told you that." He pursed his lips together.

I touched his arm. "It's okay, Will. It actually helps me."

"How?" Will asked, scratching his head.

Sighing, I looked up at the sky. "It lets me know I need to give up hope of ever getting my mother back."

"I'm sorry, Emmie," Will said.

"Don't be," I said, turning back to him. "It's not your fault. Everything she's done has been her own choice."

Will nodded. "I know, but no one should have to deal with stuff like that."

Oh, I was dealing with a lot worse than an adulterous mom who didn't want me. I reached up to touch my necklace, only to realize it was gone. I stopped in my tracks.

"What's wrong?" Will asked.

"My necklace. It's gone." I must have lost it in the fight.

"What does it look like?" Will asked, scanning the ground around us.

I shook my head. "It wouldn't be here. I think I lost it

back near River Springs."

Will's gaze settled on my face. "It meant a lot to you, didn't it?" He must have seen the sadness in my eyes. Not only was Eric gone, but the only possession that reminded me of him was also gone.

"Yes, it did," I said.

As we started walking again, I looked back up at the gray sky. The threat of rain hung in the clouds. We walked at a brisk pace, which was good because it was cold. I was looking forward to spring in the next month or so.

I could feel someone watching me. Looking to my right, a girl I met in Recruitment glared at me, just like she had the first time she met me. I smiled at her and she let out a little huff. From the look in her eyes, she was debating whether she should come over and talk to me. She finally rolled her eyes and came over.

"It's nice to see you again, Rachel." I was glad I remembered to use her real name and not the nickname I gave her during Recruitment: Thunder Thighs. She was thick and muscular, and very intimidating. Not someone you'd want to cross.

Thunder Thighs grunted. "Yeah, I guess it's nice to see you, too. Even though you look like crap."

Will inhaled a sharp breath. He was a kind, considerate type of person, whereas Thunder Thighs was painfully blunt.

I laughed. "Yeah, I got into a little fight."

"Well, they obviously won," Thunder Thighs said.

I moaned. "Don't remind me."

"So, this place we're going," Thunder Thighs said. "Is it nice?"

"It is." I wasn't sure if Thunder Thighs would appreciate the beauty of it as I did.

Thunder Thighs cracked her knuckles. "As long as I get my own bed, I'll be fine." She gave me a weird look. It took me a moment to realize she was smiling. At least her version of a smile. She almost looked pained. "See you around, I guess."

"See you," I said.

She gave Will her version of a smile and left.

"That was weird," Will said.

I looked over at Will, taking him in. He was a cute guy and extremely sweet. Dee came to my mind, making me smile.

Will shifted his eyes uncomfortably. "What?"

I gave a little laugh. "Nothing, there's just someone I want you to meet when we get to New Haven."

Will raised his eyebrows. "Who?"

"A friend of mine," I said. "You'll like her."

Will started to say something, but we were interrupted.

"What happened to you?" Gideon asked, coming up to me.

"Amber," I said.

"Amber Johnson?" Gideon asked.

"That would be the one," I said.

"She always seemed a little ..." Gideon didn't finish his thought. He was too nice of a guy.

But I had no problem finishing it. "Bratty, selfish, conceited, arrogant, ugly, annoying ..."

"You must be talking about Amber," Tina said, falling into step next to us.

She'd been back talking with some old friends of hers from her previous precinct in River Springs. She was trying to get information about Luke and see how he was doing.

"I wish I could've met her," Santiago said. I turned around to see him and Joshua walking behind us. "She sounds interesting."

"Oh, trust me, you'll get a chance to meet her by the end of all of this," I said. "She can't help but get herself involved in everything."

Tina laughed. "So true."

"I need some more training," I said, touching a cut above my eye. "She's a lot stronger than the last time we fought."

"You've fought her before?" Joshua asked.

I looked at Tina and we both laughed.

"A few times actually," I said.

"But fighting isn't allowed in our city," Gideon said. "I mean, our old city."

"You couldn't fight?" Santiago asked. "That sucks. We had fights everything Thursday night. It was awesome."

"You had scheduled fights?" Tina asked Santiago.

Santiago stretched his arms. "Yeah. Well, it's called boxing. It's a sport."

"I'm learning new things every day," I said. "Fighting for fun. As a sport. Crazy." I turned to Gideon. "I know we weren't allowed to fight. But Amber took every opportunity to start something."

"How did you not get in trouble?" Will asked.

"Her dad," Tina and I said at the same time.

Amber never got in trouble because she was Dean

Johnson's daughter. And since Dean was President Randall's personal advisor and head of Recruitment, apparently the rules didn't apply to him or his family.

"She can get away with anything," I said. "Plus, Dean was in on Whit's plan to kill me. There was no point in disciplining us if I was going to be dead soon anyway."

Joshua coughed. I couldn't even imagine what he thought about all of this.

"Is that what you call him?" Joshua asked me.

I turned around. "What?"

"Whit. Is that what you call him?" Joshua asked.

I nodded. "Yes. Sorry if that bothers you."

"It doesn't," Joshua said. "I'm just not sure what to call him myself. I don't want to call him dad, but President Randall seems weird. So does Whit."

"You'll think of something." I slowed my pace down, so I was walking next to Joshua. "Do you guys mind if I talk with Joshua alone?"

"Sure," Tina said. "Hey, Santiago, tell me more about boxing."

"You'll love it, Tina," Santiago said, walking up next to her. "I was thinking of starting it up in New Haven."

"Oh, yeah?" Tina asked.

"Yeah," Santiago said. "First fight, me and Dante. We'll see for certain who's tougher."

"Well, that's easy," Tina said. "Dante for sure."

Santiago raised his arms. "What? That guy has nothing on me." He threw out some punches. "He can't take down The Bone Crusher."

Tina, Will, and Gideon laughed.

"The Bone Crusher?" Tina asked.

"That's who I am, baby," Santiago said, flexing his muscles. "I'll crush anyone with these guns." He kissed his bicep.

I looked at Joshua. "Do you see what I have to deal with day in and day out? You sure you want to be a part of this?"

Joshua laughed loudly. "Trust me, this is way better than dealing with my family every day."

CHAPTER 11

I waited until we were out of hearing range of the others before I spoke with Joshua. "When I was talking with Austin earlier, he said something about giving you a lie detector test. What is that?"

"They put these patches on you that can detect your pulse," Joshua said, tugging on his blue tie. "When they ask you a question, it tells them your heart rate so they can tell if you're lying or not."

I couldn't help but laugh. "For years and years, they hide all this technology from the city residents, not letting any of us know they have stuff capable of doing things like that."

"When behind the scenes, they have way more than you can imagine," Joshua said, his voice quiet.

"So not only are we outnumbered ..."

He looked at me. "Your equipment doesn't even compare to what they have."

"Could we build our own lie detector test?"

Joshua smiled and patted the strap around his shoulder

that held his bag. "I brought some things with me that I thought would be helpful. Lie detector included."

"Thought we'd have a bunch of liars?" I asked, a small smile forming on my mouth.

"If I have learned anything from my … our … father … whatever, is that you never know who you can really trust. There are two types of people in this world: Those who are willing to do whatever it takes for the good of mankind, and those who are willing to do whatever it takes for the good of themselves." He rubbed the back of his neck. "I don't think you know what type of person you are until you're put in a situation that will prove it."

I thought back to Recruitment and the challenge where I thought Tina and Eric were killed. Shivers ran through me, causing me to rub my arms. I still had nightmares about it.

"That's what that challenge was for," Joshua said.

Startled, I looked at him.

He gave me a small smile. "We all went through that challenge, Emmie. I figured that's what you were thinking about."

"Oh."

"Austin and I looked back at the tapes of that challenge. We checked everyone who has left River Springs." He loosened the tie around his neck and unbuttoned the top of his white button-down shirt.

"So, you know what type of person everyone is?"

He nodded. "Our best guess, anyway. I mean, some didn't help their partners because they were scared. Some tried as long as they could, but then gave up at the last second."

"Like Will," I said.

He had stayed with me and Luke until the very last second. But once he realized he was about to be trapped himself, he got out.

"Yes. But some didn't try and looked like they didn't even want to try. Some just passed that room and didn't look in." His face twisted. "One even laughed when they saw their partner getting killed. They stayed to watch and then left."

I scrunched my face. "Who?"

"Who do you think?"

"Amber," I said. He nodded. And Dee was her partner. She watched Dee die and enjoyed it. Well, Dee didn't actually die since it was all simulated, but still. "She's so sick."

"Tell me about it," Joshua said, untucking his dress shirt. "I have no idea what Steven saw in her."

"Wait, what?" I lost my footing and stumbled over some small rocks. Joshua reached out and grabbed my arm, steadying me. "Steven? As in my Recruitment leader, Steven?"

"Yup. Steven and Amber. I can't tell you how many times I saw them kissing." His body shook. "So gross."

"And so wrong," I said. "Ewwww!"

Joshua laughed. "That's an understatement."

A thought came to me. "Did you check to see how Steven did on that challenge?"

"He didn't even look in the room. Just ran toward the exit and escaped."

"Well, maybe he didn't know they were in there," I said. Half of our group walked past the door before I looked in. If I hadn't stopped, we could've all just left.

"There's always one who stops," he said. "Like you. Someone stopped in Steven's group, too, but he ignored them. They yelled to let him know his partner was trapped and could die, but Steven kept running."

"I've wondered about him," I said. He wasn't in my dream about New Haven, but he was there with the original group that escaped River Springs. It had always worried me. "He's worked for your dad before."

"I know." He patted his bag. "I think we should give him a lie detector test."

"I agree. But I think we need to give everyone from River Springs a lie detector test."

A look of surprise passed over his face. "Everyone?"

"Everyone. We need to be sure we can trust all these people. We can't take any risks." I turned to Joshua. "That means you have to take the test, too."

"Of course. I have no problems with that. I think it'll be a good thing. I want you to trust me, Emmie. I know I'm a Randall, but I'm not like him."

I rubbed my arms. "That statement applies to me, too, you know." The wind began to pick up and thunder rumbled in the distance.

"It's crazy to think I have another sister." He ran his fingers through his hair, loosening the gel holding it in place. He was slowly relaxing, getting comfortable with his surroundings. "I already like you better."

"What's Tami like?" I asked, thinking of his, well, our sister.

He mulled it over for a moment. "Think of Amber, take

away the giddiness, and add our dad's viciousness, and you have Tami."

"Well, and she's cuter."

"Uh, I can't comment on that," Joshua said with his hands raised. "She's my sister."

I laughed. "Well, I'm sure every other guy would agree with me."

"Except Steven."

I shivered. "So gross." I tucked my hair behind my ear. "What did you do? In the challenge?"

"The same as you. I tried until those walls came crashing in on me." He smirked at me. "Except I didn't kiss anyone."

Heat raged on my cheeks and neck. "How many people have watched that?"

"Not too many. But it's the most replayed tape at Headquarters."

My eyes widened. "What?"

"That was quite the kiss, Emmie," Joshua said with a huge smile. "All the security guys love to watch it. It was just so intense. Then add on top of that you had another guy you liked, and he liked another girl. Then add that it's Luke. Everyone knows how strict his father is. Luke's wound up just as tight as him." He laughed, rubbing the back of his neck. "Man, I can't believe how loose Luke was with you. I'm sure if there was room to move, his hands would have ..."

I held up my hand. "Enough. I get it." Joshua was still laughing, so I punched him on the arm. "I thought I was about to die! I had just seen the guy I love, plus my partner die! Don't tell me you wouldn't have done the same."

"I was in there with another guy, so no, I wouldn't have done the same." He wiped some tears from the corner of his eye. "That moment made me respect you so much, though."

My eyebrows shot up. "Making out with Luke made you respect me?"

He shook his head. "Not that part, although I did like that you seized the moment like that. But everything you yelled out before the walls came crashing in. And how hard you fought to save your friends. I knew at that moment that you were one to do whatever it takes to protect those around you. You were the last thing on your mind. Not many people are willing to risk their lives for others. Especially at your age."

"I guess I'm not like most seventeen-year-olds," I said with a shrug.

"No, you're not," Joshua said. "Speaking of which, didn't you just have a birthday?"

"No. Wait, January has passed already, hasn't it?"

He nodded. "It's the end of February. You forgot your birthday?"

"Birthdays have been the last thing on my mind. Plus, it's not like they were celebrated back in River Springs."

"True." He smiled at me, rubbing a hand down his tie. "Well, Happy Birthday, Emmie."

"Thanks. Eighteen," I said. Glancing around at everyone walking, I thought about all the challenges that faced us ahead. We had a lot to overcome. "I can't help but think this isn't going to be a very good year."

"Probably not, but it will all be worth it in the end. It will make all the upcoming years that much more special."

"I hope." In my heart, I hoped so desperately that Joshua was right. That it would be worth it. All the losses and heartache would be for good. For freedom. "You're nineteen, right?"

"Yes."

"And Tami's twenty-one?" Thunder rolled through the sky just as the wind started to stir. Pulling my coat tighter around me, I glanced up at the sky right as a small raindrop landed on my cheek.

"Yeah." Joshua held his folded arms close to his chest. "We're not too far apart in age."

"Yes, but I'm sure adding another woman to the equation wasn't foreshadowed." I put my hands in my pockets. "I'm assuming your mom knows."

"She does. Not much she can do about it, though."

"Has she ever talked about it? I can't imagine how that makes her feel." A few more drops fell onto my face, so I wiped them off with my sleeve.

He looked at me. "My mom is just as conniving as our dad. She has her own affair on the side. Although, only I know about that one."

My eyebrows shot up. "Whit doesn't know? I would hate to be the guy if Whit ever finds out." Whit would kill him.

"I think Dean could put up a pretty good fight," Joshua said, keeping close to me as we walked.

"Dean Johnson? Amber's dad? This keeps getting worse and worse." I took one of my hands out of my pocket and patted my stomach. "We need to stop talking about this or I'm going to lose my appetite."

"That's probably a good idea. I could tell you stuff that would make your toes curl."

I held my hand up to my mouth. "Please don't."

A small smile rested on his lips as he looked up at the sky. "Hey, Emmie, I just want you to know I'm sorry about what happened to Eric. I've been trying to get a hold of Austin, but he hasn't responded."

"You have a communicator with him?"

Joshua nodded as he turned to look at me. "Please don't tell anyone."

"Why did you tell me?" I asked. A drizzle started, so I pulled up the hood of my jacket, tucking my hair in the back.

"You strike me as the type who keeps her word. If I asked you not to tell anyone and you said you wouldn't, I'd believe you."

"But I haven't said I wouldn't." I couldn't help but smile. "But I won't, I promise."

"Thanks, Emmie. I'll let you know once I hear from Austin. Maybe he can help rescue Eric."

"I hope so. I don't know what I would do if I lost him."

"You're lucky," Joshua said.

I looked at him. "How so?"

"To have someone you love that much and returns it. True love is hard to find." He stepped to the side to avoid a small puddle and then came back close to me. "Especially when River Springs wouldn't let you marry below your clearance level. Equal partners, right?" He grunted. "Bunch of crap if you ask me. Your status shouldn't define who you are."

No, it shouldn't. I touched my neck where my necklace

should've been. "No matter what happens, it was worth it. I wouldn't take back the love I have for Eric, ever. I would take the short time we've had together over a lifetime of fake love."

"I hope I find that one day," Joshua said, glancing over at me.

Nudging him in the arm with my elbow, I stuffed my hands into my pockets and smiled. "Now you will have the opportunity to search for yourself."

"I'm not sure if anyone will ever trust me with the last name of Randall."

"Change it."

He looked at me. "What?"

Some kids ran by, laughing as they splashed through some puddles. It would be nice to start hearing constant laughter throughout New Haven. That was one sound I didn't realize I would miss so much.

"Change your last name," I said.

Thunder boomed above making Joshua jump a little. He shoved his hands into his slack's pockets as he spoke. "I can do that?"

"You live in New Haven now. If you want to change your last name, all you have to do is petition it to our committee for approval."

"Who's on the committee?"

"Me, Dante, Santiago, and President Brown." I smiled at him. "And I'm the only one on the committee who knows the Randall's as we do. They don't have the same hatred as the people from River Springs do."

"What would I change it to?"

"I'll tell you what," I said as I wiped some more rain from my face. "You pass the lie detector test, you're welcome to the last name Woodard."

"Really?" Joshua asked.

I shrugged. I surprised myself with how quickly I trusted Joshua. But I liked to think I could read people well. "Joshua Woodard. Has a pretty good ring to it."

"Your family won't care?" He shook his head back and forth, flinging water out of his hair.

"You *are* my family."

"Thanks, Emmie. Austin was right about what a good person you are."

I put up my hands. "Oh, trust me, I was worried at first. You're a Randall after all."

"Even after I killed Pierce?" he asked with raised eyebrows.

"Yes," I said. "But after our talk, I can tell you're nothing like your father."

He laughed. "So, I kill someone to save your life, and you still don't trust me, but I talk to you about making out and then you do."

It was my turn to laugh. "I never said I fully trusted you. I just said you're nothing like your father. But if you pass the test, I will fully trust you. You have my word."

Joshua stuck out his hand and I shook it. I hoped I hadn't made a deal with the devil.

CHAPTER 12

Vivica was waiting for us when we got back to New Haven. She was leaning against a tree, her hand on her hip, wearing her brown military uniform.

When she saw me, she reluctantly backed away from the tree and approached me, eyeing my face. "You look terrible."

"Thanks, Vivica," I said. "I missed you, too."

She ignored my sarcasm. "It's about time you got back. A lot has happened."

"Like what?" I asked, walking toward Headquarters. Tina, Santiago, and Gideon were behind me. Joshua had stayed by my side the entire trip. Everyone was still hesitant, not sure if they could trust him.

"For starters, Lou is even worse than when you left," Vivica said. "I think it's only a matter of days until he's gone." Her voice lacked any emotion. I still hadn't been able to figure her out. I didn't know if she didn't care about anyone but herself, or if it was just a block she put up to not let anyone in. "Also, Vice President Mendes showed up."

"My dad's here?" Santiago asked.

Vivica didn't even turn around to look at Santiago. "Yeah."

Santiago left us, finding Javier on the way to join up with their father.

I looked at Vivica. "Anything else?"

"The citizens from Juniper City are here." Vivica waved her hand like it was no big deal.

I stopped. "Are you serious? How many of them are there?"

Vivica didn't stop walking. "Only twelve."

I shook my head and ran to catch up with her, who took long strides. "That's it? What happened to them?"

"Ask them," Vivica said. "Besides, both our cities only showed up with ten."

"Why did you even bother coming out here if this is how you're going to act?" I asked. She annoyed me like no other.

"I was ordered to, so I did. Go to the infirmary. They're waiting for you." Vivica walked away.

"She seems nice," Joshua said beside me.

I let out a little laugh. "She's a little rough around the edges."

Tina, Gideon, Joshua, and I hurried over to the infirmary, stopping when we saw President Brown, Dante, Santiago, Javier, and a man I took to be Vice President Mendes standing in the hallway talking.

Dante saw me, his eyes going wide. He ran up to me, quickly assessing my wounds. "What happened, Emmie? Are you okay?"

"I'm horrible." I had barely recovered from my broken thumb I received back in River Springs from the underwater challenge in Recruitment. Now I had a broken nose to deal with. I wasn't in the mood for any of this. "What's going on? Vivica said the other city showed up."

Dante nodded. "A few hours ago." He paused for a moment. "Are you sure you don't want to talk about …" He pointed to my face.

I sighed. "I got beat up by my nemesis."

President Brown joined us. "We need to talk, now. Something big has come up. We'll go to Maya's room to talk."

"Who's Maya?" I asked.

"The fourth member of our club." The corner of Dante's mouth turned up. "I'm not sure if it's going to work out, though. She's actually calm and rational."

That brought a smile to my face. "That's exactly what we need right now." I turned to Gideon, who stood a little bit behind us. "Will you find Dr. Stacey and take him to Marie? The sooner they can get to work, the better."

"Sure thing, Emmie," Gideon said. With a small nod, he left.

Tina and Joshua were standing nearby. I looked at Tina. "Could you show Joshua where I live? He can stay with us for now."

"Are you sure that will be okay with your father?" Joshua asked.

"Yes, he'll understand. Just explain it to him. I'll be there as soon as I can, and we can talk more." I eyed his bag that he had strapped to his back and he nodded in understanding.

"Emmie," Santiago said to me as Tina and Joshua walked away, "this is my father, Oscar Mendes."

Vice President Mendes smiled big, shaking my hand firmly. "Nice to meet you, Emmie." He was tall and bulky like Santiago. He had brown eyes and his brown hair was cut close to his head.

"It's nice to meet you, too," I said.

"I wish it was under better circumstances," Vice President Mendes said as he stroked his goatee. His smile faded. "I'm sorry about Eric. From what I hear, he's an amazing young man."

I nodded, holding back the tears. "He is."

"Let's go in here," President Brown said, pointing to an infirmary room. He, Javier, and Vice President Mendes walked into the room. Both Santiago and Dante stayed outside.

"Em," Dante said, walking up close to me. My heart did a little flip. Vice President Oliver used to call me Em. "I'm so sorry about Eric." He swore under his breath. "I should've been there."

"You couldn't have stopped it," Santiago said. "It happened so fast. There were too many of them."

I looked away, tears forming in my eyes.

Dante pulled me into a hug. "We'll get this figured out, Em. We will."

I nodded slowly, pulling back. I looked up at him. "Have you grown? You seem taller."

Dante laughed. "Really? You want to talk about my growth spurt right now?"

"It's better than the alternative," I said quietly.

Santiago squeezed my arm and we walked into the infirmary room.

Maya was sitting up in her bed, her hands clasped together in her lap. She looked at me when I entered, her soft smile somehow comforting. Sorrow sat in her eyes and it made me wonder what she had been through.

All her features were soft and delicate, from her smooth, clear skin to her warm, brown eyes. Her black hair was cropped short, spiking out around her head, so she still had a spunky side.

"Emmie, this is Maya Chang," President Brown said, gesturing to Maya.

Maya had her back straight, her demeanor proper and elegant. She held out her hand, her two bracelets holding charms clinking together. "It's so nice to finally meet you."

I took her soft hand in mine, shaking gently. "You too." I eyed her left leg, which was wrapped up tightly. "Are you okay?"

"I was about to ask you the same thing," Maya said with a quiet laugh.

I put my hand up to my broken nose and winced. Marie would need to fix me up soon. "It's nothing that can't be healed."

Maya glanced down at her leg. "I wish I could say the same."

Dante moved a chair close to Maya's bed and motioned for me to have a seat. I touched him gently on the arm, smiling at him. Everyone else was already sitting down.

A young boy sat in a chair at the foot of Maya's bed. He looked a little younger than her, but I could tell by his round face and brown eyes that they were related. When he smiled at me, I could see the relation even more.

"I'm Bruce, Maya's brother," he said.

"It's nice to meet you." I looked at Maya. "What happened to your leg?"

"A sword," Maya said. "It gave me a nice, long gash. We wrapped it the best we could for the journey here, but it's been a few weeks and all the walking on it wasn't great."

Bruce grimaced. "You're lucky you didn't have to see it before. It was red, swollen, and oozing puss."

"I don't think she needed all the details, Bruce," Maya said, fingering one of the charms on her bracelet. "Anyway, Marie cleaned it the best she could, but she said I'd have a permanent scar and probably a little bit of a limp."

"So, this happened back in Juniper?" I asked.

Santiago let out a whistle. "They have a full-on war happening there."

My eyes widened. "Is it really that bad?"

"It unfortunately gets worse," President Brown said.

"How could it get worse than a war?" I asked. Something wet trickled out my nose.

"Emmie, you're bleeding." Dante stood and left the room, coming back shortly with a towel and Marie. Dante handed me the towel and I put it under my nose.

Marie let out a little gasp when she saw me. "Oh, Emmie, you look terrible."

I smiled under the towel. "Why does everyone keep telling me that?

"Because you look terrible," Santiago said, clasping his hands behind his head. I rolled my eyes and then winced at the movement.

Marie put her hand under my chin, turning my head left to right. Seeing her so close reminded me how long and curly here eyelashes were. "Hold that towel there for now. When your meeting's done, come straight to me."

"Yes, ma'am." I saluted her with my free hand.

Once Marie left the room, Vice President Mendes shut the door and sat back down.

"So, what's going on?" I asked.

I felt completely out of the loop, giving me another reason why I shouldn't go on trips. I missed everything that happened in New Haven, got the crap beat out of me, and had my boyfriend taken hostage.

President Brown looked at Maya, then Bruce, then Vice President Mendes.

I groaned in frustration. "Please, just tell me. I've already had a terrible week, so I can pretty much take anything right now. Throw it on me."

Vice President Mendes smiled. "Why don't we start with something easy? President Brown suggested that we have a vote now that I'm here to see who the president should be, but he seems to have been running things smoothly, so I nominated myself for vice president of New Haven to make things easier. Santiago, Dante, and Maya have already agreed, so it's all up to you now."

I put down my towel. "What about Maya and Bruce's dad?"

Bruce shifted in his seat and looked down at the ground. Maya sighed beside me.

"They're dead," Maya said, her voice quiet.

"I'm so sorry." I ran my fingers through my hair. The bad news kept piling up and I knew it was about to continue. I took in a deep breath. "The president of your city sounds like he's probably worse than the one from mine."

Bruce let out a little laugh. "He's one of the sweetest men I've ever met."

I looked at him, startled. "What?"

"Our dad was the president," Maya said. "It was the vice president who went corrupt and turned on Juniper. He started the war."

"But I thought it was all the vice presidents who were the good guys," I said, scratching the back of my head. I pulled my hand away when I realized I was probably getting blood in my hair.

"The prophecy never specifically stated that," President Brown said. "It just came to all the vice presidents at the time. Although, we had no idea that the vice president from Juniper was bad. He's been working with us for years, acting like he was on our side and the president was against us."

A thought came to my head. "But the vice president knows where New Haven is located."

There was a collective sigh in the room, except for Dante who swore instead. I couldn't believe it. They knew where we were. They'd already shown they were willing to go to war. And we had so few residents of New Haven. We had just brought back children. We had led them into a war zone.

I put my head in my hands. "Are they already on their way?" I really didn't want to know the answer.

Maya's voice was barely audible, but I heard her. "Yes."

CHAPTER 13

I didn't know whether to cry, yell, punch something, or scream out every swear word I knew, repeatedly. I settled with slamming my hand down on the arm of my chair. "How long do we have until they're here?"

"We're not sure," Vice President Mendes said. "A week at most. Probably sooner."

I let out a few of the swear words bouncing around in my head. "That isn't enough time."

Santiago laughed. "You're corrupting her already, Dante."

"It's good for the soul," Dante said with a shrug. He leaned forward, resting his forearms on his legs. "What's our strategy?"

"We need to get Mack and Terrance in here," President Brown said. "Let's take a small break and clear our heads. We'll meet back here in twenty minutes."

As everyone got up to leave, I placed my hand on Maya's arm. "I'm glad you're finally here. I was getting so worried."

Maya smiled. "I was worried, too. There were a few times

I thought I wouldn't make it." She sat back in her bed. "I'm just glad to be here now, resting."

"Maya, is there anyone left to rescue from your city?" I asked.

She shook her head. "I don't think so. They had wiped out everyone sympathetic to our cause. We were lucky to even getaway."

"They burned down all of our homes." Bruce frowned. "The whole place is so corrupt. There isn't a single decent person left. Their thoughts and ideas on how things should be handled are so messed up."

"I know the vice president will keep on attacking us until we're completely wiped out," Maya said.

"Unless we take them out first," Bruce said.

Maya let out a strained laugh. "And how do you propose we do that? Right now, we need to focus on the soldiers who will be here any day." She looked at her leg. "If I don't get well soon, I have no idea if I'll be able to fight."

"You don't need to fight," Bruce said. "You need to recover. You have a serious injury."

"I know," Maya said, turning a bracelet around on her wrist. "Bruce, why don't you go check on the rest of the Juniper members? Make sure everyone's okay."

Bruce pouted. "What about the meeting?"

"You don't need to be here for that," Maya said.

"You can't always boss me around, you know," Bruce said, folding his arms. Maya sighed.

I stood, my presence not needed. "I'll leave you two alone to work this out."

Leaving the room, I went toward Dee's room. I passed Lou's room on the way, so I peered in to check on him. James was asleep in a chair near the bed. I couldn't imagine what he felt, watching his son in the condition he was in.

"I'm not sure who looks worse," Lou said from his bed. He wore a weak smile.

I leaned against the door frame. "I haven't checked myself in a mirror yet, but I'm pretty sure it's me. Everyone keeps telling me how horrible I look."

"At least they're being honest with you," Lou said. "Everyone's sugar coating how I look. If I look as bad as I feel, I know it can't be good."

"They're just trying to be nice," I said with a shrug. "You're a kind person. I, on the other hand, can be a brat, so they don't have any problem telling me the truth."

Lou tried to laugh, but a cough came out instead. He looked a lot worse than when I left. "You speak up for yourself. I think that's a good thing." He put his head down. "I wish I was like that."

"You can be," I said. He looked up at me, surprise in his eyes. "You just have to demand it."

"Well, then I demand you tell me the truth about my condition," Lou said, his face serious. "How much longer do I have?"

I threw up my hands. "Hey, I just got back, so I have no idea. You'll have to ask Marie."

I saw Marie down the hall, so I called out to her. "Hey, Marie! Lou needs you." Giving Lou a wink, I left his room.

"I still need to evaluate you," Marie said as she passed me

in the hall.

"I'll be in Dee's room," I said.

Right when I entered Dee's room, Marie yelled out from Lou's room. "Dang it, Emmie!"

I smiled as I sat down in the chair next to Dee's bed. Dee looked at me, her eyebrows raised. "Well, don't you look beautiful, my dear Emmie."

I took her hand in mine. "Oh, I missed you dearly."

"I get that a lot," she said, crossing her feet at her ankles. "So, who do I need to eliminate for doing that to you?"

"Do you have to ask?" I smiled at her. "But I'm not letting you take her out. I want the satisfaction of doing it."

Dee shook her head. "You need to learn to share, Emmie. You can't have all the glory."

"I'll tell you what. When I get the honor of ending her, I'll throw in a few punches for you."

"Make them good and hard. A nice sucker punch would be good."

I raised my eyebrows. "What do you know about sucker punches?"

She smiled. "Rosie Mendes has been visiting me daily. I absolutely adore her. Do you know they fight for fun in Scorpion?"

"So, I've heard."

She squeezed my hand. "We have three major things to talk about. Let's start with Eric." She took her hand from mine and ran it through my hair. "You must be in pieces."

"A billion," I said, frowning. "It's killing me being here and not being able to do anything about it. I can't stomach the thought of never seeing him again."

Dee gasped. "Where's your necklace?"

I reached up to where it should've been. "I lost it during the fight."

"Oh, Emmie," she said, stroking my cheek.

"He'll just have to make me a new one when I see him again," I said, forcing a smile.

"Do you have a plan to get him back?"

I sighed. "Not yet. There's a bigger issue now that is unfortunately going to put rescuing Eric on the back burner."

"The second major thing to talk about," Dee said.

I noticed for the first time since entering the room that she looked a little worse than when I left. I pushed the thought from my mind.

"We're going to be attacked."

She nodded. "And soon from what I hear." A small smile came to her face. "You know, that's one good thing about being in here. Rosie likes to eavesdrop on her dad and President Brown's conversations. Then she likes to report everything she hears to me when she comes and visits."

"I need to meet this Rosie," I said. She sounded a lot like me.

Dee must have read my thoughts like she always does. "She's a mini Emmie."

"I just hope we can come up with a good strategy before the soldiers from Juniper get here."

"When are you going to talk about it?"

I looked at my wristwatch. "In a few minutes. I have to go back to Maya's room."

"Seriously, Emmie?" Marie said, storming into the room. "Why did you do that to me? I had to look that boy in the eye and tell him he didn't have much longer." She turned my chair so I could face her. She wiped the blood from my nose, not being the slightest bit gentle.

"Ouch," I said, trying to swat her hand away.

Marie smacked my hand out of her way. "You're a brat, you know that?"

I tried to nod, but she held onto my chin firmly so I couldn't move my head. "I know. But he wanted to know the truth."

"He didn't need to know the truth," Marie said.

"Yes, he did," Dee said. Marie and I both looked over at her. "You don't know what it's like being in our position. Everyone tries to avoid being honest with us when that's all we want. Let us know so we can start processing the information."

Marie turned my face back toward her and started bandaging my nose. "Well, it sucks to be the one to have to tell you. It's a horrible feeling."

"It's your job," I said.

Marie looked me in the eye. "A job I was forced to go into because I'm good at it."

For some reason, I was surprised to hear Marie say that. "You didn't want to be a nurse?"

"I did and didn't," Marie said. "Look, I love being able to help people. I love all the research I'm able to do. Alexander has been so helpful and having Dr. Stacey here is going to be amazing. He's a smart man. I think the three of us together might solve this." She finished taping my nose and stood up straight. "But having to look at Dee and Lou day in and day out is draining on a person. It's the part of the job I hate. But this is the job Infinity Corp gave me, so here I am."

"I'm going to ignore the fact that you just stated that looking at me daily isn't having the grand effect it normally has on people," Dee said, "and let you know that you're amazing at your job and I'm glad you're the one helping me out."

Marie smiled. "Thanks, Dee." She shook her head. "This part makes it even worse. The two people who are sick are the two sweetest people on the planet. You're both nice to me, which helps, but then it pisses me off at the same time because this shouldn't be happening to you." Her smile twisted a little. "Now, if it was Amber sitting in that bed …"

"We'd being having a party in the next room," I finished for her. Marie and Dee laughed. I looked at my watch. "Oh, I should probably get back there."

Dee grabbed my arm. "But major issue number three!"

"Which is?" I asked.

"Um, hello," Dee said, tilting her head. "My future husband. Did you find him?"

I wiggled my eyebrows. "Actually, I might have."

Dee's eyes went wide. "Really? Are you being serious?"

I nodded.

Dee sat up tall in her bed. "Okay, what's his name? What does he look like? How tall is he? What color is his hair? What's his smile like? Does he have good hygiene? Do you think he'll want a big family? I've always wanted a lot of kids." She stroked her chin, deep in thought. "Does he like brunettes? One a scale of one to ten, how cute are our kids going to be? Alright, tell the truth right here and now. How hot is he? I know looks shouldn't matter, but let's be honest, they do. How can you be with someone you're not attracted to?"

Marie and I couldn't contain our laughter.

Dee folded her arms in protest. "I'm being serious right now! These are important things to know." She took in a deep breath. "Oh, no, this isn't good. He can't see me like this. I look terrible." She looked at me, her eyes pleading. "Will you let him know that I usually look better? You know, more color in my skin, more meat on my bones."

I leaned in and kissed Dee on her cheek before I stood. "I love you buckets full. He's going to like you, no matter what."

Dee nodded. "I guess if we're going to be married, he'll have to accept me looking terrible sometimes. I mean, I know I'm stunning, but a girl can't look perfect all the time."

I tugged on one of her curls. "But you always do." I walked to the door and then turned around. "His name is Will Sanders."

"Will," Dee said. "I like that name. Dee Sanders. My heavens, it works."

I smiled to myself as I walked back to Maya's room. Marie, Dr. Stacey, and Alexander needed to find a cure, and soon. I needed my daily dose of Dee if I was going to survive myself.

CHAPTER 14

Maya was sitting up tall in her bed, the chair where Bruce sat before now filled by Mack. So, Maya won the argument.

"She smiles," Dante said when I entered the room.

President Brown, Vice President Mendes, Santiago, and Terrance were all seated. I took my seat between Dante and Maya, giving Dante a little smack on the head as I sat down. It felt good to hit someone. I normally hit my half-brother Derek daily, but I hadn't seen him in weeks.

"We need to get started," Mack said. "We don't know how much time we have until they get here."

"Tina and Javier are on guard duty right now," Terrance said. "We're going to have at least two people up in the tower every day until they come."

"What kind of weapons will they have?" Dante asked Maya.

"Swords," Maya said. "That's the only weapons we had."

Mack nodded. "That will give us a small advantage. We

have guns and bows and arrows which we can use to stop as many as we can from even getting in."

"I think it'll be best to push them back." Terrance rubbed his head. "We need to avoid them getting into the city if we can. The more we can stop them in the canyon, the better."

"Do you think we'll have time to construct some more towers to shoot from before they get here?" Santiago asked. "I think that would help. We need to be higher up."

President Brown nodded in agreement. "Let's have Archie draw something up and get started on that. We'll need as many citizens helping him out as we can."

"We need to focus on training the new arrivals," Mack said. "Everyone needs to be able to shoot a gun and fire an arrow."

"Who are we going to have fight?" Stretching my legs out, I crossed my feet at my ankles.

"Anyone over fourteen who are willing and able," Terrance said.

"What are we going to do with the children?" Maya asked. I wondered the same thing.

"We'll keep them deep in Headquarters, back in the infirmary," Vice President Mendes said. "The enemy would have to fight their way all through the city and break into Headquarters before they could get to them. We need to stop them before that happens."

"How many soldiers are we talking about?" I asked Maya. "Will a lot be coming?"

Maya nodded. "I think so. The vice president had an army put together of about five thousand."

My heart stopped. "There's that many?" I shook my head in disbelief. "We only have a little less than five hundred residents, some of whom are children."

"He's sending half of them first," Maya said. That didn't make it any better. "If that doesn't completely wipe us out, he'll send the rest. They were planning on leaving about a week or two after we left, but with our escape, I'm sure the vice president sent them sooner so we wouldn't have a lot of time to prepare."

Wipe us out. Hearing that sent a chill through my body. With twenty-five hundred of them and less than five hundred to fight for us, it was highly possible that we'd be wiped out in a matter of minutes.

Santiago whistled. "This is going to be wild, man. You think we can pull this off?"

"We don't have any other option," President Brown said with a grave look on his face. "We have to stop them."

The corner of Mack's mouth turned up a little, his version of a smile. "I have a few fun surprises for them that will help us out."

Dante rubbed his hands together. "I love surprises. What kind?"

"Grenades." Mack sat back in his chair. "A couple of rocket launchers, too. Have a pair of men up in the tower firing those things and you'll take out multiple soldiers with each hit."

"Can I please be one of those men?" Santiago asked, sitting on the edge of his chair. "Pretty please?"

Mack nodded. "Of course."

Santiago clapped his hands together. "Now I'm excited

about this."

"Well, if he gets a rocket launcher, I'm freaking lighting my arrows on fire," Dante said, his eyes eager.

"That'll leave me and Maya on the front line." I looked at Maya. "Do you think you can fight? We'll need your sword expertise."

Maya rubbed her leg. "Yes. I have to."

"Can you help train our members?" Terrance asked Maya.

"Sure. Bruce can help, too. He has excellent swordsmanship." She smiled, running a finger over the sword charm on her bracelet. "Not as good as me, but he's decent." When she caught me staring at all her charms, her smile grew. "Every year on my birthday, my parents would give me a charm of something I mastered that year." She pointed to the sword. "I got this one when I turned nine."

Dante elbowed me. "We just need to make sure Emmie has as many magazines on her as she can for her handgun. She can just fire those babies off like breathing air."

"What about ammo?" I asked, nudging Dante back. "How much do we have? All of our guns won't do any good if there's no ammo."

"We brought a ton of shotgun shells from Scorpion," Santiago said. "We loaded up about fifty cases into the truck before we left."

"I retrieved a lot of ammo for our rifles, shotguns, and handguns from River Springs." Mack gave a small smile as he shook his head. "Everyone thought I was crazy for loading up half a bus with just ammo, but we needed that more than anything."

"What about the grenades and rocket launchers?" Dante asked.

Mack scratched the back of his head. "We have around a hundred grenades. As for the rockets, they were harder to get my hands on. Plus, we didn't have much stored in River Springs anyway. I think I ended up with ten."

Santiago frowned. "I only get to set that baby off five times? That's going to be the shortest relationship I've ever had." He smirked. "Oh wait, the second shortest."

Dante's eyes lit up. "I'm going to need to hear that story."

"Oh, it's hot," Santiago said, his smile mischievous.

Mack looked somber as he spoke. "We need to remember this is no laughing matter." He looked at Dante and Santiago. "We have to take this seriously. We're going to be outnumbered six to one and we have a limited supply of ammo. Even in our best-case scenario, a lot of people are going to die."

"Mack's right," President Brown said. "The outcome of this battle will be horrendous." The room went silent for a minute, all of us soaking in the information. After a while, the president cleared his throat. "We can have Archie get to work on making arrows. I'll have him get as many helpers as he can from Kingsland who know what to do."

"Alright, President Brown and Vice President Mendes do you mind working up an attack plan for us?" Mack asked.

"Sure," President Brown said. Vice President Mendes nodded in agreement.

Mack sat forward. "Terrance and I will round up everyone that can fight. We'll split everyone into groups and have them rotate through different training instructors. Dante, Vivica, and Terrance can teach archery. Santiago, Emmie, and I will teach them how to use a gun. Let's have Fernando, Javier, and Tina teach self-defense and fighting techniques in case it comes down to bare-knuckle fighting. I'll have Gideon walk between each group, taking note of who's good at what so we know where to put people when the time comes." Mack looked at Maya. "How many swords were you able to bring with you?"

"I think we have about twenty in all," Maya said as she ran her hand over her spiked hair.

Mack nodded. "We'll have Maya and Bruce teach the residents how to wield a sword. We don't have much to work with, but we'll acquire more swords as we kill the enemy."

"Sounds like a plan," Terrance said as he stood. "Let's get to work."

I put my hand on Dante's arm, holding him from getting up. Glancing over at Santiago, I waited until he made eye contact with me and then mouthed, "*Stay.*" Once everyone else was out of the room, I talked with my fellow revolutionaries.

"What's up, Emmie?" Dante asked.

"I had an interesting chat with Joshua Randall on the way back to New Haven."

"Who's that?" Maya asked.

I sat back in my chair, touching my nose. It still ached. "My half-brother and the son of the president of Infinity Corp."

"Are you sure we can trust this guy?" Santiago asked. "You've talked about President Randall like he's El Diablo himself and now we're just supposed to trust his son?"

I laughed. "I know, it's crazy. I'm not even sure yet if we can trust him, but I'm going to for now since Austin vouched for him." I wasn't sure if I should bring this up since I hadn't had a chance to talk to Joshua yet, but the impending battle changed everything. "He brought a lie detector test with him."

Dante folded his arms. "A lie detector test?"

I nodded as I pulled my legs in, tucking them under the chair. "It's a machine that can tell if you're lying or not. I think we need to use it on all of the New Haven residents."

Maya raised her eyebrows. "All of them?"

"All of them," I said. "We're about to go to war. We need to know who we can fully trust. All our lives are on the line and the last thing we need is someone turning on us. We obviously have a leak from River Springs."

"You think so?" Maya asked.

"They knew we were coming," I said. The scene replayed in my mind, making me cringe. "That ambush was staged."

Santiago nodded. "They were prepared for us, no question about that."

"You think now is the best time?" Dante asked. "We have so much training to do."

I sat forward, resting my arms on my legs. "I know, but I think this is pressing. I was thinking we could have Naomi and Derek run the tests while we're training. We'll just cycle all the residents through." I didn't relish the thought of Derek doing it, but he was our tech guy.

"Can we trust Naomi and Derek?" Santiago asked.

"We'll give them the test first," I said. "We can have Joshua show us how to use it. Maybe I can have my dad sit in there, too."

Dante nodded. "I think we should do it."

"Do you think the residents will get mad?" Maya asked. "We all came here to be free and the first thing we do is question everyone?"

I tucked my hair behind my ear. "They might, but I'm not sure if we have a choice right now. Time isn't on our side."

"If we all do it, the president, the vice president, and the four of us included," Santiago said, motioning to us, "they might be more willing."

"Hopefully they'll understand that we're doing this for their protection." Dante smiled. "Plus, we'll know to keep our eyes on whoever gets the most upset."

"I'll get the machine from Joshua and take this to the president and vice president," I said. "If they agree, we'll start with them and Joshua, then all of us, then Derek and Naomi and go from there."

"What are you going to ask everyone?" Maya reached out and rubbed her leg, wincing in the process.

Dante scratched his head as he sat back in his chair. "Easy. Are you an enemy?"

"Can we trust you?" I said.

"Should I take you out back and beat the living crap out of you?" Santiago said, swinging a few punches into the air. I liked that one the best.

"All we need to know is if they're on our side," I said. "We're not going to be asking personal questions about their lives. I just want to know if they've been lying to us and have leaked any information that can compromise New Haven."

Santiago snapped his fingers. "They should be in and out in no time."

Maya slowly swung her legs over the edge of her bed. "Well, let's get going then."

"Should we do something at the end of our meetings?" Dante asked. "Like some type of chant or high five? Something to unite us?"

Santiago nodded. "I like the idea. My trainer and I would say a little prayer before each boxing match. It cleared my head and got me focused on the task at hand." Santiago held out his hands to Dante and Maya. They each took one of his hands and then both took one of mine, and we all closed our eyes.

Santiago took a deep breath. "Lord, give us the strength to carry out our mission. Help us to keep our eyes clear and focused, our hearts full and open, so we can win this battle for New Haven. Amen."

Santiago and I helped Maya stand. She wobbled a little, but then steadied herself. Dante came in close, putting his arm around Santiago's and my shoulders. I put my arm around Dante's and Maya's shoulders, and she followed suit by putting her arms around my and Santiago's shoulders. We leaned in close, our foreheads touching.

"For New Haven," Dante said, his voice excited.

"For New Haven," Maya and I said at the same time.

"For New Haven!" Santiago shouted.

CHAPTER 15
Eric

The wings from the butterfly were pressed deep into my skin, my fist fastened tight around it.

By some miracle, I found Emmie's necklace on the ground as I dragged by two men toward the cave. The butterfly and the twine holding it were brown, making it almost impossible to see in the dirt. My window of opportunity to grab it was mere seconds, but it ended up in my hand.

It had all happened so fast. As I fought with one man, another approached from the back, but there was nothing I could do. He jammed the butt of his gun into my head, sending me to the ground. I tried to get back up, but the man I had been fighting with slammed his foot down on my right arm, pinning me down as the other man grabbed my left arm.

After they pulled me to my feet, Emmie got knocked down. Mack appeared behind her, shooting her attacker in the head. As the man's lifeless body fell to the ground, Mack took

Emmie's unconscious body and slung it over his shoulder, carrying her away.

Another man headed toward Mack and Emmie with his gun raised, so I shouted as loud as I could and thrashed my body all around. The two men holding me kept their grip firm, but it was enough to distract the man about to shoot Mack.

Mack noticed, shot the other man, and took off running, shouting for everyone else from New Haven to retreat. Mack gave me one fleeting glance and I nodded, telling him they had to leave.

I continued to throw my body around, yelling and kicking as much as I could. Another man approached, his gun pointed at my head, his finger on the trigger. He was about to pull it when I heard a shout.

"We take him alive!" Footsteps approached from behind and the person the voice belonged to stepped into view. Dean Johnson. "The president wants him alive." He glared at me. "For now."

Dean motioned for his men to fall back and I sighed in relief knowing my comrades had escaped. That my Emmie had escaped.

They took me underground below Infinity Corp's headquarters and threw me in a small, concrete room. A mirror resided on one wall and I was certain they were watching me through the other side. Dean and a few of his men had each taken a go at me, beating me to try to get information. But it hadn't worked.

Hours had passed. My feet and hands were bound, so I couldn't move from the cold floor. A few of my ribs were broken, along with my nose. My left eye was swollen shut. The metallic taste of blood filled my mouth from where they had knocked out a tooth.

There went my perfect smile.

I held tightly onto Emmie's necklace and pictured her beautiful face in my mind. I closed my eyes and concentrated on her green eyes, gorgeous smile, and the best set of lips I'd ever seen.

My hours alone in the room turned into days with a minimal amount of food and water and no sense of hope. I grew weaker, my heart beating slower.

The door finally opened, and Dean Johnson entered the room. He stood towering above me, puffing out his chest. I didn't know why he tried to act so manly, showing off his muscles. He wasn't my type.

Dean squatted down and grabbed a fistful of my hair, pulling my head off the ground and toward his face. A strong waft of garlic came out of his mouth when he spoke, making me heave. "I'll give you one last chance, Greene. You tell us what we need to know, and you'll live."

I'd rather die than tell them anything. I smiled, ignoring the pain from a split in my lip. When I tried to speak, my voice barely came out. My throat stung from lack of water or use in days.

"What was that?" Dean asked, coming even closer to me.

I forced the word out. "Never."

Dean slammed my head into the ground, causing a throbbing sensation to penetrate my skull. "Wrong answer." He stood and barked a command at someone. "Inject him."

"Are you sure?" The person asked. "We've never used this before. We don't know if it will work or what the side effects will be."

"I'm willing to take that risk," Dean said. "Now do it!"

When the person approached, I took every ounce of energy I had left and swung my legs under theirs, knocking them to the ground.

Dean was on top of me quickly, pinning my arms and legs down. "Do it! NOW!"

A sharp needle pricked my left arm. The pressure of Dean's body soon left and the two of them retreated from my prison.

I lay there and waited for the drug to kick in, not knowing what would happen or if I'd survive. Shifting my arms toward my side, I took Emmie's necklace and put it in my pocket for safekeeping.

A minute later the door opened, and two people came in. One of them sat me up and the other held my mouth open, pouring in water. I didn't even bother to see who the people were, I just drank the water until they pulled away and left me alone again.

It didn't take long for the effects of the injection to kick in. My legs started to tingle and go numb until all the feeling left.

Next, it was my arms. Soon, I couldn't move anything below my neck. I still had control of my head and face, but even that seemed limited.

The room spun, colors swirling in the air. I had a sudden urge to laugh. Once the laughter came, it didn't stop. I laughed so hard, tears poured down my cheeks.

I took a few breaths, trying to calm my laughter. Warmth covered my thighs. "Oh, I peed myself!" My stomach hurt from all the laughing. "I peed myself!"

A loud bang echoed in the room, but I couldn't move myself to see what had happened. "What was that? Is someone there?" Clicking my tongue against the roof of my mouth, I counted each second, waiting for a response, but only silence filled the air. "I know someone's here. Come out, come out wherever you are." The laughter boiled back up.

"What's wrong with him?" Dean asked.

"I have no idea," Mr. Man-who-injected-me said. Bad man.

Dean "Mr. Bald" Johnson sighed rather loudly. "Bring in a chair and strap him to it."

"Yes, sir," Mr. Man said.

I could see Mr. Bald's shoes in front of me. They were ugly. "I don't like your shoesies. They is ugly." Suddenly I was lifted into the air. "I'm flying! Can you see this? I'm flying!"

The room spun at a high speed as my body was turned. "No! Too fast! Slow down!"

Mr. Man tied a rope around me. Something about his face looked familiar.

"Do I know you?" I asked Mr. Man.

"No," Mr. Man said. His eyes told me he was lying.

Mr. Bald stood there watching. His head was shiny.

"Have you ever tried having hair?" I asked Mr. Bald. "You might look prettier."

"How in the world are we supposed to get anything out

of him when he's acting like this?" Another man. Lots of men in my room.

Mr. Man finished tying me up. "It's supposed to loosen him up. Make him talk."

"Talk is fun," I said.

The other man came into view. Hey, I knew him! "I know you! You're Whitty boy!" I frowned. "I don't like you. You a bad man."

"I'm not sure how long this drug will remain in his system, President Randall," Mr. Man said. "But you should have enough time to get what you need." Mr. Man left the room.

"Bye-bye," I said to Mr. Man.

Whitty Boy looked at me. His eyes didn't look happy. "I hear you haven't been cooperating."

I giggled. "Co-op-er-a-ting. Funny word."

"What's your name?" Whitty Boy asked.

"What's yours?"

"I asked you first," Whitty Boy said.

"I asked you second."

Whitty Boy said a naughty word. "How's this supposed to help me? Dean, help him out."

Mr. Bald hit me in the stomach, but I couldn't feel it. Mr. Bald glared at me. "The president asked you a question."

I wanted to shake my head, but it wouldn't move very much. "He not president. He bad man."

"Well, the *bad man* asked you a question," Mr. Bald said. "What's your name?" When I didn't answer, he punched me again.

"Okay, I'll tell you," I said. "Stop wasting your energy.

Eric is my name."

Whitty Boy bent down a little and stared me in the eye. "Can you feel anything?"

"Nope." I smiled at him. I liked to smile.

"So, we can't even hurt him to get information out of him," Whitty Boy said. He was talking to the mirror. Silly Whitty Boy. Mirrors can't talk.

Mr. Bald went and pouted in the corner.

"Are you hungry, Eric?" Whitty Boy asked.

My tummy did seem like it could use food. I think. "I guess."

"Would you like some food? Maybe some water?" Whitty Boy asked. "It'll give you strength."

I tried to raise my eyebrows. "Big strength like Mr. Bald?"

Whitty Boy looked at Mr. Bald and then back at me. "Just like Mr. Bald."

"Yes, sir," I said.

"Good," Whitty Boy said. "All you need to do is answer a few questions and then we will get you a nice, warm meal."

"What kind of meal?" I didn't want anything yucky.

"Steak, potatoes, anything you want," Whitty Boy said.

I kept my voice low. "We can't eat meat in River Springs. We get in big trouble by Infinity Corp."

Whitty Boy winked at me. "Then we won't tell anyone. It'll be between you and me."

"And Mr. Bald," I pointed out.

"And Mr. Bald," Whitty Boy said, nodding.

"What would you like to know?" I asked.

"Where's New Haven located?" Whitty Boy asked.

I laughed. "In New Haven."

I don't think Whitty Boy liked my answer. His lips pursed. "Is New Haven near water? Near a mountain? Out in the desert?"

"I not spoze to tell," I said, making sure to be quiet.

Whitty Boy squatted so his head was a little below mine. "You can tell me. I'm your friend."

"Bad man might be watching," I said. "They is always watching."

"No one is watching," Whitty Boy said. "Just tell me what the area looks like. Are there trees? Sand? Flowers? Grass?"

"Okay, I tell you," I said. "There is a sky. It blue sometimes. Gray other times."

"What else?" Whitty Boy asked.

I opened my mouth, but then closed it. My head shouted to stay silent. Did I trust my head or Whitty Boy? "I see birds sometimes."

"Good," Whitty Boy said. "What kind of birds?"

"Ones with wings," I said. "They can fly! So can I. I'm a birdy."

Whitty Boy said another bad word. "Just tell me, Eric! Where is New Haven? Who is helping you?"

"Everybody helps me," I said. "Emmie, Mack, Tina, the president."

"Who's your president?" Whitty Boy asked.

"Mr. President," I said. Wasn't he listening to me?

Mr. Bald sighed as he paced in the corner of my room.

"What's his name?" Whitty Boy asked. "His first and last name?"

I smiled at Whitty Boy. "First name Mr. Last name President."

"Someone from River Springs is helping you out," Whitty Boy said. "Who is it? Is it Austin? Luke?"

My smile left. "Luke not my friend. He always listens to his daddy."

"Okay, not Luke," Whitty Boy said. "What about Austin?"

"Do you think my legs will always be like this?" I asked. "I can't feel them. Are they still there?" I looked down and let out a breath. "Oh, good, they still there."

"I'm done with this!" Whitty Boy yelled so loud it rang in my ears. He looked at Mr. Bald. "Untie him and take the chair out of the room. Take out Carl, too. His drug didn't work. His services are no longer needed."

"Who's Carl?" I asked. I didn't know a Carl.

"He's a dead man." Whitty Boy left the room.

Mr. Bald came to me and untied me, letting my limp body fall to the floor. He stepped on my arm and turned it funny. I heard a snap but felt nothing.

"You'll feel that when you get the feeling back in your body." Mr. Bald punched me in the jaw and left the room, taking the chair with him.

The pain from that blow came. I still had some feeling in my face. The room spun again, so I closed my eyes. Emmie's face showed up and I smiled. She was so pretty.

My head became heavy and it took a lot of effort to breathe. My heart rate slowed way down. Each intake of breath was tortuous. I had to will myself to breathe. I wasn't sure why, but I felt the need to stay alive. Every cell in my body screamed for me to let go, but I clung onto life as best as I could. I wasn't sure how much longer it would last, though.

CHAPTER 16
Emmie

I knocked softly on the door to the conference room where President Brown and Vice President Mendes were working out an attack plan for saving New Haven.

Joshua stood next to me, holding his bag that contained the lie detector test. He was shaking slightly, probably from nerves. His white button-down was untucked, the top button undone, his blue tie loose around his neck. I thought he'd want to change, but he seemed to like that look.

"Come in," President Brown said.

I stepped into the room with Joshua right at my heels. President Brown eyed me and then Joshua.

"Aren't you supposed to be leading training?" President Brown asked me. He had ditched his polo and slacks, switching to his military uniform.

I nodded slowly. "Yes, sir, but I have something I wanted to bring to you. Then I'll get to training." My palms were sweating, not sure how my plan would be accepted.

President Brown pointed at the two chairs to the left of him. Vice President Mendes sat at his right, also in a military uniform.

I took a deep breath and sat down in the chair next to the president. Joshua sat down next to me, placing his bag on the floor.

"Make this quick," President Brown said.

I had to sell this the best I could. "Sir, my brother Joshua brought something from River Springs that we think will be useful."

"I don't think I've ever been introduced to your brother." Vice President Mendes stuck out his hand. "I'm Vice President Oscar Mendes."

Joshua gave me a sideways glance before he shook the vice president's hand. "I'm Joshua … Randall."

The vice president raised his eyebrows, looking at me. "Your brother from the *other* side of your family."

Even though everything in me wanted to scream that Whit Randall was not my family, I contained myself. "Yes, sir."

President Brown narrowed his eyes at Joshua. "Can I ask why you're here?" He turned his eyes to me. "And why I should trust him?"

Joshua cleared his throat. "I know, sir, that you should have no reason to trust me. We both know what my father is capable of. But I swear to you, I'm nothing like him and I'm willing to prove it."

Joshua reached into his bag, pulled out a machine, and set it on the table. It was just a small, square, black box, with a couple of cords running out from it. That was what he'd been talking about the whole time? I had a sinking feeling in my stomach that I'd made a mistake.

"What is that?" President Brown asked.

"It's a machine that can tell if someone's lying to you or not." Joshua set a round, silver disk on top of the box. "This disk contains the software for it. All we have to do is install it on one of your computers and hook up the machine to the computer." He picked up one of the cords that had a small black rectangular-shaped box on the end of it. He pressed down on one side of it and the box opened down the middle. "Just put this on someone's finger and it will be able to read their pulse."

"What use is it to know their pulse?" Vice President Mendes asked.

"You ask them some questions," Joshua said. "If their pulse is regular, they're telling the truth. If it's beating out of control, they're probably lying."

"Probably?" President Brown asked, arching an eyebrow.

Joshua shrugged. "You can never really be one hundred percent certain, but it's pretty accurate." He looked at me. "President Randall used them all the time on people he didn't trust."

"What are you suggesting we do with this?" President Brown asked, looking at me.

Wiping my sweaty palms on my pants, I took a few deep breaths before I spoke. "Use it on the residents of New Haven."

Vice President Mendes laughed, the sound strained. "That's madness. We can't do that."

"Why not?" I asked.

President Brown intertwined his fingers, pressing his thumbs together. "It's a matter of ethics, Emmie."

I shook my head. "I couldn't give a crap about ethics right now."

President Brown started to say something, but I cut him off. "Look, I understand that this sounds like we're invading everyone's privacy but that's not what we'll be doing. I just want to ask everyone that has entered our city if they truly want to be on our side. I want to know if we can trust them and if they've leaked anything that can hurt our city or our people in any way."

"This is for everyone's benefit," Joshua said. "We're only thinking about the safety of everyone here. If there's a traitor in your city, don't you want to know about it?"

Vice President Mendes pointed at the machine. "And that little box is supposed to tell us if someone is a traitor?"

"It will tell you if they're hiding something," Joshua said. "You can do whatever you want with them after that. Interrogate them. Search them or their home for any evidence."

"Now you want us to invade our citizen's homes?" President Brown asked, his voice not hiding his anger. This wasn't going as I had planned.

"Sir, please," I said. "Let's just start with the test. Ask a couple of questions. It'll take just a minute for each resident. Once we have the results, we can decide what to do from there."

President Brown stood and paced the room—never a

good sign. "I'm not sure why we should even do this in the first place. The point of New Haven was to get away from the politics and restrictions all the cities had. We've only been here a few months and you want to start questioning everyone and their motives?"

"Under normal circumstances, I'd say no." I sat forward in my chair, clasping my hands together on the table. "But we have a leak here. We have a traitor amongst us, and that traitor led us into an ambush. We're lucky no one died." I closed my eyes and took a deep breath, trying to calm my nerves. "That traitor got Eric taken hostage by River Springs. They might even end up getting him killed."

"I still think there are better ways to go about this," President Brown said.

"Maybe," I said, "but I think any other solution will take a lot of time that we don't have. If that traitor stays out there, more lives could be at risk. We promised to protect the citizens of this city. How are we protecting them by letting a traitor run loose?"

The president stopped walking. He sighed and leaned down, pressing his palms against the edge of the table.

I looked at the box, then at Joshua, and then at the president. "Do me first."

President Brown raised his eyebrows. "You're volunteering to do this and go first?"

"Yes, sir," I said. "Ask me anything you want. Once I'm finished, you can decide if you want to continue."

"And it will just take a couple of minutes?" President Brown asked Joshua.

Joshua nodded. "Yes, sir. I just need a computer to install the software and hook it up to."

President Brown looked at Vice President Mendes, but the vice president just shrugged. "This is your decision, Wallace. I have no idea what to think."

"Fine, let's just do Emmie for now," President Brown said. "But if this proves to be a waste of my time, I'm destroying that machine and will hold Emmie personally responsible."

"Yes, sir," I said.

We left the conference room and headed down the hall. I had only gone two steps when a small sneeze came from behind me. When I turned around, someone quickly stepped back into the room across from the conference room.

"I have to use the bathroom," I said to the others. "I'll meet up with you in just a couple of minutes." They all nodded and continued down the hallway.

I waited until they were far enough away and went to the door, slowly opening it. I flicked the light switch on to reveal an empty room. I was about to turn away when another sneeze sounded behind the door. I stepped into the room and closed the door.

Standing there was a beautiful young girl, probably around nine. She had long black hair that had the slightest curl to it. Her round, hazel eyes lit up when she realized saw me.

"Emmie?" she asked, her voice soft and sweet. I nodded and the next thing I knew, her arms were around my waist, squeezing tight.

I held her close and laughed. "You must be Rosie." She

nodded against my stomach. I pulled her back, putting my hands on her shoulders. "Well, let me get a good look at you."

Rosie stood tall, straightening out her white, knee-length dress. Purple flowers were embroidered on it, and a purple sash was tied around the waist. Her dress poofed out as she did a twirl for me.

"That is the most beautiful dress I've ever seen," I said, running my finger along one of the flowers on her shoulder.

Rosie beamed. "Thank you. My nana made it for me."

"Your nana?" I asked.

"Yes." Rosie smiled at my confused expression. "It's what I called my grandma."

"You said called. Has she passed on?"

She nodded. "Yes, just last year. She was an amazing seamstress."

"It sure looks like it."

"My daddy said Joshua was from your other side of the family. What does that mean?"

I smiled. "Were you listening at the door?"

"Always," she said, her smile huge.

A laugh escaped my mouth. I had the same bad habit. "Joshua and I share the same dad, but not the same mom."

She scratched her chin. "And Derek?"

"Same mom, different dad."

"I knew a family like that back home." She looked up at me. "So, do you like my brother?"

Her question threw me off guard. I tucked my hair behind my ear. "What do you mean?"

"Do you like Santiago?"

"Yeah, he's a nice guy."

Rosie shook her head. "I mean, do you *like like* my brother."

I pursed my lips, wondering why she would ask such a thing. "No, I have a boyfriend."

"I know." She twisted her hips back and forth making her dress sway. "Dee told me all about you two. She said it was love at first sight."

I smiled. "It kind of was. We did hit it off pretty fast."

"But you don't like my brother, right?"

Why did she keep asking me that? "No, of course not. I love Eric."

She nodded. "That's what I keep telling Santiago, but he won't listen. He just keeps talking about you. All. The. Time. It's annoying." She blushed. "I mean, I like hearing about you, it's just the way he talks about you."

I scrunched my eyebrows together. "Santiago talks about me?"

"Yes. My mom says he's smitten."

I bit my lip. "But he must talk about girls all the time. He flirts with everyone."

Rosie giggled, enjoying this conversation. "Oh, he'll flirt with any girl. But he never talks about them with us. He brings you up any chance he gets. Emmie said this. Emmie did that. Emmie's tough. Emmie's hot. Emmie would look good with her nose pierced."

I touched my bandaged nose and shook the thought from my head. "Well, I'm sure he'll get over it soon. There are plenty of pretty girls here and the numbers will keep growing."

She shrugged. "Whatever you say."

"Well, I have to get going." I brushed back some hair that had fallen over her eye. "I'm so glad I finally got to meet you."

"Me, too." She hugged me. "I'll tell Santiago you don't like him. It probably won't do any good, but I'll still tell him." She pulled back and looked up at me. "Just watch out for him. He can be forward sometimes. And he usually doesn't stop until he gets what he wants."

I stroked her hair. "That's good to know. But I'm sure it's no big deal." I gave her another quick hug and left the room, trying not to think about Santiago having a crush on me. It was just a phase. It had to be.

CHAPTER 17

We walked into the security room where Naomi sat at a computer up against the wall, her back to us, typing feverishly.

Derek sat next to her, gazing longingly into her eyes, completely oblivious to anything around him. He scratched at an itch on his chest—right over the camera lens shaped as a shield on his shirt—not taking his eyes off her.

I looked at Joshua and rolled my eyes.

"Derek," President Brown said, making Derek jump in his seat.

Derek pressed his hand against his chest. "Scare the crap out of me, why don't you?" He looked up at the president, his cheeks turning red. "I mean, hello, sir."

"We have a task for you and Naomi," President Brown said.

Vice President Mendes found a seat near the door and sat down, making himself comfortable.

Naomi turned around in her seat, facing us. "What can I

help you with, sir?"

"We have a machine we need to hook up to a computer," President Brown said. "Do you have one you can spare?"

Derek pointed to an unused computer near where I stood. "You can use that one."

President Brown looked at Joshua. "Hand the software to Naomi. She can install it for us."

Naomi stood and went to the computer, sitting down in the chair in front of it. She held out her hand and Joshua placed the disk on her palm.

Derek came over and stood near me, almost in a protective way. "How do we know there isn't some virus on that disk?"

"Who cares?" Naomi said. We all looked at her. "This is a standalone computer. It's not hooked up to our network in anyway. If there's a virus, it'll only affect this computer, which happens to be a piece of crap anyway which is why we don't use it." She shoved the disk in the drive and began the installation.

Derek looked Joshua up and down, standing up taller and straighter as he did. Derek was already a lot taller than Joshua, so I didn't know what the point of it was.

"What's he doing here?" Derek asked me, his voice quiet but still loud enough for Joshua to hear.

"What do you think?" I asked Derek. "To be a part of New Haven."

"And you trust him?" Derek asked, puffing out his chest a little, the shield shaped lens on his shirt looking like it was zeroing in on Joshua. It was Derek's favorite shirt because security was his way of protecting people.

I eyed the machine in Joshua's hands. "I'm about to find out."

Joshua pulled up a chair for me. "Have a seat."

As I sat down in the chair, Joshua set the box on the table near Naomi and clamped the pulse detector over my finger. Naomi plugged the machine into the computer and turned it on.

"So, what's this supposed to do?" Naomi asked, picking it up with her hand and looking it over.

"Tell us if Emmie's a liar or not," Joshua said, smiling at me.

Derek snorted. "Well, we all know the answer to that. She has no problem giving you her honest opinion."

President Brown sat down. He looked at Derek and Joshua. "You boys can have a seat."

"I'm good," Derek said, making sure his back was straight and his head high.

"I don't mind standing," Joshua said. At least his stance seemed more relaxed and normal looking.

I shook my head. Boys.

"It's ready to go," Naomi said.

I looked at the president. "Ask me anything you want."

"Start with a basic question we all know the answer to," Joshua said, running his hand down his tie. "It'll give you a sense of what her normal heart rate is. Stick to questions that have either a yes or no answer."

President Brown looked at me. "Is your name Emmie?"

"Yes," I said.

Derek looked closely at the screen, pressing his chest up against Naomi's shoulder. "She's telling the truth."

Naomi pushed Derek away as she sighed. "Well, obviously."

"Are you a resident of New Haven?" President Brown asked.

"Yes," I said.

"Do you think I'm the coolest person ever?" Derek asked.

"Yes," I said.

Derek smiled, looking over at Joshua. "I thought so."

"She's lying," Naomi said, pointing at the screen.

Derek's smile faded as he glanced over at the screen. "That's impossible."

"I just wanted to make sure it could detect a lie," I said. Joshua laughed, making Derek glare at him.

"Fine, do you think Joshua's cool?" Derek asked.

I tried to control my smile. "Yes."

"Truth," Naomi said.

Derek groaned in frustration and went to sit down on the other side of the room. Joshua leaned against the wall, smiling, tucking his hands into his pants pockets.

"Have you leaked any information that could threaten New Haven in any way?" President Brown asked.

"No," I said.

Naomi had watched Derek walk away. She pried her eyes away from him to look at the screen. "Truth." She looked over at me, but I couldn't read her expression.

"Do you believe in what New Haven's doing?" President Brown asked.

"Yes," I said, ignoring Naomi's gaze and keeping my eyes on President Brown.

"Do you trust me and Vice President Mendes?" President Brown asked.

"Yes," I said.

"Would you ever do anything to harm New Haven, me, Vice President Mendes, or any of your fellow revolutionaries?" President Brown asked.

I shook my head. "No."

"All truths," Naomi said.

President Brown leaned forward, looking me straight in the eye. "Do you think this test is necessary for the good of our city?"

My gaze on the president stayed firm. "Yes."

"Truth," Naomi said.

President Brown sat back in his chair and nodded. "That's good enough for me." Pointing to the chair I was in, he looked over at Joshua. "You next."

I stood and switched places with Joshua. His hands shook as Naomi hooked the machine up to him, so I gave him a reassuring smile when he looked at me.

When Naomi nodded at the president, he started. "Is your name Joshua Randall?"

"Yes," Joshua said. His leg bounced as he tapped his fingers against it.

"Truth," Naomi said.

"Do you trust your father?" President Brown asked.

"No," Joshua said.

"Are you here as a spy?" President Brown asked.

Joshua looked me straight in the eye. "No."

"Would you do anything to harm New Haven, me, Vice President Mendes, or any of the revolutionaries?" President Brown asked.

"No," Joshua said. His leg had stopped moving and his eyes held a fierce determination.

President Brown took a deep breath. "Do you believe in what New Haven is doing?"

"Yes," Joshua said.

"Are you on President Randall's side?" President Brown asked.

"No," Joshua said, shaking his head.

"One more question," President Brown said. He leaned in close to Joshua, his eyes intense. "Have you ever done anything in your life that you're ashamed of?"

Joshua winced. After a moment, he cleared his throat. "Yes."

Naomi looked at the president. "All truths."

President Brown nodded in approval. He volunteered himself to go next and then Vice President Mendes went. They both passed, which didn't surprise me. Derek went and passed, and then Naomi went. She passed, but there was one thing that surprised me.

Partway during her test, Derek interjected with a question.

"Do you think you could ever like me as more than a friend?" Derek asked.

"No," Naomi said. She didn't hesitate with her answer, but there was a slight blip on the screen, making me wonder if that answer would one day change. I shook my head in disbelief.

When I saw the sad look on Derek's face, I felt sorry for him. He couldn't help the fact that he was born socially challenged.

President Brown clasped his hands together. "I want to make one thing clear. This test is voluntary. I will not force any resident to take it. I don't want to make a big deal out of this and don't want any resident to feel pressured to take it. Does everyone understand?" When we all nodded, he continued. "I'll leave Naomi and Derek in charge of the rest of the tests."

"We can have Rosie bring the residents back and forth," Vice President Mendes said. "With her sweet demeanor, no one should feel guilty about saying no."

President Brown nodded. "Sounds good." He looked back and forth between Derek and Naomi, I'm sure unsettled about leaving just the two of them in charge. I knew that had to do with Derek more than Naomi.

"I can ask my dad to sit in here and help," I said to the president.

"I like that idea." President Brown's shoulders relaxed. "We'll have Rosie go get him first. He can take the test if he wants and then he can stay and supervise."

President Brown, Vice President Mendes, and Joshua all left the room. I was about to leave, but I looked at Derek one more time which I instantly regretted.

I sighed and went to his side, keeping my voice low. "Don't give up, tiger."

Derek grunted. "Like you care."

"I do." I put my hand on his arm. "Dad always told us to never give up on what we wanted. Maybe you can just ease up on her a little. She doesn't seem to like the direct approach."

Derek looked at me, hopeful. "Do you think she could like me one day?"

I nodded. "Just take it easy. Be subtle. And kind."

"Kind?" His eyebrows were scrunched together.

"Yes, kind. Do nice things for her. Bring her coffee in the morning but don't make a big deal about it."

"She likes coffee," Derek said, nodding.

"Just set it down in front of her and go to work."

He rubbed his head. "And don't say anything?"

I sighed. "Derek, for once you just need to learn to keep your mouth shut. It gets you in trouble more often than not."

"Okay," he said, glancing over at Naomi. "I think I can do that. So be thoughtful, but not pushy."

"Exactly," I said.

Maybe there was hope for the guy. I hugged him and left the room.

CHAPTER 18

Training seemed to be going well. Everyone who was old enough and healthy enough to fight was more than willing to help New Haven.

Gideon was quick on picking up on our resident's talents. Once he figured out what they were best at, he put them in that group for the rest of training. With so little time to prepare, we figured might as well train someone to be good at one thing than alright at a lot of things. Besides, you couldn't hold a gun, a bow and arrow, and a sword all at once while fighting.

It didn't take long for me to see how well Will was with a gun. His grip was steady and firm, his aim accurate. He was able to figure out adjustments for wind and distance without hesitation. He tried to explain his reasoning and the calculations he used in his head. After about a minute, I shook my head and gave up. I had no earthly idea what he was talking about. But it worked for him and that was all that mattered.

During one of our breaks, I went to check on Dee. She was asleep when I entered her room. I went and sat down in the chair next to her bed, taking her hand. She looked so peaceful as she slept. As gently as I could, I moved one of her curls back from her face.

"That better be a handsome young man who has come here to woo me," Dee said, her eyes closed.

I laughed. "Sorry, love, it's a beautiful young woman who has come here to check on you."

"Marie?" She opened her eyes. "Oh, sorry Emmie, I thought you were someone else." Even though she was trying to be serious, playfulness danced in her eyes.

"You're lucky that I'm too tired from training to slap you," I said, squeezing her hand.

She squeezed my hand back. "How's training going, anyway?"

"Pretty good, actually. Everyone has been so willing to learn and so focused on doing well. I'm impressed."

"And how's my future husband doing?" she asked with a smile on her lips.

"Amazing," I said. "He's great with a gun."

She raised her eyebrows, her smile faltering. "Remind me to never tick him off."

"Thankfully he's too sweet of a guy to ever hurt you." I thought back to Recruitment and the challenge he and I were in together. He'd jumped on top of me to protect me from being attacked by bats, getting himself bit in the process. Adding the fact that I'd only known him for a couple of hours showed even more about his character.

"He hasn't met me yet," she said, biting her lip. "He may not like me."

I rolled my eyes. "He already seems smitten by everything I've told him about you."

Dee straightened out her sheets. "What can I say? I'm amazing."

I smiled at her and then looked over my shoulder at the door. "He should be here soon."

She shot up in her bed, grabbing my arm. "What? He's coming right now? Oh, Emmie, what should I do? How should I act? How's my hair?" She reached up and started fixing her curls.

"Dee, you look beautiful as always. Your hair's perfect, which totally sucks because you were just lying on it. You should get bed head like me, with your hair flying all over the place."

She laughed. "Your hair is pretty wild in the mornings. The trick's not moving your head when you sleep."

"Please, I've seen you sleep before, woman. You toss and turn like a wild animal and still wake up with perfect hair."

Dee's spunky attitude left. She looked me straight in the eye, genuinely concerned. "Do you think he'll like me? I mean, I know we've been joking around about it, but I'm really nervous."

"He's going to love you, Dee, trust me on that. Just be yourself. He'll like your fun attitude."

"How's my skin?" she asked, touching her face. "How pale am I right now?"

I scratched my head. "Uh, you want the truth?"

She pinched her cheeks. "Maybe this will give me color. My mom used to do it all the time when I was younger."

Her face fell when she mentioned her mom. Her parents and her brother hadn't come back with us on either of the trips to River Springs. Austin said he'd investigate it, but I hadn't heard anything from him. She wanted her family with her, especially being in the state she was in.

Our moment of silence was interrupted with a knock at the door. I turned around and saw Will standing there, completely nervous. He had one hand in his pants pocket, the other holding onto a bunch of blue flowers that had started to spring up near the mountainside.

I smiled at him. "Hi, Will. Come on in."

Will stepped slowly into the room, pausing when he looked at Dee. I couldn't read his face to know what he was thinking. Dee sucked in a deep breath.

When he started walking again, Will tripped over his foot, causing him to stumble. With bright red cheeks, he muttered something under his breath as he moved forward.

I motioned to another chair in the room, near the foot of the bed. "Why don't you have a seat?"

Will came to the side of the bed and held out the flowers to Dee. "I brought these for you."

Dee took them from him, a huge grin on her face. Her cheeks had some color in them, and I knew it wasn't from the pinching. "They're beautiful. Thank you, Will." She held them up to her nose, smelling the fragrance.

"You're welcome," Will said, taking a seat. "The spring's finally starting to show up."

"Do you want me to get you a vase?" I asked Dee.

She shook her head. "No, not yet. I want to hold them for

a while. I haven't seen the outside world in months. How's the weather been?"

"Nice." Will adjusted his glasses as sat forward in his seat. "The past few days have been perfectly clear and a nice temperature. You weren't missing anything before that, though. It's been a rough winter."

"That's what Emmie's always telling me," Dee said. "I thought she was just being nice."

"Please, when have I ever been nice to you?" I asked.

Dee laughed. "True."

"So, I told Will your idea about starting a school," I said, looking at him.

Will's eyes widened in excitement. "I think it's a brilliant idea." He pulled out a piece of paper from his back pocket. "I talked with Archie last night and we drew up a rough plan." He scooted his chair around, so it was next to mine and closer to Dee.

"Really?" Dee couldn't hold back her smile.

"Yeah." Will flattened out the paper. "We thought we could start with a small building with a few classrooms for different subjects. I thought it would be good to put it right outside Headquarters near that alcove. That way the kids could have lunch up there on nice days."

"That would be lovely," Dee said, looking at Will. I scooted my chair back quietly, trying to make myself invisible.

Will pointed to a spot outside of the building on the drawing. There was some type of structure there, but I didn't know what it was.

"Rosie told me about these playgrounds they had in

Scorpion," Will said. "We want to put one outside on some grass." He pointed to each item as he spoke. "There will be slides, swings, walls for the children to climb, and monkey bars."

Dee furrowed her eyebrows. "What are monkey bars?"

Will laughed. "I asked Rosie the same thing. It's a structure the kids can swing around on with their arms."

"Like monkeys," Dee said.

"Yes," Will said. "Just like monkeys." He pointed to another spot. "We could put picnic benches out here for lunch. Or even to have class outside sometimes."

"This is amazing," Dee said, setting her flowers down on the bed next to her. She teared up. "Wow, this is embarrassing. Sorry. This is just something so dear to my heart. Something I hope to be a part of one day."

Will placed his hand on Dee's. "It means a lot to me, too. And you can be a part of it. Archie and I just came up with the structure. We'll need your help on what to put in the classrooms, course material, all sorts of stuff."

As Dee wiped a few tears from her eyes with her free hand, I slowly stood and left the room, leaving them alone. A smile found its way to my face as I walked down the hall.

I found Marie, Dr. Stacey, and Alexander in a room at the end of the hall. Papers were all over the place and computers and microscopes were set up on a desk in the middle of the room.

Alexander pulled back from a microscope when I entered. He came to me, giving me a big hug. He missed Eric as much as I did. He had barely reunited with his son after years of being held captive and now his son was the one being held captive, without knowing if they'd ever see each other again.

Alexander released me from the hug, putting both his hands on my arms. "How's our Emmie doing?"

"I'm all over the place right now," I said. "My emotion changes every few seconds."

"You're a teenage girl." Marie smiled at me. She had her hair back in a ponytail, showing off her high cheekbones. "It's expected."

"Yeah, well take a normal teenage girl's emotional state and times it by a hundred," I said. "Because that's where I'm at."

"I'll make sure to keep my distance, then," Alexander said, giving me a wink.

Some vials were sitting on a shelf inside a cabinet against the wall. I picked one up, its pink liquid catching my attention. "What's this?"

"Oh, don't touch that," Dr. Stacey said. He looked older than Alexander by a few years. All his hair had turned gray and he wore glasses that sat low on his nose. Walking over, he took the vial from my hands, placing it gently back on the shelf. He closed the cabinet door and locked it. "I didn't even realize this was open."

"What is it?" I asked, my curiosity now piqued.

"It's very dangerous, is what it is," Dr. Stacey said, going back to the table where he was working. "It's a virus."

My eyes widened. "A virus?"

"Yes," Dr. Stacey said. "One that could kill thousands of people with just a few drops. Not something you want to mess with."

"Why do you have it?" I asked.

Dr. Stacey looked at me. "I didn't want it left at Infinity Corp. President Randall is the type who'd use it. He was the one who wanted it created in the first place."

I walked up to the table Dr. Stacey was at. "Why not destroy it?"

"We're still at war," Dr. Stacey said. "You never know if it may come in handy."

I looked down at some of the papers on the desk. I had no idea what any of it meant, but I glanced over them anyway. "How's the research going?"

Excitement lit up behind Dr. Stacey's eyes. "It's been incredible. The knowledge we've gained over the past few days have been monumental. Studying everything we've received from Dee and Lou has taken us further than we ever got in River Springs."

A little bit of hope sprung up in my heart. "That's wonderful."

Alexander nodded. "It is. I'll spare you the boring, technical details ..."

"Which I thank you for," I said, looking down at all the papers with numbers and formulas that I couldn't pretend to understand.

"And let you know," Alexander said, smiling at me, "that we know where it stems from and how it starts. With that knowledge, we're putting together a formula of compounds that should fight off the disease."

"I brought back several medical supplies from River Springs that we need to formulate the compound," Dr. Stacey said. "I think we have everything we need to start getting it ready."

My heart swelled. "I'm speechless."

Marie laughed. "Well, that's a first."

"Emmie," Alexander said, "do you think Dee will allow us to test the drug on her? We can't sample it on anything, and we don't know if it'll work for sure, but we have to test it out."

I nodded. "Dee would be willing to do anything to help find a cure. She's the type who'd sacrifice herself so others could be saved in the future."

"There will be risks," Dr. Stacey said. "We can't be one hundred percent certain how her body's going to react to the drug."

"At least she'll be here with you when she takes it," I said. "That way if anything goes wrong, you'll be at her side in no time."

A loud beep rang out from down the hall. I looked at Marie, wondering what it meant. She pulled out a pager from her pocket, her face turning serious.

"It's Lou," Marie said as she ran out of the room.

Dr. Stacey and I followed her out, running down the hall to Lou's room.

"He can't breathe!" Marie shouted from the room. "He needs oxygen."

As Dr. Stacey and I entered, Lou was on the bed, his face turning blue. His body was so fragile as if it could break apart at any moment. A few seconds after Marie placed an oxygen mask over Lou's mouth, he started convulsing.

I backed out of the room, unable to watch. Leaning up against the wall, I slid my back down until I was sitting on the floor. I pulled my legs in close, the sounds of machines and

Marie and Dr. Stacey shouting ringing in my head.

"Emmie." Someone touched my shoulder and I looked to see Will crouched down next to me. He put his hand on my arm. "Emmie, what's going on?"

I opened my mouth to speak, but nothing came out. I just stared at Will, not being able to wrap my head around what was happening. I could see Alexander in my peripheral vision, looking into Lou's bedroom.

Taking a deep breath, I closed my eyes and leaned my head against the wall. After a few minutes, Will's hand tensed. I opened my eyes and looked at him. His whole face had gone pale. I focused myself back on the noises and heard the distinct sound of a flat line. Marie swore loudly, followed by a loud bang, the noise of something being punched.

I tried to get up, but I was too weak. Will placed his hand on my back and helped me stand. When I looked at Lou's door, Marie stormed out. She walked up to her desk, which sat in an opening in the middle of the hall. Letting out a scream, she pushed everything off her table, file folders and office supplies flying everywhere. Marie leaned her hands up against the edge of the table and cried.

Dr. Stacey walked out of the room, his face grim. He looked at me, shook his head, and walked down the hall past Marie.

"I'll tell Dee," Will said to me. He hugged me tight before he left.

I stood there for a few seconds, stunned by the sudden turn of events. Just moments ago, hope had filled the air. The wonderful idea of a cure sat in our hearts. And now ...

I ran down the hall, grabbed Marie and pulled her into a hug. She squeezed me tight, her tears falling on my shoulder. I let my tears flow and we stood in the middle of the hall, hugging fiercely, letting every emotion pour out.

CHAPTER 19

irds chirped softly as they flew overhead. A couple of them landed on a tree nearby, their tweets coming out like a song. The air was nice and warm, the sky clear. The smell of blooming flowers wafted through the air, along with the sap of the trees that sat on the mountain.

When Dante, Santiago, Maya, and I went around our city the day before looking for the perfect spot to start a cemetery, we instantly settled on the location. The sun cast a spotlight on the open area of grass a few hours before sunset.

Every resident came, all of us lined up in a few rows, forming a semi-circle around the gravesite. We let James pick out the spot where he wanted to bury his son. President Brown and Dante stood to the left of the opening Dante and Santiago had dug for the casket. Vice President Mendes stood on the right.

We'd been able to take Dee out in a wheelchair. Marie was worried because the night before she'd given Dee the first injection of what they hoped was a cure. The day Lou passed away, Marie stayed up all night putting together the drug. She didn't stop until it was ready.

We had no idea how Dee's body would react to it, but so far, she had some color back in her skin and her energy level had gone up. She even demanded I bring a dress for her and made me help her into it.

I stood to the left of her, holding her hand. Will was on the other side, holding her other hand. My dad stood next to me, his arm around my shoulder, squeezing me tight. Tina stood behind me, holding my other hand, and Derek and Joshua stood on either side of her.

We were all back in our fifties-style clothing, trying to look as nice as possible.

We'd never had a funeral before. Not in New Haven, and certainly not in River Springs. We never saw what happened to the bodies after someone died. The leaders of River Springs didn't want us to focus on death.

In only one day, we had to figure out what we wanted to do during the ceremony and what traditions we wanted to start, if any.

President Brown and Dante spoke about Lou's life. They each shared stories, some personal, and some they had gathered from other Kingsland residents. James sat in a chair in front of the casket, his head down as the stories were told. Archie was able to put a casket together for Lou. It wasn't anything grand with such limited time, but it worked.

We had asked James if he wanted to share a few words, but he refused. His wife and daughter didn't want to leave Kingsland. They didn't agree with James and Lou on the state of their city. James had said once that it was like he'd already lost two members of his family. And now he'd lost the only member left, so I knew this was extremely hard for him.

Vivica stood behind James, her hand on his shoulder. I could tell she was fighting back tears, which was the first time I'd ever seen her show any amount of her soft side. She'd borrowed a black dress from Tina, and it fit her surprisingly well.

Once President Brown and Dante were done with their stories, the Mendes family joined the vice president up front. Rosie sprinkled some flowers on top of Lou's casket and then went to stand in front of her mom and dad, with Santiago on her left and Javier on her right. Together they sang a beautiful song, bringing tears to every member of our city.

Vice President Mendes closed the services with a prayer. I was surprised by the comfort it brought to my heart, knowing that Lou was in a better place.

The whole ceremony brought the city of New Haven together. It bonded us, the ties strong, which was just what we needed.

After the ceremony, the residents slowly trickled away, going back to training. Marie took Dee back to the infirmary. As she was wheeled away, Dee's eyes remained unfocused, her lips forming into a frown. The whole experience must have hung heavy on her heart. If the new drug didn't cure her, she might be the next person we'd have to dig a grave for.

Before going back to training, I changed back into my military uniform and then went around the different groups, watching everyone practice. Two very different emotional states came from the trainees. Some looked grieved, most of them from Kingsland who knew Lou well. Their hearts weren't in it.

Then there were others, including Vivica, who were fighting with every ounce of strength they had. Their eyes held determination, as if their life depended on the mock battle before them. Like they now had something to fight for.

We needed to keep the city of New Haven intact and continue the research on the disease. We had to find a cure.

Not long after training had gotten back in full swing, our scouts we had sent out the day before came back, parking their vehicle near the watchtower on the east side. Dante, Santiago, Maya, and I met them as they stepped out of the jeep.

"What's the news?" Dante asked.

One of the scouts we sent was Gideon. I wasn't sure if he'd want to go since he'd just gone on our trip to River Springs, but he was excited about the opportunity.

The other guy we sent, Hiro, was one of the few members from Juniper. We wanted to send him since he knew the way and was in the best condition from his city.

Gideon folded his arms and leaned against the jeep. "With the large number of soldiers, and their pace, I'd say about fifteen hours, maybe less, until they get here."

"They looked hungry," Hiro said, shaking his head, "for blood." His brown eyes were weary. He wasn't much taller than me, but he was well built and very capable of taking care of himself if danger were to cross his path. He kept his black hair perfectly trimmed.

"Who's leading them?" Maya asked Hiro.

Hiro sighed, rubbing the back of his neck. "General Ming."

Maya kicked at the ground with her good leg. A few quiet, but still audible, swear words escaped her mouth. For some reason, they didn't sound right coming from her mouth. "That's not good."

"No, it's not," Hiro said. Still rubbing his neck, he looked up at the sky. "The man, if that's what you want to call him, is ruthless."

Gideon looked at me. "From everything Hiro told me, President Randall pales in comparison to General Ming."

Maya cringed beside me. "Once during a training exercise, a man in my friend's unit failed to beat the time the general wanted them to reach. General Ming took the soldier by the hair and knelt him in front of the entire unit. With everyone watching, he beheaded the guy."

Santiago whistled. "For not reaching the desired time? That's insane."

"And this General Ming's going to be entering New Haven?" Dante swore. "We can't have someone like that issuing commands." He looked at Maya. "Where does he usually go during battle? Does he fight? Does he stay back?"

Maya gave a strained laugh, rubbing her thumb over her violin charm like she was playing it. "He keeps in the very back, surrounded by at least ten men. He'd be the last one you'd have to kill."

"We have to find a way to take him out as early on as we can," I said.

Hiro nodded. "If we could, that'd be best. He's constantly

issuing orders through earpieces to all the unit leaders. If he wasn't barking anything out, it would throw everyone out of sync."

"How do you propose we do that?" Dante stood tall, his arms folded, and his feet square with his shoulders. His demeanor and stature were becoming more like Mack and Terrance's every day. But he still had his youthful, fun side which was endearing.

"Come from behind," Gideon said. We all looked at him. "We know where they're coming from. If we could have someone waiting at the other end of the canyon, hiding somewhere, they could take him out right away."

"They'd have to get through at least ten other soldiers first," Hiro said.

I looked at Dante and smiled. "Unless they have a rocket launcher."

Dante nodded, his smile mischievous. "It could work."

"Even if it did work," Maya said, "as soon as that launcher's set off, the person's location is exposed. It's a suicide mission."

"I think it's worth it," Santiago said. "If this general is as vicious as you say, we need him killed right away no matter the cost."

"Even if the cost is someone's life?" Maya put her thumbs in her back pockets, swaying slightly.

"We're already sacrificing lives," I said. "We know we're going to have casualties on our side, no matter what. If there's the possibility of lowering the causality rate, plus a better chance of victory, we have to take it."

"I agree," Dante said, nodding.

"Me too," Santiago said.

"I'll volunteer," Gideon said, surprising all of us. His voice was confident, but fear lingered in his eyes.

I looked at him. "Gideon, are you sure you want to do this?"

He nodded. "Yes, Emmie. I'm willing to sacrifice my life for New Haven. For the chance for Marie to continue her medical research." He got a little choked up. He and Marie had grown close since he first came here. They complimented each other very well.

A thought came to my mind. "What if you didn't stay?"

Gideon scratched his forehead. "What do you mean?"

"What if you had a vehicle hidden that you could use to escape?" I asked. "Set off the rocket launcher, make sure it worked and then take off in the other direction?"

"And go where?" Dante asked. "It's a long way around the mountain."

The wheels were turning in my head. "He could go to Juniper."

Santiago laughed. "So, he could be tortured and killed there?"

"No." I looked at Maya. "You said your city is really bad off, right?"

Maya nodded. "It's pretty much hell on earth."

"And no one good is left?" I asked, reading her face.

"Not that we know of," Hiro said.

I turned to him. "And they'll keep on attacking us, no matter what, right?"

"Seriously, Emmie, where are you going with this?" Dante asked, looking at me with raised eyebrows. "Just get to the point, woman."

I rolled my eyes and then punched him in the arm. "While I was in the infirmary, I noticed a vial of pink liquid. When I touched it, Dr. Stacey freaked out. He told me it was a deadly virus and that it could kill thousands of people with just a few drops."

"And you want to use that on Juniper?" Santiago asked. A huge grin came to his face. "I like it."

Dante rubbed his arm where I hit him. "If we could take out the rest of Juniper and the other half of the soldiers, along with General Ming, we might have a chance at winning this thing."

"How would you spread the virus?" Hiro asked. "I think they'd notice some random white guy walking into the city."

Maya smiled. "Through the water supply. I know where he could put it without even entering the city limits."

"The underground tunnel on the south side of the mountain," Hiro said, nodding at Maya. "That's a brilliant idea."

Maya looked at Gideon. "I can draw you a map. You could easily sneak in without being seen, drop the virus in the water, and leave."

"Hopefully by the time you make it back, we'll be done here," Santiago said.

Maya sighed. "I just thought of something."

"What?" I asked.

"About a month ago, there was an explosion near the

tunnel that caused a collapse," Maya said. "When my dad went to go investigate, he couldn't even get through. It was too narrow. He had to send someone small in."

"Who?" Hiro asked.

"Me." I startled at the voice. I turned around to see Bruce come out from behind a tree. He'd been hiding there that whole time. The little sneak. "I can go with Gideon."

"No," Maya said, shaking her head. "No way. Bruce, we already lost mom and dad. I can't lose you, too."

Bruce shrugged. "You just said it would be easy. That he could sneak in without being seen. So could I. Besides, I'm way smaller than this giant." He smiled at Gideon, craning his neck to look up at him.

Gideon let out a laugh. "He has a good point."

Maya took a deep breath and ran her hand along her spiked hair, her bracelets clinking together.

I put my hand on her arm. "This could help us win this war. Gideon and Bruce are both smart and capable of this task."

Maya sighed. "I know. I'm just being the protective big sister."

"It takes an hour to get through the canyon by jeep," Dante said. "Let's get them the supplies they need, show them how to use the rocket launcher, and get them on their way."

"Yes," I said. "You'll need time to find a good cover for the jeep, plus a spot for you to hide out before the army gets there."

We went to find Mack to tell him of our plan. It took us a while to convince him to part with one of the rocket launchers.

He didn't like the idea of only having one left for us to use, but the thought of killing General Ming right away intrigued him.

We decided not to tell the president and vice president for now, just in case the plan went horribly wrong. We didn't want it resting on their shoulders. We needed every resident of New Haven to trust them.

I also thought it best not to tell Dr. Stacey we were taking the virus. Since he freaked out just from me picking it up, I figured he wouldn't like us taking it from New Haven.

Santiago was thrilled that I gave him the mission to break into the storage container that held the virus. Dante, Maya, and I made sure to distract everyone else in the infirmary during this time, telling them of the plans for the children and other residents who weren't going to fight.

When we met back up afterward, Santiago had a vial that was only a quarter full.

"Where's the rest?" I crossed my fingers he wasn't about to tell me he spilled some and that we'd all be dead soon.

Santiago laughed. "I see the look on your face, Emmie, but you can relax. I thought I shouldn't take all of it, just in case we need some of it again. There are three other cities, after all."

"You opened it?" I asked, my eyes wide. "What if you'd spilled some during the transfer of vials?"

"I was careful," Santiago said with a shrug. "There were some gloves in the room that I put on while I did it. I disposed of the gloves afterward. Not a single drop escaped."

I shook my head. "That was still foolish of you."

"I'll have you know that I opened the storage container

without any evidence that I did," Santiago said, pointing at me. "Dr. Stacey won't even notice unless he unlocks it and looks specifically at the bottle."

"Alright, let's get Gideon and Bruce on their way," I said to Maya and Dante.

Santiago raised his arms. "I think a thank you is in order. What I just did was awesome."

Dante slapped Santiago on the back. "Nicely done."

Santiago looked at me expectantly. I couldn't help but smile as I hugged him. "Thank you, Santiago."

"You're welcome," Santiago said, squeezing me tight. He held onto me as the others walked away. "You doing okay? I mean, with Eric being gone and everything else going on?"

I sighed into his chest. "I'm just worried that it's too late. But with New Haven about to be attacked, there's nothing we can do about it right now."

Santiago kissed the top of my head. "You have my promise, Emmie, that once we kick some Juniper butt, we're drawing up a game plan to get your man back. I'll go in with guns blazing if I have to."

"Thanks, Santiago."

I hoped there was some way we could win the battle and get Eric back, but I wasn't going to get my hopes up. In reality, they both seemed impossible.

CHAPTER 20

We wanted to send Gideon and Bruce on their way before anyone could realize what we were doing. Gideon wouldn't leave without saying goodbye to Marie, but I told him he couldn't tell her anything since we'd stolen the virus from the infirmary.

Gideon marched into Dee's room where Marie was checking her vitals, placed one hand on the small of Marie's back, the other on the back of her head and pulled her close. He kissed her with a heated urgency, his lips moving in hunger, and then walked out, leaving Marie breathless and Dee fanning her face.

As I watched Gideon walk down the hallway toward Bruce, someone cleared their throat behind me. I turned around to see Will, his face beet red. He looked wide-eyed at me, then Marie, then Dee, and then Gideon.

Will straightened his glasses. "Um." He looked at Dee again—who was talking with Marie—and then looked back at me, keeping his voice low. "I've never kissed anyone before.

I've seen my parents kiss a couple of times, but nothing like that. Is that normal?" His neck suddenly matched the color of his face. "I mean, is that what's expected?" He looked at Dee again.

I shook my head, trying not to laugh. "No, those kinds of kisses should usually be done in private. This was a ... special circumstance."

Will scratched his head, still looking at Dee. Dee must have noticed Will's stare because she looked over at him, her cheeks turning red. Seeing color in her cheeks again made me smile. Even if it was from embarrassment.

Will quickly looked at the ground and shifted uncomfortably where he stood. I patted him on the shoulder. "Hang in there, Will. It'll all work out in the end. Just don't think about it too much."

Will nodded and then walked away. Dee looked at me with her eyebrows raised. I just winked at her and gave Marie a thumbs up before I turned and left.

I wanted to catch up with Gideon and Bruce to make sure they got off okay, but I was stopped as I was walking back through Headquarters.

"Emmie," Derek said, stepping out from the security room.

I stopped in the hallway, folding my arms. "Can this wait? I have something important to do right now."

Derek shrugged, shoved his hands in his pockets and leaned against the doorway. His green tee had the caption, *I can't adult today.* "Depends if you want the results of the lie detector tests or not."

I did. My head debated whether I should ignore him and leave, but the way he looked at me made me curious. I sighed. "Did everyone pass?"

His smile was smug. "Let's make this interesting. We need to have a wager to see if you can guess right."

"Really, Derek? I don't have time for this. Just tell me the results."

"Come on, Emmie Let's have fun for once."

"Yes," Naomi said from inside the room.

I peered in to see her at her normal station, watching all the security feed, backs to us.

Derek sighed. "Thanks, Naomi. Yes, everyone passed."

"Wonderful," I said, walking away. Derek mumbled something that I couldn't understand. I stopped and turned back to him. "What?"

"Oh, nothing." He pulled his hand out of his pocket and ran his finger along the door frame, stopping to pick at a piece of wood that had splintered. "Nothing important or possibly life-threatening."

"Derek, you're killing me."

He shook his head. "Nope, I'm not the one who will be doing any killing."

I walked back to him, a frown forming on my face. "Are you saying someone will be?"

"Maybe," he said with a shrug.

"You just said everyone passed." Irritation boiled inside, an emotion Derek had no problem evoking from me.

He looked at me. "They did." I waited for him to continue, but he walked back into the security room, sitting down in his chair.

I stared into the room, thinking he'd sense my penetrating glare and just tell me what he was hiding from me. When that didn't work, I went in and walked up next to him. Putting my hands on the armrests of his chair, I turned him so he faced me. "Spit. It. Out."

Derek just sat there, smiling. I looked past him at Naomi for support, but she ignored us. I stood up straight, folding my arms. "What do you want?"

He leaned back, clasping his hands behind his head. "I want you to tell me how awesome I am."

It took every ounce of strength I had to not roll my eyes. "We both know it would be a lie. You were there during my test."

"I asked if you thought I was cool. Being awesome is different than being cool."

"Well, I'd still be lying."

"What I'm about to tell you could change everything." He moved his hands dramatically as he spoke. "Lives could be altered. Trust could be broken. Hearts could be shattered."

I thought I heard a small laugh from Naomi. Derek must have noticed too, because his smirk left for a second and he looked at me, his eyes asking if I'd heard it too. I nodded. His smirk was back. He mouthed, *"She wants me,"* making me roll my eyes.

"So, all I have to do is tell you that you're awesome and then you'll tell me what you're keeping from me?"

Derek sat forward, pointing his finger at me. "But you have to say it like you mean it."

I closed my eyes, mustering up the courage to say it. Taking a deep breath, I let the words leave my mouth, trying not to think about the consequences that would come from it. "Derek, I think you're awesome."

He smiled and pressed a button on the computer next to him. My voice rang out from an overhead speaker, repeating the words I had just said.

"You recorded it?" I shouldn't have been surprised.

"Of course, Emmie." He intertwined his fingers, pushing them forward until they cracked. "I need everyone to know that one of the revolutionaries thinks I'm awesome."

"*Think*," I said. "They'll think that. Not know it, because it's not true."

Derek shrugged. "Doesn't matter. So, you want to hear the juicy gossip?"

"Yes, please."

"Well, as we've already confirmed, thanks to the way cool lie detector test your *other* brother brought with him, everyone passed."

"Just tell her," Naomi said. So, she was paying attention.

"That is, everyone that took the test." Derek's eyes bore into mine, waiting for my reaction.

I didn't give him the reaction he wanted when I just shrugged. "This was voluntary. We assumed some wouldn't take it."

"Well, what if I told you it was just *one* person who didn't take it?"

His statement surprised me. "Only one person didn't want to take it?" I smiled. "That's good, isn't it?"

He sighed and shook his head. This wasn't going the way he'd hoped it would. "They didn't just say no. They refused."

That caught my interest. "Someone refused?"

"Yes, dear half-sister of mine," he said, moving his fingers along the controls on the desk. "He refused. Very adamantly, too, I might add."

"Who was it?" I hated that he was dragging this out. He loved it, though.

"You'd like to know that, wouldn't you?" he asked, crossing his feet at his ankles.

I gave him the nicest smile I could. "Yes, Captain Awesome, I would."

Derek's eyes lit up. "Love it. Changing my name. I'm Captain Awesome from here on out."

I shook my head, mad at myself for the monster I'd just created. I took a deep breath. "Well then, Captain Awesome, would you please tell me?"

"Why, I would love to tell you, Ms. Illegitimate."

"No," I said, wagging my finger at him. "Not happening."

Derek threw his hands into the air. "Fine. I was just trying to give you a cool nickname, too, but whatever." He scanned some files on his computer. "I need to find something. Like a sound of some sort for my big reveal."

I looked at Naomi. "Please, just tell me. I'm begging you."

"I'm not getting involved this time," Naomi said.

She eyed a cup of coffee on the table, and then glanced at Derek. So, my idea had worked. I knew being nice to Derek that one time was going to come back and haunt me.

"I think I've got it," Derek said. "I found this earlier and

I think it's brilliant. It's called a drum roll." He looked at me. "Ready for this?" He pressed the button dramatically and flicked his wrists along with the beat.

I stared at him, waiting for the name. How long could the drum roll possibly go on for? Well, at least two minutes because that's how long it was until Derek told me.

"Steven." He turned off the drum roll, stood and bowed. "Captain Awesome has done it once again."

CHAPTER 21

I wasn't really surprised that it was Steven. I had been wary of him being in New Haven. A part of me wanted to give him the benefit of the doubt, but he'd worked with President Randall before at being a spy. Maybe he still worked as one.

Ignoring the shouts from Derek demanding praise for his awesomeness, I ran out of the security room. When I went out to the training area where Steven should have been, I couldn't find him. I searched every single training group, but he wasn't there. If it had been any other resident who refused, I probably wouldn't have cared so much.

But it was Steven.

My adrenaline raged at that point, so I sprinted to the home he'd been sharing with a couple of other guys. I stopped at the entrance, pounding on the door with my fist. A small noise came from inside the house, but no one opened the door.

I pounded so hard, the side of my fist burned. "Steven, open the door." More noises came from inside. I tried the knob, but it was locked. "Steven, open the door!"

The sound of a zipper and then shuffling of feet sounded on the other side of the door. A slight twinge ran through my arm when I rammed my shoulder into the door. My shove had done nothing more than make the door rattle. A window opened, catching my attention, so I walked around to the side of the house.

Steven had thrown a duffel bag out his window and was now awkwardly trying to get his lanky body out of the window, too.

I stepped forward, drawing my gun from its holster. Holding it up, I pointed it directly at his chest. "Steven."

He fell to the ground, stumbling to grab his bag and stand. He stared at me, his eyes terrified.

I took a couple of steps forward, keeping my gun steady. "Steven, put down the bag and slowly lower yourself to the ground." He looked behind him and then back at me. I shook my head. "Please don't try anything stupid. We don't need this to be harder than it has to be."

He rubbed his head with his free hand. "I'm sorry, Emmie. It wasn't supposed to be like this." He turned and ran.

Lowering my gun, I ran after him, my adrenaline giving me the fuel I needed to pump my legs as fast as they would go. Steven was a lot taller than me, making his strides long. I wasn't sure what was in his bag, but the weight of it seemed to be slowing him down.

We weaved back and forth between houses, our pace not slowing. The streets were quiet since most of the residents were training. Most of the moms and children not training were in their homes, putting together food and supplies that would be needed after the battle.

A part of me wanted to raise my gun and just shoot him to stop the pursuit, but I didn't want the sound of my gun to alarm anyone.

Plus, I wasn't certain Steven was a traitor. The whole situation made it seem like he was, but I still had no evidence and he hadn't confessed to anything.

A little boy ran out from his house just a few yards ahead of Steven. I shouted as loud as I could. "Get back in your house!"

The boy stopped and looked at Steven and then at me. He stood there in confusion, not knowing what to do. His mom stepped out and saw me holding my gun as I ran, her eyes lighting up in fear. She sprang forward, picked up her son and ran back into their home, slamming the door.

I ignored the protests from my legs, demanding me to slow down. As we continued to run, Steven headed for the canyon on the west end of New Haven. The one that would take him back to River Springs.

Reaching into my pocket, I pulled out my communicator. I tried to be as clear as I could, but it was hard with my heavy panting. "In pursuit of Steven. Headed into the west canyon."

A few seconds later, Dante's voice rang through. "What's going on? Why do you sound like you're out of breath?"

I rolled my eyes. I didn't have enough oxygen to engage in a conversation right then. "He's trying to escape!"

"Why?" Dante asked.

"I don't know!" I yelled. "I. Just. Need …" My lungs were

burning, shouting at me to stop. "HELP!"

I shoved the communicator back into my pocket, paying no attention to whatever Dante said. I put my gun back in my holster so I could pump both of my arms faster.

We ran out of New Haven and into the canyon. A little way in, Steven tripped over a rock, slowing him down. I mustered all the strength I had, begging my legs to go as fast as they could.

Steven was only a few yards ahead of me. A large boulder was ahead, just to the right of the path we were on. Right as he passed it, I sprinted toward it, ran up, and threw myself off the boulder, my body hitting Steven in the back, sending us both to the ground. We rolled a few times, his bag hitting me in the head twice.

Steven tried to get up, but I took hold of his bag, pulling tightly on it so the strap choked his neck. He stumbled back, giving me a chance to jump on top of him. I took two swings at his face before he twisted to the side, causing me to fall off him. He swung his leg at me, his foot hitting me full force in the stomach.

He stood and took off, kicking up some dirt. I debated for just a moment, but my tired legs and my orneriness of everything that had happened the past few weeks made my decision for me. I couldn't let him get away. But I couldn't catch up with him and his long legs again.

I reached for my holster, pulled out my gun, took aim, and shot his right leg. Thank the revolutionaries, my aim held true. Steven screamed out in pain as he fell forward. He landed on top of his bag and reached forward to grab his leg. I slowly stood, keeping my gun aimed at Steven.

When he saw me coming, he scooted away, his jaw clamped together. He tried to stand, but he stumbled backward, landing on his butt. He threw his hands into the air. "Please don't shoot me!"

"Stop moving and I won't."

When I walked up to him, he turned his head away from me, shielding his face with his arms. Grabbing the strap on his bag, I yanked it off him. I set it on the ground, knelt, and unzipped it.

On top, there were just clothes and some food items. I threw them out and continued to rifle through the bag. Inside were a flashlight, a knife, and a handgun in the bottom of the bag. A side pocket revealed a small communication device, like the one Steven and Jen, my dorm leader, used during Recruitment.

Pointing my gun at Steven's head, I put the device in front of his mouth. "When I press the button, you're going to say hello and that's it. If you say anything more than that, I'll shoot you."

Steven stared at me for a moment, his eyes wide with panic. Sweat dripped down his face, his breathing ragged and shallow. I pushed the barrel of my gun into his forehead.

Once Steven nodded, I pressed the button. "Hello." He kept his mouth open like he was going to say something else, but I pushed my gun harder against his forehead, making him close his mouth.

I pulled the device toward my ear, waiting for a response. A few moments passed until I heard the shrill voice. "Hey, baby! What took you so long? You were supposed to contact me an hour ago. Daddy isn't going to be happy." Amber.

I put the device back in front of Steven. "If you want to live, you better make this convincing."

Steven nodded, his motion causing some sweat to fly off his face. I pressed the button again. "Sorry, things have been a little crazy here."

Amber giggled. "Oh, I've missed your voice! I mean, I know it's only been a few hours, but still."

"I've missed yours, too," Steven said, his eyes locked with mine. "Listen, I don't have time to talk right now. I just wanted to touch base."

"That's okay, sweetie," Amber said, her voice high-pitched and baby-like. "With all that training going on, I understand." My head shook in fury. How much had he told her? "I don't know why they even bother trying. It's not like they're going to win. Just make sure you get out in time, okay? I'm going to see if daddy will let me meet you halfway."

"That sounds good," Steven said. "Have you told him yet?"

"No, not yet. They're going to be so happy, though, to finally find out where New Haven is. What a stupid name, anyway." She giggled, the sound crawling over my skin. "I think they're going to be mad, though, that they aren't the ones who are going to destroy Emmie's stupid town. But hey, less work for us, right? Now we can concentrate on destroying the other three cities and forget about that dinky little town. Oh, and don't forget our deal."

Steven looked at me. "I won't. I have to go."

"Okay, but don't wait long to contact me again." The tone of her voice switched to a lower, more seductive one. "Oh, I can't wait to see you again. I have a big present for you. I think I'm ready to ... you know." Steven's eyes widened as I tried to keep the bile from coming up my throat. I really didn't need to know that.

Steven cleared his throat, his cheeks red from more than just exertion. "I can't wait. Bye babe."

"Bye! Love you!"

"Love you, too," Steven said.

Sighing, I pulled the device away from him. So, he was the traitor.

A few moments passed before I tried to say anything, but her voice rang out from the device again, catching my attention. I had closed my hand around it, but it was still close enough to hear what she said. "Seriously, though, remember I want Emmie alive. She's mine."

Every part of my body wanted to destroy the device in my hand, snapping it into tiny pieces, but I did my best to control myself. We could need it in the future.

I looked at Steven, sitting on the ground, holding his wounded leg. His pants were soaked through and a pool of blood filled the ground beneath him. Standing up, I ran my free hand through my hair. I kept my gun aimed at Steven, just in case he tried anything stupid.

"So, you've been working with them this whole time?" My voice was shakier than I'd wanted. I swore, kicking a rock on the ground. "Why, Steven? Why did you do this?"

He shook his head. "I've only been talking with Amber, I

swear. Her dad just barely found out, and that's because he walked into her room when we were having a conversation."

I picked up a rock from the ground, turning it over in my hand. "But you were going to tell them where New Haven is."

"After the battle, Emmie." He looked at the ground. "You must know we can't win this battle with Juniper. New Haven will no longer exist in less than twenty-four hours."

"You told her you'd bring me to her." Clenching my jaw, I threw the rock at his head, hitting him in the eye. Even with my left hand, I was surprised how well I threw it. "You were going to hand me over to that horrible excuse of a person. That beast."

His face turned red. "Don't talk about her like that!" His left eye watered from where I hit it. He rubbed his eye with his hand. "Don't ever talk about her like that! I love her!"

My laugh came out a little wild and panicked. "How can you love her? She's a horrible person! A psychopath. The things she's capable of ..."

"You don't know her like I do!" He yelled loudly, the veins popping out from his forehead.

I resisted the urge to hit him. "She's evil, Steven! I know her well enough." I shook my head, running my fingers through my hair again. "But now that I know what you're truly capable of, you two were made for each other." I bent down, leaning my face in close to his. "Too bad you'll never see her again." I held my gun up to him, my finger on the trigger.

He closed his eyes. "It was worth it. She's worth it."

I took a deep breath, my finger itching to pull the trigger. He was a traitor. He was going to reveal New Haven's location.

He'd been working with Amber. He was going to take me prisoner and hand me over to her. He also let her know we were coming, which lead to Eric being captured. I took another breath, pressing the barrel into his forehead.

"Emmie, don't!" Dante's voice sounded behind me, but I ignored it, keeping my gun where it was. Out of the corner of my eye, I saw Dante come up next to me. He gently placed his hand on my arm. "Emmie, don't do this. This isn't you."

Choking back on my tears, I licked my lips. "He's a traitor, Dante. He's been working with Amber."

"That doesn't matter," Dante said, his voice soft. "This isn't how we operate in New Haven. You know that. We're better than them."

"He was going to take me to her," I said, my voice barely a whisper.

Dante's voice pleaded with me. "Emmie, please, put the gun down. We'll deal with this the right way. He'll get his reckoning, I promise. But you can't just execute him like this."

The word *execute* bounced around in my head. I closed my eyes, thinking of Vice President Oliver and how he'd been executed right before my eyes. I shook the image from my mind. I couldn't do this. I wasn't President Randall. I would never be him.

Lowering my gun, I thrust it back into my holster and looked at Dante. "You'll have to take him from here. I need to get away from him."

He nodded in understanding.

I turned and walked away, not daring myself to look back.

CHAPTER 22

They'd taken Steven to the infirmary to get his wound treated. President Brown made sure that he was handcuffed to the bed so he wouldn't attempt another escape.

Marie let me know that she'd been less than gentle when she bandaged him. She took my hand, the remnants of the bullet landing softly in my palm. "It got lodged in his bone. It took forever to get all of it out; I'm not even sure if I did. There could still be some pieces of the bullet in there."

"Thanks, Marie," I said, squeezing her arm. I stepped into the room, shutting the door behind me. Dante and President Brown were the only other people in the room besides Steven.

Dante gave me a small, sympathetic smile. "Feeling better?"

I'd gone up to our alcove above Headquarters to cool down. Staring out over the city, I reminded myself of why we were truly there. It helped calm me.

I nodded at Dante. "Yes, thank you."

Steven was laying down, his face completely pale. I'm sure

the pain was unbearable for him, but I didn't care.

President Brown stood at the foot of Steven's bed, his arms folded. "I need you to tell us everything you told Amber."

"I didn't tell her much," Steven said through gritted teeth. He took a couple of deep breaths. "We mostly just had normal boyfriend/girlfriend conversations."

I stepped up to his bed. "She knew we were going to war with Juniper. She knew they were on their way."

Steven looked at me. "I mentioned the training, which led to the people of Juniper coming here. But what's the big deal? I was just stating a fact."

"You have no idea the implications that can come from telling her that," President Brown said. Anger flashed in his eyes. "River Springs knows when and who we will be fighting. They know that we will be at our weakest afterward. They could even be on their way here right now to attack us from the other side."

"No," Steven said, shaking his head. "I never told Amber where we're located. I promise."

"Why should we trust you?" I asked. "You've been lying to us. You've lied to me before."

"I don't care whether you believe me or not," Steven said, rubbing the top of his head. "It's the truth. She doesn't know where we are."

Dante stepped forward, leaning in close to Steven. "You were going to hand Emmie over to Amber. You were going to take her hostage and send her to her death." He slammed his hand down on the back of Steven's bed. "We should sentence you to death just for that!"

Steven looked up at Dante, startled. "You said you wouldn't execute me."

Dante shook his head, his face livid. "No, I told Emmie not to execute you out in public like that. Not without a proper discussion among the other revolutionaries and a trial with the president and vice president. But believe me when I say that we have enough evidence now to convict you of treason, attempted kidnapping, and attempted murder."

"What?" Steven looked flustered. "You can't be serious."

"I don't think you comprehend the trouble you're in," President Brown said.

"I didn't do anything!" Steven shouted. "Nothing bad is going to happen because of my communication with Amber. River Springs isn't coming here. Emmie's safe."

I couldn't wrap my head around the fact that Steven didn't truly understand what he did. I balled my hands into fists, fighting back the desire to hit him. "Nothing's going to happen because I stopped you." Stepping forward, I pressed my knees up against the side of Steven's bed. "If I hadn't shot you, you would've gotten away. You would've told them everything!"

"You don't know that!" Steven's face was red, his breathing fast and heavy. "I just wanted to talk to my girlfriend. I missed her."

I pointed my index finger at him. "If you think for a second that I'm going to believe you, you're out of your damn mind. If you wanted her so badly, you shouldn't have come here in the first place. You're a worthless, pathetic human being. You're weak. I've seen you crumple under pressure. All Amber would have to do it bat her stupid eyelashes at you and you'd reveal everything."

Steven looked away, fighting back tears. Just looking at him disgusted me. I turned away and walked back toward the door. Closing my eyes, I took deep breaths, trying to calm myself down.

"I think this should be obvious," President Brown said, "but you're under arrest, Steven. Once Marie clears you, we'll send you to lock up. We don't have time right now to fully address this situation, so your trial will have to wait until the battle with Juniper is over."

I didn't wait to hear if there was any more to be said. I opened the door and left and almost started running down the hall, but President Brown's voice stopped me. "Emmie, we need to talk."

"Can it wait?" I was trying to keep my emotions at bay, and I didn't think talking right then would help.

President Brown shut the door to Steven's room and came up next to me in the hall. "Do you want to tell me what you were thinking?"

Dante was standing near us, but when he heard the irate tone in his father's voice, he stepped back.

I looked up at President Brown. "What do you mean?"

"You shot a resident." President Brown had his jaw clenched together, doing everything he could to not yell at me.

"He was trying to get away," I said, my voice a little shaky. "And he would've gotten away if I hadn't stopped him."

President Brown rubbed his forehead. "Emmie, why were you even chasing him in the first place?"

"He refused to take the lie detector test." When I said it

out loud, I realized how stupid it sounded.

President Brown lowered his hand, looking me straight in the eye. "That is why you chased him?"

I bit my lip and slowly nodded.

Taking me by the arm, President Brown dragged me to the conference room. He slammed the door and threw me down in a chair. He didn't control the volume in his voice. "I told you it was voluntary!"

"I know, it's just …"

President Brown held up his hand to stop me. "I don't want to hear it. You can't just chase down residents like that and threaten them. You didn't even know if he was guilty of anything."

Heat flared in my cheeks. "I didn't have to know. I trusted my gut. I've never trusted the guy. I knew something was off."

President Brown slammed his hand down on the table. "I don't care about your gut. We aren't running this city off gut feelings! You need proof of guilt before you pull a stunt like this." He sighed and sat down in the chair next to me. "Emmie, I like you. You're a strong woman and most of the time you think rationally. But lately, you've been thinking with your emotions. You can't base your decisions on your feelings."

"But I was right." I was being stubborn. I had a hard time backing down or admitting I was wrong.

"You were lucky. There's a huge difference. Emmie, what if an innocent bystander got hurt? What if you'd been wrong?"

"So, I was just supposed to let him get away?" I tucked my hair behind my ear and focused on keeping my breathing even.

"He may have never run in the first place if you'd never gone to question him."

I shook my head. "He was already packing a bag. He was ready to go when I got to his home."

President Brown sat back in his chair, his face full of disappointment. "Next time, if you don't have absolute proof of someone's guilt, you let them go."

"Are we done here?" I didn't feel like talking anymore. I was on the verge of a breakdown.

President Brown nodded. "For now."

Leaving the room, I ran until I was out of the infirmary and out of Headquarters. I sprinted to my house, went to my room, slammed the door, and curled up on my bed.

So many thoughts raced through my head. If Amber had taken me prisoner, I had no idea what she'd do to me. That was if Whit and Dean didn't have their way with me first.

Lou's face entered my mind, followed by Dee's. We'd already lost such a sweet, innocent boy and the thought of digging a grave for Dee was too much for me to even process. With thousands of soldiers on their way to destroy our city, the number of graves would just pile up.

I thought about the disappointment in President Brown's eyes and how I'd let him down. I'd been so foolish, making irrational decisions and not thinking about the consequences.

Then I thought of Eric and how much I missed him. I wanted him there with me so badly to give me the comfort I needed. The fact that I might not ever see him again cut me to the core. Just the thought of never again being in his warm embrace left me hollow on the inside. I lay there, sobbing, unable to control my emotions.

I cried until there were no more tears. I cried until every negative emotion and thought left my body. I had to get through this on my own. I needed to stay strong for New Haven. I needed to fight for our freedom.

Slowly sitting up, I wiped my cheeks until they were dry. I said a silent prayer in my heart asking for the courage and strength I needed to win the war.

When I finally had myself put back together, I stood, telling myself I could do this. I needed to be brave. I *was* brave. I was a fighter and I'd stop at nothing to get what I want.

I opened my door, my heart now lighter. For the first time, I felt courageous. And then I stepped into the front room to find Dad, Tina, Dante, Santiago, Maya, and Joshua all waiting for me and my heart softened all over again.

Tina was the first to me, wrapping me in a bear hug. "I'm here for you and I always will be."

"I know," I said into her ear. "Thank you. You have no idea how much that means to me. I love you."

"I love you, too." Tina pulled back and smiled at me, tucking my hair behind my ear.

Dad came up next, giving me a big hug. "Be strong, my sweet girl. You're going to get through this." He pulled back, kissing me on the cheek in the process. "I love you so much, Emmie. I want to look at you and see my little girl, but all I see now is a beautiful, strong woman."

"Thanks, Dad," I said. "I love you, too." I looked at everyone else in the room. "I truly appreciate your support. It's something I need right now. But I think I just cried out every little girl emotion I had, so I'm good to go."

"So, you're ready to fight?" Dante came up, kissed me on the cheek, and pulled me into a hug.

"Yes, I think it'll be good therapy for me right now," I said with a small laugh. Maya tightly hugged me. When we pulled away, I looked at her. "Did Bruce and Gideon get off okay?"

Maya nodded. "Yes. They should be to the end of the canyon soon. Once they're settled, they'll contact us."

"Are you going to be okay?" I asked her. It was hard for her to send her little brother away, knowing there was a chance he may not come back.

"I think so." Maya smiled. "I just need to remind myself that Bruce can take care of himself. He's strong, just like our dad."

"We should all get some rest," Dante said. "It's getting late and the soldiers will be here tomorrow morning."

"That's a good idea," Dad said. He excused himself from the room, and then Dante and Maya left.

Tina moved to leave, but I stopped her. "Do you mind staying with me tonight?"

She smiled at me. "Of course. I could use a good snuggle."

Santiago wrapped his arms around me. "Remember for tomorrow, all you need to do is picture every soldier that comes at you as someone who's pissed you off. President Randall, Steven, Amber, Dean ... whoever you need to lash out at."

"I like that idea. I have a lot of aggression to get out."

"I'm just excited at getting to use the rocket launcher."

Santiago kissed the top of my head. "You know, if you ever need someone to hold and comfort you while Eric's gone …"

I pulled away and looked up at him. "Really, Santiago?"

He laughed, raising his arms. "I'm just giving you options."

"That's what I have Tina for," I said, pointing over at her.

Santiago looked at Tina and then at me. "I'm up for that, too."

"I'm glad I have your humor at times like this to cheer me up," I said dryly.

"Who's says I'm joking?" Santiago asked, his smile a little twisted. "I have a softer side, I'm a great listener, and I love to snuggle."

I sighed. "We really need to find you a woman." One that wasn't me.

After countless times of telling Santiago that Tina and I were fine on our own, he finally left.

Joshua had been standing in the corner of the room, his hands stuffed in his pockets, quiet the whole time. When we made eye contact, he stepped away from his corner and came to me, rocking back and forth on his heels as he scratched the back of his neck. "I know we're in a new and awkward family situation, but would a hug be out of line or too …"

I threw my arms around his neck, cutting him off. "It's only going to be awkward if you make it awkward." I was about to pull away, but Joshua held on so tight. It made me wonder when he'd last been hugged by a family member.

Joshua's voice was quiet in my ear. "Thank you, Emmie, for everything."

"Of course," I said. "That's what families are supposed to be for, right?"

Joshua laughed. "That's what I hear." He pulled away and stuffed his hands back in his pockets. "So, are we good, on trust and everything else?"

"Yes," I said, nodding. "I told you I'd trust you if you passed the lie detector test and you did."

"Were you serious about me being able to change my last name?" Joshua asked.

Tina looked at Joshua. "You want to change your last name?"

"I don't want to be linked with the Randall name anymore," Joshua said.

Tina nodded. "Makes sense. I wouldn't want to, either. What will you change your last name to?"

Joshua looked at me. "Would it be okay if I took yours?"

"Of course," I said. "You can take Woodard. After the battle, I'll get the committee together and we'll write up the papers and get everything signed off."

Joshua hugged me. "Thanks again, Emmie."

"You're welcome."

As Joshua went to his room, Tina and I went into my bedroom and lay down on the bed, facing each other.

"I think I finally know how you feel," I said to Tina. "I can't believe how much I miss Eric. It just makes my heart ache."

Tina sighed and rubbed my arm. "It was harder at first. I thought about Luke every day. But then I finally realized that I'd lost him for good." She scooted closer and wrapped her arms around me. "We still have a chance to get Eric back, Emmie."

"If they've kept him alive. I don't know why they would. It's been so long now."

"He's still leverage for them. They don't have what they want yet."

I grunted. "What they want is me."

"I know. But we aren't giving you to them and we still have a chance to rescue Eric. As soon as we win this battle with Juniper, we're going after Eric. It's been decided."

I looked at her. "What? When?"

"When you were having your meltdown," Tina said. "Which was heartbreaking to listen to, by the way."

"Sorry," I said with a frown.

She laughed. "You have nothing to be sorry for. You needed to get that off your chest. But me, Dante, Santiago, Maya, and Joshua are all going with you to get Eric back. It won't be hard to talk Mack and Terrance into coming, too."

"Us four revolutionaries aren't allowed to go on trips together. We can't all die at once."

"Screw that. Eric's more important."

Running my fingers through my hair, I raised my eyebrows. "More important than keeping the four of us alive?"

"Let me rephrase that. You're important and Eric's a part of you. We all love you and want you to be happy." She pulled away and lay on her back. "And if I happen to have a side mission of kidnapping Luke, then so be it."

I laughed. "I like that plan."

CHAPTER 23
Gideon

We found the perfect hiding spot for the jeep. We made sure it was nestled behind some trees and used tree branches to conceal it. Since we knew it would be a while until they came, we decided to get a few hours of shut eye to renew our strength.

When we woke, Bruce stayed in the jeep, using a pair of nighttime binoculars to look for the troops. Mack had made sure we both had communicators so we could talk to each other when we were separated. Bruce said he'd contact me as soon as he saw something.

I went up the side of the mountain, hoping to find a spot that was high enough so I could see but would still conceal me. I had the launcher in my arms, the rockets in a pack on my back. Mack had given me two rockets, but I was hoping to only use one. Once I set it off, it wouldn't take long for the enemy to come for me.

I found the perfect spot not too far up where I could clearly see the opening to the canyon. There was a giant sequoia tree that I could hide behind, so I rested my equipment up against it.

When I was settled in, I contacted Mack. "We're here. Bruce is hidden in the jeep. I'm up the side of the mountain, ready to go."

"Good," Mack said. "Try to keep your communication with Bruce to a minimum. Only talk to each other when needed. You both need to be as quiet as you can."

"Yes, sir," I said. "Anything else I need to know?"

"Don't be too hasty," Mack said. "Make sure you have your sight set on General Ming. Only take the shot if you're certain it'll hit him. Try to keep your mind clear and focused, and your breathing steady."

"Will do," I said.

"Don't contact me again until you've set off the launcher and you and Bruce have made your escape," Mack said. "Wait until you know you're out of danger of pursuit. Good luck."

"Thanks," I said. "We won't let you down." I put the communicator away and pulled out a pair of binoculars, searching the valley below. It was still dark, but I hoped the sun would come up soon.

While I waited, large gray clouds rolled in, casting a gloomy feeling over me. Time seemed to move slowly, the minutes dragging on like hours.

As if sensing the impending battle, the air had shifted dramatically. A fog came in, thick and heavy. The temperature dropped at least fifteen degrees. I could smell the incoming rain and I hoped it would wait until after I accomplished my goal.

The weight of my choice suddenly came crashing down on me. The whole tone of the war balanced on this moment. Killing General Ming meant throwing off our opponent. It would shake them up; give them something they weren't expecting. It would give the New Haven warriors hope. Hope of victory. Hope of survival.

Bruce's voice interrupted my thoughts. "They're here. About fifty yards out."

I heard them before I saw them. Their march was in sync, each step firm and concise. I was surprised Bruce could see where they were with all the fog. I kept my binoculars pressed firmly against my eyes, searching all around until I finally saw them. My breath caught for a second, taking in the full sight of their army. A couple thousand soldiers lined up perfectly in rows were coming toward us.

As quietly as I could, I put the binoculars away, picked up the rocket launcher, and loaded one of the rockets. Steadying the launcher on my shoulder, I leaned against the tree for support. We had attached a scope on the launcher so I would be able to clearly see General Ming.

As they drew closer, passing by my tree, faces came into view. Each soldier looked fierce and determined. There wasn't an ounce of doubt on any face. They were here to win, and they knew they would.

Steel armor covered their chests, abdomens, and legs. They wore steel helmets with a red feather sticking up from the top. Each soldier held a long silver sword in one hand, a bronze shield in the other.

Each row of soldiers that past filled me with despair. There were so many of them and so little of us. They looked like they had years of training, their bodies perfectly sculpted for battle.

I shook the negative thoughts from my mind, trying to stay focused on getting my mission done. If I dwelled on the numbers and odds, there was no chance of success. I needed to center my thoughts on one thing at a time, looking at the end of one goal, not the end of the entire war.

I stayed perfectly still, keeping my breathing quiet and even. Minutes passed, and the soldiers kept on coming. The weight of the launcher multiplied as time went on.

Bruce's voice was barely a whisper. "In the back there's a group of soldiers clustered together."

We both agreed beforehand that I wouldn't respond to anything he said unless I desperately needed to. I was much closer to the enemy than he was.

"You can tell the imperial soldiers apart from the others because they wear silver cuffs, their shields are silver, and they have red and silver feathers in their helmets."

I trained my scope toward the back of the army, looking for the men with Bruce's description.

"They're the biggest, toughest, and cruelest soldiers we have. You'll see them in a square. Three in front, three in back and two on each side. General Ming is in the middle."

I spotted the group of soldiers, spaced well back from the others. The fog had eased, making it easier for me to see. A big mass was in the middle of the group, a man covered head to toe in armor.

Focusing my scope, I narrowed in on the center. The armor was made completely from silver. Elegant artwork was engraved on each piece. The feathers on his helmet were thicker and the colors more vibrant than anything I'd ever seen.

He held his head high, his hand beating against his chest as he marched. The only part of his body I could see were his eyes. They were chilling, slicing right through everything in front of him.

Taking a deep breath, I made sure I was focused on the center of the group. I put my finger gently on the trigger, waiting for the right moment to pull. I had to set off the launcher at the right moment or the whole plan would be ruined. I couldn't mess it up.

I remembered Mack's words to only take the shot if I knew I'd hit him. Lightning filled the air, giving me a clear view of General Ming. I took a deep breath, exhaling as I pulled the trigger.

Thunder roared in the sky as the launcher recoiled against my shoulder, but I kept myself steady, watching the rocket soar straight through the air toward General Ming.

Drops of rain fell, a few landing on my face. I let them slide down my eyes and cheeks, not daring to look away.

The sky filled with light again, only this time it was from the explosion. The rocket hit dead center, directly onto General Ming. His surrounding soldiers flew back, their bodies breaking into pieces.

Without hesitating, I took the launcher off my shoulder, grabbed the bag with the other rocket, and made my way swiftly down the side of the mountain. Soldiers were shouting in the distance, confused by the sudden turn of events.

I sprinted as fast as I could back to the jeep, willing myself to keep my eyes forward. I didn't want to know what lay behind me. Bruce had the jeep started and taken off the branches for concealment. I threw the launcher and my pack into the back of the jeep, jumped into the driver seat, put the jeep into drive, and slammed on the gas.

It was pouring rain by then and I was glad that Bruce had thought to put the cover on the jeep before we went to sleep. Bruce bounced beside me, his energy buzzing in the air. He turned around, facing the aftermath of the explosion.

"That was so freaking awesome," Bruce said. "Your aim was perfect." He turned his head toward me. "Did you see their bodies flying everywhere? I'm so glad I wasn't next to them. There were probably body pieces falling from the sky."

I was too worked up to respond, so I just let Bruce ramble on, getting out all his excitement. "I wish I could've seen the look on the other soldiers' faces. They probably had no clue what was going on. No one even came after you. I think the timing of the rain, lightning and thunder was perfect, helping to cover up the noise of the jeep."

Bruce finally turned so he faced forward. He had his hands on his head trying to process everything that just happened. "Seriously, I don't care what else happens to me on this trip. I'm just glad I got to live to see that." He started laughing. "General Ming is dead. General Ming! The man who can't die is dead. How is that possible?"

Bruce playfully punched me on the arm. "It's possible

because of you! You're amazing! Man, I can't wait to get back to retell the story." I could feel his eyes on mine. "Do you mind if I tell the story? I mean, I know it's yours to tell, but I don't think I'll be able to control myself."

It took me a minute to respond. My stomach churned, my heart racing faster than it ever had before. The thought of blowing someone up wasn't sitting easy with me.

I cleared my throat. "I'm sure you'll tell the story way better than I would."

Bruce pumped his fists into the air. "Thank you!"

"Why don't you contact Mack and let him know the news?" I shook my head as I drove, completely baffled by what had just happened.

"Mack!" Bruce shouted into the communicator. "Mack! Mack!"

"By the excitement of your voice," Mack said, "I'm guessing you have good news?"

"Man, you totally missed it!" Bruce exclaimed. "Gideon is awesome! Seriously. He just sat up there, calm as can be, and fired off the launcher like it's something he does every day."

"Did he hit General Ming?" Mack asked.

"Dead center. Literally." Bruce moved his arms around as he spoke, reenacting the event with his hands. "The rocket soared perfectly through the air, colliding with General Ming's head. Gideon completely obliterated the evilest man on the planet. The explosion lit up the sky and smoke filled the air. And his ten buff guards? In pieces, landing on other soldiers. Freaking awesome."

Mack coughed. "Sounds like you enjoyed the show." I

could tell by the tone of his voice that he wasn't sharing the same excitement Bruce had. Neither was I. Bruce was still too young to truly understand the consequences of war and the impact it had on a person. The kid was only fourteen and had a lot of growing up to do.

"You. Have. No. Idea," Bruce said.

"Did anyone come after you?" Mack asked.

Bruce shook his head even though Mack couldn't see him. "Nope. The other soldiers had no idea what was going on. They were so confused. The rain and thunder helped cover up our exit."

"Good," Mack said. "I'm glad to hear that. Good work, Gideon. You were born to be a warrior."

A small smile formed on my lips. "Thanks."

"He's so humble, too," Bruce said. "If I were him, I'd be screaming at the top of my lungs, telling the world how awesome I was. He's even letting me tell his story. And not just to you! To everyone!"

"Sounds about right," Mack said. "For both of you."

"Hey, I'm okay with being a showoff," Bruce said. "That's how I am. But I'll exclaim Gideon's praises to everyone. They'll know how amazing he is." He looked at me. "Seriously, you're my hero. If you weren't a dude and there wasn't a huge age gap between us, I'd totally kiss you right now."

"Well, then I'm glad I'm a dude."

Bruce laughed. "It's weird to hear the word 'dude' come out of your mouth."

"Keep me informed on the rest of your trip," Mack said.

"We will," I said.

"Gideon, I'm proud of you," Mack said. "I think you deserve a promotion."

"To what?" I asked. It wasn't like there were multiple ranks in our small army.

I could hear a smile in Mack's voice. "I'll think of something. I'll talk to you guys later."

"Bye, Mack," Bruce said.

Bruce's high faded pretty fast. He fell asleep not long after, giving me time to think on my own.

The first part of our mission was a success. The cost would be several sleepless nights with an image I'd never be able to get out of my head, but it was a price I chose to pay and a choice I'd make over again. This would give New Haven the hope it desperately needed.

Now we just needed to make sure we did the next part right so we wouldn't have a whole other army coming to attack us.

If we succeeded at spreading the virus in Juniper, the safety of those living in New Haven would increase dramatically.

We needed to succeed.

CHAPTER 24
Emmie

We were all excited to hear the news of Gideon's success. Mack woke all of us up early to tell us. Gideon was made for excellence. He was brilliant.

We debated whether we should tell the news to the president and vice president, but in the end, Dante and Santiago couldn't contain their excitement. They had to tell their fathers.

"You did what?" President Brown asked, folding his arms, his eyebrows furrowed together.

We had found him and Vice President Mendes sitting in the conference room, drawing out plans.

"We killed General Ming," Santiago said. If his smile got any bigger, his face might have broken.

"Well, Gideon killed him," I said. "The guy's a hero."

Vice President Mendes had his hands clasped together, resting on the table. "I think the president was referring to the part where you broke into the infirmary and stole something. That's against the law."

Dante laughed. "I'm not sure the law applies to us." He gestured to us four revolutionaries.

President Brown shook his head. "The law applies to you four more than anyone else, Dante. This isn't a game. This is war. A lot of lives are at stake."

"I know, Dad," Dante said, "but we, well Gideon, killed General Ming, along with his ten toughest soldiers. And if they succeed in the second part of the mission, it'll end Juniper for good. They won't come after us again."

President Brown stood and paced the room, walking around the table. He made eye contact with each of us as he passed by, stopping in front of Santiago. "The worst part is, you didn't even steal something small or insignificant. You stole a virus."

"You're going to wipe out an entire city," Vice President Mendes said. "What if there are innocent people there?"

Maya shook her head. "There aren't. The only good people left got out and are here in New Haven. Everyone else was murdered."

"Do you know that for certain?" President Brown asked.

"Yes." Maya twirled the violin charm on her bracelet. "I'm about ninety-nine percent sure."

President Brown slammed his fist down on the table, making Santiago jump in his seat. "That's not enough! You need to be one hundred percent sure before you make a decision like this."

"How come you didn't talk to us about this?" Vice

President Mendes asked, eyeing Santiago.

Santiago smiled, looking at his father and then at President Brown who still fumed beside him. "Because I knew this is how you'd react."

"And General Ming would still be alive if we did come to you." I sat forward. "And we wouldn't have the chance to end Juniper."

"They'll keep coming for us," Dante said.

"And they won't give up until New Haven's finished," Maya said.

"That doesn't give you the right to make this decision without consulting us," President Brown said. "I think you're forgetting who's in charge here."

I looked at President Brown. "We're not trying to insult you or question your authority. We saw a chance to put the odds of winning this war in our favor, so we took it."

President Brown leaned forward, resting his hands on the table. "You took it without asking me or the vice president. I know what you four have been chosen to do, but you aren't in charge yet."

"Isn't this why we were chosen?" Dante asked. "We come up with ways to win the war and keep New Haven alive and we seize them." He looked at me and then Santiago. "We aren't the type to ask before we do something."

"You still need to recognize authority," Vice President Mendes said. "If the residents of our city see the four of you ignoring us and the laws we've created, why would they want to live by them, too? You four have the right mindsets to fix this world and restore it to its proper order, but you aren't invincible."

"You're still young and naïve," President Brown said. He paced the room again.

I stood and went to President Brown, stopping him in his tracks. "Listen, I understand what you're trying to tell us, and I understand your reasoning, but we aren't going to change. We're willing to do whatever it takes to win not just this upcoming battle with Juniper, but the entire war with the rest of the cities. We're fighters. Yes, we make rash decisions. But they're the right ones."

President Brown looked down at me, his eyes a mix of disapproval and pride. "We won't know that until Gideon and Bruce make it safely back to New Haven."

"They will," I said. "Bruce is tough, and Gideon was born to do this. It's in his blood. He's logical and can put his emotions aside at the snap of a finger."

President Brown smiled softly. "So, the complete opposite of the four of you."

"Hey, we can think logically," Dante said. "Sending the two of them to kill General Ming and wipe out Juniper was completely logical."

Santiago clasped his hands behind his head. "As for the emotions, we just happen to wear ours out on our sleeves. Yeah, it gets us in trouble sometimes, but it fuels us. It makes us the fighters we are."

"President Brown," Maya said, her voice soft and gentle, "it was the right choice. Trust me. I've lived with the people that are still in Juniper my whole life. They aren't good people. I'm not even sure if they're human anymore. They're monsters."

"You'd better be right," President Brown said, "for the sake of their city and ours."

Vice President Mendes smiled. "He really killed General Ming?"

"With a rocket launcher." Santiago whistled as he flew his hand in the air like a rocket and then he made the sound of an explosion as his hand hit the table.

"Don't encourage them, Oscar," President Brown said.

Vice President Mendes cleared his throat. When the president wasn't looking, the vice president winked at me. His playfulness reminded me of Vice President Oliver. He was serious when he needed to be, but he was still able to have some fun now and then.

President Brown looked at his watch. "We don't have a lot of time. Let's get Mack, Terrance, Derek, and Naomi in here. We need to go over our strategy."

When everyone was settled into the room, the president spread out a map on the table. It showed the east entrance to New Haven and the canyon leading to it.

"We have five towers now constructed on the east entrance," President Brown said, pointing to the towers. "I want as many men and women up there as we can who know how to use a bow and arrow. They're our first line of defense. As soon as the army is in range, we need to fire. The sooner we lower the enemy number, the better."

"Archie has already placed a whole bunch of arrows on each tower," Mack said. "We'll need to designate one person from each tower to oversee weapon control. As soon as the number of arrows gets low, we'll need to move on to guns."

"We aren't going to start with guns?" I asked.

Terrance shook his head. "We need to conserve ammo. We've been able to make thousands of arrows the past few days, so we'll use those first."

"Gideon said they have armor," Mack said, running his hand over his beard. "On their chest, abdomen, legs, and head."

"That doesn't leave us many areas to aim for," Dante said, frowning.

"But now you know where to aim," Mack said. "Neck, arms, and face."

Dante sat forward. "That won't kill them."

"No," Terrance said, "probably not, but it will slow them down. Injure them. If they get to our front line and they're wounded, it'll be a lot easier for our swordsmen to get close and finish them off."

"What about fire?" Dante rubbed his hands together. "Can we light the arrows on fire?"

"No," Mack said.

Dante's face fell. "Why the hell not?"

"The last thing we need is for a fire to spread and burn New Haven down," President Brown said, his eyes scolding his son. "Everything's made of wood and easy to burn. We don't want to help the enemy."

Dante folded his arms and swore under his breath. He nodded his head toward Santiago. "His rocket launcher could start a fire."

President Brown sighed. "This isn't a time for an

argument, Dante."

"Speaking of my precious rocket launcher," Santiago said, his eyes lit up, "I have eight rockets, right?"

Mack nodded. "I only sent two with Gideon."

President Brown glanced at Mack. It probably bothered him that Mack knew of our plan and didn't say anything. Not only had we'd done something major without permission, but we'd also gotten an adult to agree and help us.

"When can I use it?" Santiago asked. His smile reminded me of Derek's whenever he found Vice President Oliver's stash of candy in his office.

"You'll be up with the archers," Mack said. "I want you switching back and forth between your shotgun and the rocket launcher. Space the rockets out. We want them to think that the rockets could keep coming at any point."

Santiago nodded and ran his fingers through his shaggy hair. "Works for me."

"I'll also put some grenades on each tower," Mack said. "The designated leaders of each tower will be responsible for using them as needed."

"Once we're done with arrows," Vice President Mendes said, "we'll move on to rifles on the towers."

"Is the ammo already up there?" Santiago asked.

"Only for your shotgun," Mack said. "You'll be on tower two, so that's where your shells are. The person on weapon control in each tower will oversee changing ammo. We want to minimize the amount of weight on the towers as best as we can."

"What will we be doing down below?" I asked.

The thought of being down below, completely exposed, made me feel weary. But I needed to be strong. New Haven depended on us and I didn't want to let any resident down. I would die for any of them.

Terrance pointed at the map. "We'll also have our shotgun experts lined up on the mountain on either side of the canyon. They won't start shooting until the enemy's close and the archers have already started."

President Brown looked at Maya. "You'll be down in front with all the sword experts. You're in charge of them. We don't have a lot of swords yet, so there won't be many of you at first."

I raised my eyebrows. "Yet? Are you planning on getting more swords?"

"I figure as soon as we kill an enemy," President Brown said, "we can take their sword and use it."

Santiago whistled. "Think about it. If we kill all twenty-five hundred of them, we'll have that many swords. That will surely put a boost in our weapon supply."

Maya nodded. "Yes, it would." She looked over at President Brown. "How are we communicating with each other? Am I just supposed to shout commands to my line, or do we have devices?"

"We have some earpieces," Vice President Mendes said. "You will each be given one. All the others will be spaced out among the residents so they can spread around whatever commands any of you give out."

Mack stood, stretching his back. "Once the fight starts, there really won't be much communicating going on. It's going to be loud. You'll have to rely on visual signals."

"Speaking of that," I said, "what are we going to do about the noise? All those guns going off, someone's bound to go deaf."

Dante laughed. "I think you mean everyone."

Terrance pulled out a box from under the table and placed it next to the map. "Earplugs. Everyone's getting a set. Archers included."

Santiago reached into the box and took out a set, placing them in his ears. He swatted my arm since I was sitting right next to him. "Say something."

"You're a dork," I said, smiling at him.

"Did you say I'm hot?" Santiago smirked. "I know."

I rolled my eyes. "I think they'll work just fine."

"What?" Santiago asked, his voice loud.

I pulled out one of his earplugs. "You don't need those in here."

"Anyone have any other questions?" Terrance asked.

Derek shifted in his seat across the table from me. He was wearing his camera lens shield shirt. He'd made one for Naomi as well. She surprised me—and Derek—when she suggested they wear them to work, like unofficial uniforms.

"Why am I in here?" Derek asked. "And Naomi."

"You're our security detail," Mack said, punching Derek in the arm. Derek tried to act cool, but when Naomi wasn't looking, he rubbed his arm, a grimace on his face.

"Now that we have cameras installed on the east entrance," Terrance said, "you'll be our eyes during the battle. Let us know of things we can't see."

"Also, you're in charge of keeping anyone from getting into Headquarters," President Brown said.

Derek went pale. "What?"

"If, in the worst-case scenario, an enemy gets by and gets all the way through town to Headquarters, you have to stop them," Vice President Mendes said.

"Uh," Derek said, scratching his head. "How?"

"I thought you were a big tough guy," Naomi said, looking at Derek's puny arms.

Derek glanced over at me and then looked down, his face red.

Mack placed two handguns on the table in front of Derek and Naomi. "The chances of someone getting through the steel door and into Headquarters are slim, but if they do." He pointed at the guns.

Naomi picked hers up, dropped the magazine and pulled back the slide, examining the inside. Nodding in satisfaction, she put the empty magazine back in.

Derek just stared at her, his eyebrows raised and his mouth slightly agape. I tried repeatedly to teach him gun safety, but he never thought it was necessary. He was convinced he'd never have to hold a gun. He was a tech guy, after all.

Derek looked up at me, sweat forming on his brow. I took a deep breath, telling him with my eyes to do the same. Derek nodded and took a long, very noticeable, deep breath. I sighed.

Mack leaned over the table, placing the palm of his hands down, looking right at Derek and Naomi. "You can't let the enemy past you. They can't get to the infirmary or any of the children." He paused until both Derek and Naomi were looking right at him. "Do I make myself clear?"

Naomi nodded. "Yes, sir." She looked at her gun in front of her. "You're giving us ammo, I assume, and not just expecting us to whack them over the head with the gun."

"You'll be getting ammo," Mack said with a small smile. He looked at Derek, still waiting for his response.

Derek wiped the sweat from his eyes and forehead. He looked at me, still uncertain of what to do. Derek had a serious problem. He was good at technology. Amazing at it. But when he had to do something outside of his comfort zone, he broke down. His ability to think rationally flew out the window. It made me fear for the sick and the children he needed to protect.

"I asked you a question, Derek," Mack said. He glared at Derek until I thought Derek might burst into tears.

Derek licked his lips. "Yes, sir." His voice was barely audible.

Naomi suddenly stood, looking at her pager she always kept on her. "The security cameras have picked something up." She dashed out of the room before anyone could respond.

As everyone else left the room to see what was going on, Derek stayed frozen in his seat. He stared at his hands in front of him, which were shaking uncontrollably.

I stood and went to the other side of the table, sitting down next to Derek. I gently placed my hands over his. "Derek, you're going to do fine."

He looked at me, his eyes desperate and pleading. "Emmie, I ... I ..."

"The chances of anyone breaking into Headquarters are

so small. There's a good chance you won't have to use the gun. Mack just wants to be prepared."

"But if they do ..." He stopped, the words getting stuck in his throat. Tears started to form in his eyes as he pointed at the camera shield on his shirt. "I can't do this, Emmie. I'm a tech guy. I'm not you."

It was the first time in my life I'd ever heard Derek mention that I was better at something than him. I clasped his hands tightly. "Derek, look at me." It took him a second, but he finally did. "You can do this. I know you can. All you have to do is point the gun at the enemy and pull the trigger. Naomi knows how to use a gun, so if you have any questions, ask her."

Derek shook his head. "I can't be responsible for all those children." He paused, looking down at the table. "And Dee. How could I ever look at you again if something happened to her?"

I wanted to make a joke, asking when he had started caring about me, but I refrained. "The trick is to not think about it so much. Just do it." I smiled at him. "Show Naomi how brave you are."

"I'm not brave. You of all people should know that. I'm a total wimp." He looked up at me. "Those words aren't leaving this room."

I nodded and smiled. "Sometimes in life, you just have to suck it up and do it. Don't question yourself, don't think about the outcome or consequences, just do it."

He raised his eyebrows. "Remind me to never let you advise anyone under the age of sixteen."

"This is a special circumstance. And the outcome will be

you saving a bunch of lives. I just don't want you to think about that part. Your ego's big enough as it is."

Derek picked up the gun, placing his hand over the barrel.

I quickly pulled the gun away from him. "First of all, never put your hand over the barrel."

"But it's empty," he said, shrugging.

I sighed. "How do you know that?"

"Naomi's was."

"And she checked first. You always check that first. Just because you think it's empty, doesn't mean it is." He stared at me. "Just pick up the gun, the barrel pointed down and your hand *not* over it, press this button to take out the magazine, and then pull back the slide." I showed him how to do it and then let him have a go at it.

When he was done checking, he shoved the magazine back in. "Okay, I can do that."

"Never point a gun at a person unless you want to shoot them, and never, ever put your finger on the trigger until you're ready to pull it."

"Where do I put it in the meantime?" Derek asked, looking at the gun.

"Just along the side." I pointed right above the trigger. "That way, you can slide your finger down and pull the trigger in a heartbeat."

"You really know a lot about this, don't you?"

I nodded. "That's what training is for, stupid. Something you should've done a long time ago when I asked you to."

He shrugged. "I never thought I'd have to use one."

"And yet here you are, holding a gun."

"With a very, very, very small chance of using it, right?" Hope sat in his eyes.

I laughed. "Very small. In fact, let Naomi do most of the shooting if anyone breaks in."

Dante stepped into the room. "We have to go. The cameras spotted the army not too far out. We need everyone at their posts."

I stood and placed my hand on Derek's shoulder. "You good?"

Derek nodded as he stood. "Yeah. Just do me a favor and do your job right so no one gets back here."

"I'll do my best."

Derek gave me a big hug. "I love you, little half-sister."

I squeezed him tight, taking the breath out of him. "Love you, too, big, annoying half-brother."

Dante sniffed. I turned around and he pretended like he was crying, waving his hand in front of his face. "That was the sweetest thing I've ever witnessed."

Derek released me from the hug and walked out of the room. He slapped Dante on the back on the way out. "You really need to get out more if you consider that sweet."

CHAPTER 25

"Marie, don't let anyone past your desk," I said as all the children, men, and women who weren't fighting were passing us in the hall. They were all headed to the back of the infirmary where we had a large storage room.

Marie nodded as she watched everyone walk by. "I won't." She stopped a kid who was running. "Slow down, okay? No running in the infirmary." She looked at me. "This is crazy, Emmie. I can't believe it's finally happening."

"We knew it would someday," I said. Someone threw their arms around me and I looked down to see Rosie. She flashed me a big grin. "Hi, Miss Rosie."

"Hi, Miss Emmie," Rosie said. "You ready to fight?"

I stroked her hair. "You bet I am. I have your cute face to protect."

"And mine!" Dee shouted from her room. Rosie and I laughed as we went to Dee's room. She was sitting up in her bed, her color fully back. I still couldn't believe how well she was doing. The treatments were going so well. Dee rolled her eyes when we walked in. "Marie won't clear me to leave yet."

"You need to trust her," I said, taking a seat on her bed. "She knows what she's doing."

Dee scooted past me and stood, doing a little dance in her hospital gown. "Look, I'm a young spring chicken. I'm good to go."

"Where would you go anyway if she let you get out of your bed?" I asked.

"Um, hello, to fight," Dee said with her hands on her hips.

I shook my head. "You've been in a bed for a couple of months now. You can't just expect to go out there and fight in a battle. You'll pass out."

Dee sat down on the bed and groaned. "I'm just so antsy. I'm going crazy being cooped up."

Taking her hand in mine, I turned my body to face her. "Look, we'll get through the battle and then Marie will probably release you." I tucked one of her curls behind her ear. "You can go live with her and Tina. You can go on dates with Will."

Rosie sat down on the bed, bouncing up and down a few times. I was glad she'd be with Dee during the battle. They both needed each other's company. Dee put her arm around Rosie, squeezing her.

"Has he said anything about me?" Dee asked, biting her lip.

"I talked to him the other day." I smiled at her. "He really likes you, Dee. Like a lot."

Dee's eyes lit up. "I like him, too." She shimmied. "You didn't tell me how hot he was."

Rosie snickered, so she covered her mouth with her hand to control it.

"I wanted you to make that judgment for yourself," I said. A huge smile came to my face.

"What?" Dee asked. "What's that smile for?"

"Emmie." Dante's voice came from my communicator. "Where are you?"

I pulled my communicator out of my pocket. "I'm with Dee."

"You don't have time for chit chat," Dante said. "In case you've forgotten, an army that wants to destroy our entire city will be here any minute."

"I know, Dante," I said. "I'll be there soon."

"Will's already on his way over there," Dante said. "I'll tell him to give you a ride."

"Thanks." I shoved my communicator back in my pocket.

"What was the smile for?" Rosie asked, looking at me.

My smile came back. "Will told me that Dee was the prettiest woman he'd ever seen." I looked at Dee. "He said his breath caught when he first saw you. That's why he took a little pause after he walked in."

"I noticed he did that," Dee said, "but I wasn't sure why." She blushed. "Did he really say that?"

"Yes," I said.

Rosie threw her arms around Dee. "I'm so happy for you. You two make a cute couple."

"Thanks," Dee said, resting her head on Rosie's.

Seeing how happy she was made me think of Eric and how I'd felt when we first met. I reached up to stroke my necklace, only to touch my empty neck.

Dee took my hand. "I'm sorry, Emmie."

"For what?" I asked, tucking my hair behind my ear.

"That you lost your necklace," Dee said. "And that Eric isn't here with you."

I looked down at my lap. "Do you think he's dead?"

"I don't know," Dee said, her voice quiet. "He could be. But there's also a chance you can still save him, Emmie. With everything that's happened to me over the past few days, I believe anything's possible."

I closed my eyes and nodded, trying to hold back the tears. I needed to focus on the upcoming battle, not my love life.

"I have something for you," Dee said. She motioned to a package sitting on the chair at the foot of her bed. Rosie picked it up and handed it to me.

"What is it?" I asked.

Dee smiled. "You'll have to open it up and see."

Ripping open the package, I took out the present. It was a belt made of leather with empty pouches all around. Two leather shoulder straps connected to the belt, both with the same pouches lined along them.

Dee fingered one of the pouches, rubbing her thumb along it. "Each pouch is for a magazine for your handgun." She pointed to a loop on the left side of the belt. "I made a spot for a sword, too, since you'll probably need one of those. And of course, a spot where you can strap your holster to."

I put them all on with Dee helping me out. Once everything was in place, I looked at her. "How do I look?"

"Like a warrior," Dee said.

"Thank you, Dee," I said, pulling on one of her curls. "I love it."

There was a small knock at the door. I looked up to see Will leaning against the door frame.

"Dante said you needed a ride," Will said. He looked so official in his black military uniform.

"Yes, thanks." I gave Dee a big hug. "I love you. Always."

"I love you, too," Dee said. "Now go kick some serious butt out there.

Smiling, I kissed her on the cheek.

I stood and took Rosie by the hand. "Come on. Let's give these two some privacy." Rosie gave Dee a one-armed hug before we left the room.

I shouldn't have spied, but I did. Rosie stood with me as we hid behind the door, just barely peering in. Will had sat down next to Dee and taken her hand. They were talking too quietly, so I couldn't hear what they were saying.

After a couple of minutes, Will leaned in and kissed Dee on the lips. I covered Rosie's eyes with my hand, but she pulled my hand down over her mouth to keep herself from laughing. I could feel her smile under my hand, making me smile.

When Will finally pulled away, Rosie and I stepped away from the door. I shooed Rosie away, making her go find her mom in the storage room. I casually leaned against the wall, waiting for Will to come out.

Will's smile couldn't have been any bigger when he stepped out of the room. He looked at me and cleared his throat. "You ready to go?"

I nodded. "Yes." As I walked past Dee's room, I peered

in to see her lying on the bed, her hands over her face.

"You were right, you know," Will said, making me look over at him.

"About what?" I asked.

"That I shouldn't think about it too much and it would all work out."

I smiled at him. "So how was it?"

Will's cheeks and neck turned red. "Uh, amazing."

"Good," I said, linking my arm through his. "I swear you two were made for each other. I can't believe I hadn't thought of it before."

"This is so weird," Will said, straightening his glasses. "I never thought I'd ever feel like this." He sighed. "And now we have to go fight in a battle. One I may not come out alive in."

"Don't say that, Will," I said. "Just think positively. When you're fighting, just remember what you're fighting for."

Will nodded but said nothing. We walked in silence through Headquarters and out to the jeep. I got in the passenger seat and looked around at the emptiness as we drove through town. There wasn't a person in sight. The stillness made me shiver.

Every house and building we passed reminded me of what we were fighting for. We had worked so hard to get New Haven where it was. The survival of the city and the people depended on the outcome of the battle. It would set the tone for the entire war. Winning this would give us the encouragement we needed and the strength to continue.

When we pulled up on the east side, Dante came running over to the jeep. "Finally. What took you so long?"

I patted him on the shoulder as I stepped out of the jeep. "Some of us have what we call 'friends.' You should look into it sometime."

Will waved goodbye and set off for his post.

"Very funny, Emmie," Dante said. "Besides, my best friend is standing right in front of me." He looked at my belt and straps. "Where did you get that?"

"Dee made it for me to hold all of my magazines. Like it?"

"Like it?" Dante asked, running his hand over his fro. "It's sweet. And perfect. I made sure a whole bunch of magazines were already loaded up for you and now we have a convenient spot to put them all."

"You'll have to help me put them all in."

Dante nodded. "Sure thing."

Maya handed me a sword. Its bright polish sheen caught the reflection of the sun. The handle had flowers and vines engraved in it. I noticed a small engraving on the tip of the handle. I ran my finger over it, tracing the letters LC.

"LC." I looked at Maya. "What's the LC for?"

"Lilly Chang," Maya said, looking at the sword. "It was my mom's."

My eyes widened. "Oh, Maya, I can't take this."

"Yes, you can." Maya put her hand around mine. "I want you to use it during the battle. My mom would want you to. It's a good sword. Bruce sharpened it before he left."

I stared at Maya, still unsure if I should use it. It meant a lot to Maya and Bruce and I would've felt so bad if something happened to it. "Don't you want to use it?"

Maya shook her head. "I'm a lefty. You and my mom are

right-handed." She smiled. "It's okay, Emmie. I trust you. And if anything happens to it, no big deal. It's a sword. It was made for battle. I'd hate to think of it just sitting there not being used. I'd also hate to think of some random person using it."

"Thanks, Maya," I said. "This means a lot." I sheathed the sword in my new leather belt on my left side so I could draw it across my body. My gun sat in its holster opposite of the sword.

Santiago walked up, holding a box. He placed it on the ground and pulled out a magazine. "Dante said you needed these."

"Yes, I do," I said.

Dante and Santiago immediately went to work, filling all my pouches with the magazines.

Maya looked out at all our citizens lining up in their spots, twirling the bracelets around her wrist. "This is finally happening."

Taking a deep breath, I ran my fingers through my hair. "I just hope we're ready."

"We have to be ready," Dante said, putting in a magazine on the back of my belt.

Santiago bounced around as he loaded up my magazines. "I'm so pumped. This is going to be awesome."

"Of course, you'd be excited about going into battle," I said, laughing.

Santiago looked at me. "You aren't?"

"I'm excited and terrified at the same time." I looked out at all our warriors, seeing the mixed emotions throughout them.

Dante patted me on the shoulder. "You're going to be awesome."

I looked at him, a small frown forming on my face. "I just wish we could all be together. I don't like all of us being in separate areas." In training, we worked best when the four of us were together. An unseen power pulled us close, enhancing our strength and accuracy.

"It makes sense to be apart," Maya said. "We all have different skill sets."

"I know," I said.

"Besides," Santiago said, "if we're all grouped right next to each other, we could all be killed at the same time."

"I think she was just referring to moral support," Dante said, looking at me.

I nodded. It was comforting to think of having my friends right next to me. But it wasn't logical.

Santiago tapped his ear. "We can still communicate. I'll throw out all the words of encouragement you need, baby."

When Santiago and Dante finished loading me up, I adjusted the straps, the weight making me stumble. "This is some heavy stuff. I hope I don't fall over."

"The faster you get the ammo out, the lighter it will get." Dante pointed to a small platform on the south side of the canyon. "I had that made for you. That way you'll be a little higher up and can just keep on shooting any soldier that gets near." He put his hand on my arm. "I'll be up in the tower right behind you. I'll be your eyes, Em."

"Just try not to get too flustered," Santiago said. "Make each bullet count."

I nodded, letting it all sink in. "I will." I squeezed Dante's arm. "Thank you. I'd hug you, but I don't think it would be comfortable for either of us."

Dante leaned his cheek right up next to my mouth and pointed at it. I smiled and gave him a big wet kiss on his cheek.

"Seriously, Emmie?" Dante said as he wiped off his cheek.

Santiago and Maya were laughing.

Santiago threw his arms around Dante and Maya. "Come on, guys, let's bring this together." I put my arms around Dante and Maya, and we all leaned in. Santiago kept his voice soft. "Lord, give us the strength to carry out our mission. Help us to keep our eyes clear and focused, our hearts full and open, so we can win this battle for New Haven. Amen."

"Amen," Dante, Maya, and I said.

At the same time, we all shouted at the top of our lungs, "For New Haven!"

CHAPTER 26

Dante helped me to my platform. For the first time, I found myself hoping the enemy soldiers would just get there so I could start firing off the rounds. I wasn't sure how long I could bear the weight.

"You set?" Dante asked.

I looked down at my straps and belt, glancing at my gun and sword. "I think so."

Dante tapped my head. "What about up here?"

"I hope so."

"You can do this, Em." Determination sat in his eyes. "You have it in you. Just stay focused. You have amazing aim, so use your talent well. Aim straight for the face since most of their body is covered in armor."

I nodded, running my fingers through my hair. Dante pulled something out of his pocket and put it in my hand—a ponytail holder. "Dante, why do you have one of these?"

He laughed. "I got it from Vivica. She said you could use it to keep your hair out of your face."

"That's a relief," I said, pulling my hair back and putting it on. "I wouldn't want you growing your hair out like Santiago. It's already getting too long." I looked at his hair. "Well, big."

"What, I wouldn't look good with long, flowing hair?" Dante asked, running his hand over his mini fro.

"No," I said. "Not at all. You look great with short hair."

"Then don't cut your hair like Maya's," Dante said, eyeing my long blonde hair. "I don't think short hair would suit you."

"Well, then that's settled."

Dante looked up at his tower. "I better get up there." He hugged me tight, both of us ignoring the magazines squished between us. "I've got your back, Emmie. We're going to win this."

"I know."

We pulled back and kissed each other on the cheeks. Dante gave me one last look and left, leaving me all alone. I put my earpiece in my right ear and an earplug in my left. Thankfully, the earpieces had been made to muffle any outside noises.

A wind passed over me, sending a chill through my body. Tina had contacted me through my communicator on my way out of Headquarters and tried to talk me into grabbing my coat since it had been raining off and on all morning. At the time, I had so much adrenaline in me, I didn't feel the slightest bit cold. Now, I regretted the decision.

A drop of rain landed on my cheek. I looked up at the dark, gray clouds looming over us and sighed. The rain was going to make it so much harder.

As I stood there, I took the time to look around. We had

about a hundred and fifty warriors up in the towers, their bows and arrows ready to go. In each tower, half of the warriors kneeled while the others stood behind them.

Dante was in the middle of the tower that stood behind me. He was staring straight ahead, his posture showing his confidence. His father was in the middle tower using binoculars to keep an eye out for the army headed our way. We had all insisted that the president and vice president stay in the infirmary so we could keep them safe, but they both refused.

Santiago was on the tower to the north of President Brown. Even from down where I stood, I could see his smile. His rocket launcher was leaning up against his leg. Santiago drummed the launcher with his fingers, eager to get started. The vice president was a few guys down from him.

Vivica was on the south tower and Terrance was on the north tower. Both of them, plus Dante, President Brown, and Vice President Mendes were the command leaders on their towers.

James stood next to Vivica, his face showing no emotion. The president told him he didn't have to fight since he'd just lost his son, but James wanted to. He said the battle was the only thing worth living for now.

When I looked up at Vivica, she glanced down at me. I pointed to my ponytail. "Thank you."

A small smile formed on Vivica's face as her voice came through my earpiece. "You're welcome."

Tina had a group of around a hundred and thirty warriors with her on the north side of the mountain. Javier and Fernando stood next to her, all of them gripping their shotguns.

To the right of me, on the south side, Mack was up on the mountain with around a hundred and fifty warriors, all with various rifles and shotguns. Will stood near him, holding a rifle. He bounced around in nervousness.

Joshua stood to the right of Will, one hand around the grip of his rifle, the other hand on the forend. Joshua was one of the few residents we had that knew guns inside and out. Whit had taught him how to use a gun when he was little.

My dad stood near the back. Unfortunately, Dad didn't have great aim. He was also terribly uncoordinated, so everything we tried to train him in didn't go well. He kept saying that he was just a computer guy. But he also wasn't willing to stay behind and not fight. We needed every person we could get, and Dad wanted to help. Mack had given him a rifle and told him only to shoot when necessary.

Mack looked down at me and smiled. His voice came through my earpiece. "You ready, Emmie?"

I nodded at him. "As ready as I'll ever be."

"You're going to do great. Just remember everything we went over in training." Mack pointed to his heart. "During battle, less of this." He pointed to his head. "And more of this."

"Uh, we can't see you from where we are," Santiago said. The earpieces were an open communication to all that had one. "Where did you point? That sounded a little dirty."

I laughed. "Less heart, more mind."

Santiago sighed. "That's not so dirty."

"Of course, it would be my son to make that comment," Vice President Mendes said.

"Who do you think I got it from?" Santiago asked.

Vice President Mendes laughed. "Touché."

Lightning streaked through the sky, the booming thunder following not long after. Rain trickled down. I looked down at the warriors on the ground. They were all lined up, spaced evenly apart between the mouth of the canyon. Maya stood in the middle, her hand gripping the handle of her still sheathed sword.

There were only around eighteen warriors down with Maya, since that was the number of swords we had. The members of Juniper that came with Maya only had their swords, plus some spares they had taken before they left their city. When the ammo ran low, the warriors up higher would be ordered to join Maya down below, removing swords off the fallen enemies for use.

Thunder Thighs stood right next to Maya, her face and stature ready for battle. She had her hair pulled back in a braid and had covered her face in warrior paint that some of the residents were using.

When we started training, Thunder Thighs was immediately drawn to the sword. She didn't even bother with any other weapon. When I asked her about it, she told me only sissies would use a gun or bow and arrow. She liked being in the action, the enemy falling right before her eyes. I feared for any soldier that came across Thunder Thighs.

A faint sound in the distance caught my attention. As it grew closer, the steady beat of the soldiers stomping echoed through the canyon. I could make out the group coming toward us in the distance. My heart raced as the reality finally set in.

This was it. They were here. In a matter of minutes, the battle would be underway. I glanced around at our warriors again, thinking that we were going to lose so many of them, if not all. There were only around four hundred and fifty of us. There were twenty-five hundred of the enemy.

Well, eleven were dead thanks to Gideon eliminating General Ming and ten of his imperial soldiers. Of course, that didn't make me feel any better.

"Everyone hold steady," President Brown said. "No one moves until I give the command."

I stood straight, trying to clear my mind of any negative thought or emotion. I took my handgun out of its holster and held it at my side, the barrel pointed down.

"Santiago, get your first rocket ready," President Brown said.

The excitement in Santiago's voice radiated through the earpiece. "I've been waiting my whole life for someone to say that to me."

I shook my head, trying not to laugh.

As the soldiers came closer, a clanking sound grew. They were all beating their hands against their chests. Their swords were already unsheathed, ready to strike.

"Aim for the front of the group, Santiago," President Brown said. "Let me know when you're ready."

After a few moments, Santiago spoke. "Ready, sir."

"On my command," President Brown said. "Ready." The stomps were getting louder, the vibrations from their armor being hit filling the air. "Set." It made me wonder how loud it would be if I didn't have the earplugs in. "Fire!"

A faint whistling hummed as the rocket soared through the air. I kept my eyes focused on the front line of the soldiers.

Moments later, the rocket landed in the middle of the second line of soldiers, sending them flying away from the blast, some hitting into nearby trees. A cloud of smoke rose into the air. The soldiers nearby the blast scrambled around, flustered.

A soldier from the front line shouted something at his fellow soldiers and they quickly regained their composure, going back to the perfect motion.

"Archers, ready," President Brown said. The command leaders repeated the order. I wanted to turn around to see them release their arrows, but I forced myself to keep forward. I didn't want to lose my concentration.

"Fire!" President Brown shouted. I stood firm as the arrows flew, connecting with the soldiers. Some stumbled a little and a few fell to the ground. Their fellow soldiers just marched over their fallen comrades.

The arrows continued to fly at each issuing command. Every now and then, a grenade would be thrown. Despite the soldiers that were falling, the others kept steady, not missing a beat. Their level of discipline amazed me. Some didn't even bat an eye when a soldier fell right in front of them.

As the archers continued, President Brown ordered Tina and Mack's groups to fire their guns. The enemy soldiers flinched more at the sound of the guns. Maya had said they only had swords as weapons, so they may have never seen a gun or bow and arrow before.

General Ming had prepared them well. The way they were

synchronized, and the precision of their movements almost made them seem not human.

They were only twenty yards out now. Maya shouted for the warriors down below to unsheathe their swords and prepare to fight. The arrows and bullets continued to fly, each volley taking down a few soldiers.

I pulled my handgun up, gripping it tightly. There was a soldier only a couple of yards away from me. My aim settled on his face, right between the eyes. I took a deep breath and pulled the trigger. The bullet connected with the soldier and he fell to the ground.

From that moment on, I didn't stop. I kept firing round after round, continuously releasing and reloading the magazines in my gun. My mind was clear, concentrating only on where I needed to strike. I had pretty much drowned out any sound around me, focusing only on my duty.

The weight on my body lightened as I continued to use up my magazines. My belt and left strap were already empty and there wasn't much left on my right strap.

I faintly remember hearing commands being issued through my earpiece, none directed at me. Two of the towers had been moved over to rifles and shotguns. Anyone out of ammo had come down and continued with a sword.

Dropping an empty magazine from my gun, I reached for another one. I fumbled around until I found one and loaded it. I glanced over at my right strap to see that I had just loaded my last magazine.

Until then, most of the enemy soldiers had ignored me. They were concentrated on our warriors with swords coming at them on ground level. I was also wearing my dark brown shirt and pants, somewhat blending in with a tree right behind me. The clouds had covered up the sun, taking away most of the natural light. The rain continued, the intensity increasing with each passing minute.

Two enemy soldiers came right by my platform, spotting me immediately. They both went to jump onto my platform, but I pulled the trigger, putting a bullet in each soldier. As I watched them fall back, a noise came from the right of me.

Before I had fully turned, an enemy soldier barreled down on me, screaming at the top of his lungs. I stared into his wild eyes, no sense of human empathy or compassion behind them. He looked ruthless and disconnected from any emotion besides determination.

He drew back his sword, thrusting his arm into the air. Taking hold of my shirt, he let out another yell. I put my gun between the two of us and pulled the trigger. Nothing happened. I was out of ammo.

As I watched his sword come toward me, I let go of my gun and threw my arms at his face, pushing back with all my might. I kept pushing until his helmet came off, crashing onto the ground. I squirmed my body the best I could, trying to get away, but it was useless. He was much stronger than me.

When his sword was only inches from me, lightning rippled through the sky, the flash reflecting off his sword. It threw him off for only a second, but during that moment an arrow hit him in the forehead. His body came down on top of me, knocking the breath from my body.

"Em, are you okay?" Dante asked through my earpiece.

I struggled for words. "I. Can't. Breathe." I tried to push him off me, but he was too big. My hands kept sliding off his wet armor, making it hard to get a good grip.

The next thing I knew, he was being pulled off me. I was so relieved until I noticed it was an enemy who had pulled him off. He licked his lips and threw his fellow soldier's body to the ground. I unsheathed my sword as he came at me.

Turning my body to the side, I fell off my platform, his sword barely missing me. I got to my feet as fast as I could and drew back my sword. As the soldier jumped off my platform, I drove my sword through his throat, blood squirting all over me.

I yanked my sword out and ran my hand over my face. When I looked at my hand, it was covered in rain and blood. I did everything I could to hold back the bile that came up my throat.

Stunned by what had just happened, it took me a second to register Dante's voice. "Emmie! Behind you!"

I turned around just as an enemy soldier thrust his sword at me. His sword connected with me, cutting a long gash down my arm. I clenched my teeth and tried not to scream as he came at me again. Holding my sword up, I blocked his strike from hitting me, the force sending a vibration through my arm, startling me.

I dodged a few more thrusts until I slipped on the wet ground and fell. As I lay on the ground, I noticed a small opening on the side between his armor. I gripped my handle with both hands and drove my sword into his side.

Pulling my sword out of the dead soldier, I looked over

just in time to see another soldier coming at me. He was twice as big as the one I had just killed. "You have got to be kidding me." There was no way I could take that guy. So, I stumbled to my feet, turned around, and ran.

"Run faster, Em!" Dante yelled. "I'm almost there." I saw him running toward me, now off his tower.

When Dante reached me, he put his arm out in front of me, pushing me back and away from the enemy soldier. He and the enemy went at it, their swords ringing as they connected. I stayed behind Dante until I saw the perfect opening. Dante and the enemy both had their arms raised in the air, their swords locked together, both of them pushing. I took my sword and drove it through the gap in the armor of the soldier. He fell back sputtering for breath, the life leaving his eyes.

"Thanks," Dante said as another soldier came at him. We continued to fight side by side, working together to destroy the enemy. My arms were getting tired, my left arm growing weak from the slash it took.

Dante and I continued to push forward, falling deep into the enemy soldiers. I could tell they were getting tired, I'm sure the weight of all their armor taking an effect.

"Towers are cleared," President Brown said. "Everyone's down below, fighting."

Some of our residents were struggling to find dead soldiers so they could take their swords. I prayed they would find one before they were killed themselves.

The adrenaline that I had taken me this far into the battle started to fade. I wasn't sure how much longer I could last. My body wasn't ready for a battle like this. None of ours were.

It felt like we'd killed so many enemies, but when I looked down the canyon, I could still see hundreds and hundreds more. Another enemy came at me and it took every ounce of strength I had to drive my sword into his side. Once I'd figured out there was a gap in their armor, I continued to aim for that spot on each enemy.

Dante and I had been separated a little while earlier. I tried desperately to look for him but couldn't spot him anywhere.

As I turned around, my foot slipped on the muddy ground and I fell. Before I could get back up, one of our residents fell on top of me. Their lifeless eyes stared into mine and I screamed.

"Em, behind you," Dante said.

I wasn't sure where Dante was, but he must've been close by. I turned my head around and saw an enemy only a few feet away. I struggled to get my fellow warrior off me, making me lose my grip on my sword. As I reached out for my sword, I looked over my shoulder to see the enemy right behind me.

Mere moments later, the enemy fell to the ground, a sword impaling him through his side. Mack pulled his sword back out and came over, pushing our warrior off me. He held out his hand and helped me up.

"Emmie, that doesn't look good," Mack said, holding onto my left arm. "We need to get this treated."

Before I could say a word, Mack's eyes grew wide and blood poured out of his mouth. I looked down to see a sword protruding from his chest. As the sword pulled back out, Mack slowly fell face forward to the ground.

Bending down, I picked up my sword, screaming as I went straight for the soldier who'd stabbed Mack. I had both hands around the hilt as our swords collided with one another. I swung at the enemy over and over, but he continued to block my wild swings. Dodging a thrust from him, I turned my body around until I was behind him. I kicked him as hard as I could in the back of the legs, sending him to the ground.

The soldier was on his stomach, so he moved to get onto his hands and knees. Before he could stand back up, I kicked him in the side. He immediately curled onto his side, revealing the opening in his armor. I held up my sword with both hands and drove it down, screaming the whole time.

Once I was certain the soldier was dead, I ran over to Mack, who lay on the ground, blood covering his chest and mouth. I knelt next to him and put his head in my lap. More soldiers came toward me, but Dante, Maya, and Santiago were all there, fighting them off.

He was barely breathing as I held onto him. I bent down, resting my forehead on his. "Mack."

"Emmie." Mack's voice was barely audible. "Em, I'm so proud …" He wheezed. "Proud of you."

I pulled back and looked into his eyes, wiping the rain off his forehead and cheeks. "Oh, Mack. Please don't leave me."

Mack took his hand and put it on my cheek. "Win this. For me."

"I will, Mack." My tears were flowing, blending in with the rain. "I promise."

"You." Mack gasped for breath. "You can do this."

I watched as the life slipped out of him and his hand fell to the ground.

CHAPTER 27
Gideon

We made it to Juniper in a little less than eight hours. Bruce kept saying how much faster it would've been on the way to New Haven if they'd had a motor vehicle. It'd taken them a week to walk.

There was a spot on the foot of the mountain that we picked to hide the jeep. Juniper was up the mountain, so we figured the best way up without announcing our presence was to hike. We left the guns in the jeep, only taking swords with us. The noise from a gun would surely catch attention from the city.

I debated for a while whether I should take the rocket launcher with me. Its weight would slow me down and using it would make our presence known. In the end, I decided to carry it with me just in case something happened.

Bruce took us up a less-traveled path. It was a hard hike because of it, but there wouldn't be anyone in the vicinity. The area was tightly packed with trees, helping our concealment. As we drew closer to the city, the smell of ash and smoke filled the air. Smoke billowed up from the fires.

When we were almost there, Bruce slowed us down, motioning for me to keep quiet. We crept slowly through the trees, watching our steps to avoid creating too much noise. Bruce stopped us a few yards out from the entrance we needed to take.

Huge rocks and boulders covered up most of the entrance. I could see a small opening on the right-hand side where someone small, like Bruce, could crawl through. I pulled out my binoculars, searching the area. There was no one nearby.

Near the entrance of the city, I spotted a huge mound. A few men were carrying out stuff from the city and throwing it in the pile. I focused my binoculars on the mound, trying to make out what was in it. My quick intake of breath made me cough. Bruce put his finger over his mouth, telling me to zip it. I nodded my head toward the mound and handed Bruce my binoculars.

He glanced at me sideways, then pulled the binoculars up to his eyes. He adjusted them to fit his face and pointed them where I told him to. "Holy ..." Bruce cut off, dropping the binoculars from his hands. He stood and went behind a tree nearby, releasing all the food from his body.

I couldn't imagine what Bruce was thinking. The mound was all the dead bodies from their battle, and they were throwing them in a pile like garbage. They must have killed so many people and done so much damage to the city to still be cleaning up over a week later.

I gave Bruce some time to finish what he was doing and process everything he saw. When he came back, I put my hand on his shoulder, squeezing it. "I'm sorry, Bruce. I know that must be hard to see."

He just nodded, wiping some tears from his eyes. I suddenly regretted showing him. I kept forgetting he was only fourteen.

Bruce wiped his mouth and then nodded his head at the entrance to the cave. "I'm going in. I want to get this over with."

I reached into my bag I had carried up with me and carefully took out the bottle containing the virus. "Just drop all of it in the main water source." I tapped my earpiece. "You can reach me at any time."

Nodding, Bruce put his earpiece in. He handed me his sword. "I can't fit in with that."

He took a deep breath and went toward the entrance, creeping over in a squatting position. When he reached the boulders, he climbed to the opening and crawled his way in.

A few moments later, Bruce's voice sounded through my earpiece. "I'm in."

Then it went silent for a good five minutes. I tapped my foot impatiently on the ground, hoping everything was okay.

"Bruce," I said, keeping my voice low.

"I'm still here," Bruce said. "I'm just being careful where I walk and going slow. This flashlight isn't exactly bright. Oh, I see the opening to the water container just up ahead." Silence again. "Alright, I'm right above it with the vial in my hands.

I'm taking off the lid, hoping I don't spill any on me, and ... done." I heard a small clink. "Uh, you didn't want the vial back, right? Because I just dropped it in, too."

I smiled. "No, we don't need it. It's probably better left here than coming back with us."

"True." Bruce took a deep breath. "Well then. That was easy. I'm coming back."

I stood up straight, adjusting the rocket launcher on my back. Using my binoculars, I checked the entrance to the city again. They were pouring something on the sides of the mound, but I couldn't tell what it was. At least they were still preoccupied, and no one had noticed us yet.

"Wait," Bruce said. "I hear something."

"What is it?"

He sighed. "I don't know. I think it sounded like banging. Give me a minute. I want to look around."

"Just be quick. We need to get out of here while we still can."

"Yeah, yeah," Bruce said. There were a few minutes of silence. "I can't see anything, but I can definitely hear something. I see a small opening in one of the walls here. I'm going to look in. Uh, it's too dark, let me get my flashlight. Okay, looking in and ... oh."

"What?" I asked. "What's there?" He was silent. "Bruce? What's going on?"

I could barely hear his voice. "We were wrong."

"What do you mean?"

"It's not just bad people left," he said, his voice a little more audible.

I shook my head. "I don't understand. How do you know?"

"Because I'm looking at a cell full of prisoners. People I know. Old palace guards and maids. Kids I went to school with. They're still alive. They've been keeping them prisoner down here." He swore. "I don't believe this. I had no idea."

"How could you have known?" I asked. "It doesn't matter right now. We need to think of a way to get them out of there."

"How?" Bruce asked, his voice defeated. "I can barely fit through the opening into here, so no one bigger than me will make it through. And they're in a locked cell behind a mountain wall."

I touched my rocket launcher and shook my head. That wouldn't work. It would just cause more damage. "Can you create a bigger opening? Are any of the rocks loose?"

"Uh," Bruce said. "Yeah, a little. Let me work at it and see if I can get an opening big enough for me."

"Good," I said. "I'll work on creating a larger opening out here." I took off my rocket launcher and set it down. Very softly I walked toward the entrance, watching where I stepped. Once I made it there, I felt around to see if I could loosen any of the rocks. Some could be moved but taking them out would create another collapse.

Taking hold of a rock, I pulled myself up, climbing toward the top. If I could create an opening up there, it might work.

"I'm making progress," Bruce said. "I think this might work. If I just ..." He went silent. I waited a while until he spoke again, his voice a whisper. "There's a guard in there. I just spotted him. It doesn't seem like he's heard me yet."

"Keep at it, Bruce. Just be careful. We can't leave all those prisoners there to die." I reached the top and moved some rocks around, trying not to drop any. I needed to carefully rearrange them to create an opening and not cause a collapse. The sound of falling rocks would be heard.

It took me a while, but I finally created an opening I could fit through. I scooted my body through the hole, climbing down the rocks once I was inside. I turned on my flashlight and walked, taking the lightest steps I could.

"Bruce?" I kept my voice low. "I'm inside."

"Good," Bruce said. "I'm almost done here. Just keep walking down the main path. Take a right when you get to the water container."

It was freezing inside the cave. I clamped my jaw together so my chin wouldn't chatter. After a few minutes, I saw the water container sitting in the middle of a large opening in the cave. I made a right, shining my light down the path. Bruce stood a little way down. Pointing my flashlight on the ground, I walked toward him.

When I got to him, I noticed he'd made a pretty big opening, enough to even get me through. I patted him on the shoulder and nodded. Smiling at me, he brushed off his hands.

He leaned in close to my ear. "Please tell me you brought a sword with you."

I turned so he could see my left side where my sword was sheathed. I took it out and handed it to Bruce.

He looked at the opening. "I'm going to take out the guard." He quietly went through the hole, holding my sword at his side.

When I peered in the opening, I saw a large cell holding at least a couple hundred prisoners. Some of them were lying down and I couldn't tell if they were still alive. The ones who saw us kept quiet, not wanting to warn the guard.

Bruce snuck up behind the guard, placed his hand over the guard's mouth, and drove the sword through his back. He kept his hand over the guard's mouth as he lowered him to the ground. Taking out the sword, he nodded to me.

Grabbing a hold of the sides of the opening, I picked myself up and swung my feet through until they landed on the other side. I straightened myself and joined Bruce.

There was a door opened near where we were standing, so we both peered out. There was a long hallway to the left, but no one was there.

I bent down next to the guard, feeling around his belt and pockets until I found a set of keys in his chest pocket. I went over to the cell door and started trying all the keys.

The fifth one worked, the door clicking as it unlocked. I pulled the door open so the prisoners could get out. When no one moved, I looked in to see them all staring at me, some with their mouths agape.

I looked at Bruce. "What's wrong?"

Bruce couldn't hold back his smile. "I think they're surprised by you, that's all. You're a big guy."

I smiled at the prisoners, trying to let them know I was nice. "Hello. My name is Gideon. I know this is probably shocking to you, but we need to hurry and get going before someone figures out we're here."

An older lady stepped forward, placing her hand on my

arm. "Nice to meet you. I'm Lana."

Bruce hugged Lana tightly. She squeezed him back, rocking side to side. When they pulled back, she pinched Bruce's cheeks. He looked at me. "Lana was my watcher growing up."

"Watcher?" I asked.

Lana brushed some of her graying black hair out of her face. "I watched over him. Made sure he was taken care of, looked proper for all public and important events." She looked at him. "Made sure he ate his vegetables."

Bruce gagged. "Gross."

"I hate to cut this reunion short, but we need to go." I looked around the cell. There were still some people lying on the floor not moving. "Are they …?"

Lana's eyes lit up in anger. "Yes, they're dead. They've hardly fed us, and they've just left anyone who dies in there with us. It's completely unacceptable. We've done nothing wrong."

Bruce squeezed Lana's arm. "Now isn't the time, Lana."

Lana huffed. "Look what they've done to them! To us!"

Bruce smiled and took Lana by the arm, escorting her back to the opening we created. The prisoners gradually piled out, some moving quite slow. They were all very thin, their clothes torn and tattered. All of them were dirty and I could smell sweat and urine as they passed by.

I counted their heads as they exited. Two hundred and sixty-eight prisoners. When the last one was out, I took in the view of the cell floor. There were at least a hundred dead, some of them small children. It would have been nice to give them all a proper burial, but we didn't have time. Thinking about how many people we were trying to help escape and their horrible condition, I wasn't even sure if we could make it out of there. It was going to take forever.

Bruce had already started helping people through the first opening, telling them to continue, making a left at the water container and heading toward the exit.

I went up to Bruce, who had already gone to the other side of the hole to help. "Go to the exit. I'll keep helping everyone here." I sighed. "The next opening's going to be harder. I had to make one at the top."

"I'm not sure if they can climb," Bruce said as he helped a young boy through the opening.

"We'll have to assist them," I said. "One by one. It's the only way."

Bruce nodded. "Alright. See you at the other opening."

It ended up taking me forty minutes to get the rest of them through the first hole. When we made it to the other opening that would lead us outside, a big group of people was just standing there. Bruce wasn't in sight.

I went to the front and looked at a man who seemed to be around my age. "Where's Bruce?"

"Helping someone down the other side," the man said. Out of everyone there, he seemed to be in the best condition. By his stature, I assumed he must have been a palace guard at one point. "I've been helping them up and he's helping them down."

"How many have you gotten through so far?" I asked.

The man scratched his beard. The black hair on his head

was a tangled mess. "Maybe twenty."

I sighed, looking at all the prisoners who had hope in their eyes. Hope of freedom and life. If we continued at this rate, we would be there for hours. But what other option was there?

Bruce came back through the opening and climbed down. He gritted his teeth. "They've started a fire." He looked at me, his eyes lit with anger and disgust. "The mound."

Shock ran through me. "They're burning them?"

Bruce nodded. He looked like he might throw up again.

I gently put my hand on his arm. "Bruce, I know this is hard, but we have to continue. All of this means they're distracted right now. This is the best time to do this."

"I know," Bruce said.

"Get back up there. I'll start helping people up." I looked at the man I talked to. "I'm sorry, I didn't get your name."

"Ren." He stuck out his hand and I shook it.

"Gideon. Nice to meet you." I looked up at the opening. "Would you mind staying up there, helping people through? I'll help them up and Bruce can guide them down."

Ren nodded. "Of course."

With Ren's help, we got everyone through in two hours. I was glad we still hadn't caught anyone's attention. If anything, we were downright lucky. They must have rarely checked on the prisoners or the guard.

I was the last one down. Everyone stood in a group, huddled together near the entrance. I looked out over them. "We need to head down the mountain. Unfortunately, we're taking a path that isn't used very often, so it won't be easy. But it's the only way." I looked at Bruce. "You take the front. Ren can keep to the middle. I'll stay in the back. Let's get going."

Bruce immediately took off, all the freed prisoners at his heels. I kept a watch out, using my binoculars to glance at the entrance to the city now and then. A huge billow of smoke came up from the mound, making me shiver.

When the last person had started down, I grabbed my bag and rocket launcher, strapping it to my back. I took one last look at the mound and then started down the mountain.

I had only taken two steps when a voice came from behind me. "Who are you?"

I turned around to see a soldier standing there, his sword in his hand. He looked me up and down, sizing me up. He suddenly shouted, "Intruder!"

Unsheathing my sword, I lunged at him. He dodged a few of my thrusts, but I connected with his arm. He stepped back, losing his balance. I drove my sword through his abdomen, twisting it until he fell. When I pulled it free, I could hear shouting in the distance. I looked up to see more soldiers running toward me, my presence now known.

The soldiers were coming from the entrance to the city, running alongside the mountain. I glanced down at our escaped prisoners. They must have heard all the commotion, because they had picked up speed, going down as fast as their weak bodies would let them.

But they were still too slow. I had to think quickly. I looked back at the soldiers running toward me and then at the side of the mountain. Their city was surrounded by a large wall made of rock. If I could knock down part of the wall so it blocked their path, it would slow them down, giving us time to escape.

Since the soldier I had just killed had only shouted

"intruder," he didn't know there were others with me. He must have just walked up and only saw me walking down. Which meant the men coming toward me thought I was the only one there. I could use that to my advantage.

"Bruce, we have a slight problem up here." I tried not to move my lips too much just in case the enemies could see my face clearly.

"What is it?" Bruce asked through the communicator. "We were going down when all of a sudden all the prisoners in the back started pushing everyone forward, telling us to go faster."

"Someone spotted me."

He swore. "What do we do?"

"You keep going back toward New Haven." I looked at the soldiers and they were getting closer, all of them shouting at me.

"What about you?"

"They only spotted me. I'm taking another direction." I took off running diagonally down the mountain, the opposite way Bruce went, which would take me closer to the entrance of the city.

"I can't lead all these people by myself!" Bruce shouted.

I weaved around trees, looking back now and then to make sure all the soldiers were still only following me, which it looked like they were. "You have to, Bruce. I'll try to make it to you, but you must keep going. Notify Mack of what's going on. Maybe they can send a bus to you. Have Ren help you. You'll be fine."

"Okay," Bruce said. "But I want you to know I'm not

happy about this situation at all." He paused. "But good luck, anyway."

"Thanks." I tried not to smile. I was really starting to like the kid. "You too. See you soon."

Looking back again, I noticed I had made good progress, creating a bigger gap between me and the soldiers. I was directly down from the entrance to the city. There were only ten to fifteen people outside the gate.

I immediately stopped, taking off my rocket launcher. I pulled the rocket from my bag and loaded it up. Placing the launcher on my shoulder, I pointed it toward the opening.

The gate was open, revealing an alleyway leading into the city before it opened. If I could just hit those rocks walls, it might close off the exit making it so no one could get out. For now.

Looking through my scope, I found the perfect spot to hit. I took a deep breath and pulled the trigger, watching the rocket fly toward its target. The soldiers running after me stopped, watching the rocket go through the air.

While they were preoccupied, I hid my launcher and bag behind a tree and ran to the left, away from the path to New Haven. I heard the rocket explode, so I glanced up the mountain and stopped to watch. The rock wall fell just like I'd hoped, sealing off the entrance.

The soldiers looked down where I should've been and panicked. I made sure they saw me before I moved. As I looked back at the soldiers, I counted them. Twelve in all. Somehow, I needed to eliminate all of them so I could get back to Bruce.

I ran until it was obvious I was headed north, but still close enough to the city so the dead soldiers could be found. Stopping in the middle of the path, I turned and waited for the soldiers. I unsheathed my sword, ready for battle.

I took slow, even breaths, trying to calm my nerves and heart. I thought about Bruce and how he'd need my help. I thought about all those people we rescued. I thought about New Haven. I thought about Marie and how much I loved her and wanted to spend the rest of my life with her.

When the first soldier was only a few steps away, I yelled out and charged at him. With my mind clear of thought, I continued to swing my sword around, connecting with any enemy that came at me.

I counted as they went down.

One. Two. Three. Four.

I took a slash to my left leg, but it fueled me. I drove my sword through the culprit's side, quickly released and spun around, ramming my sword through another's abdomen.

Five. Six.

These soldiers weren't ready for battle like the others. They didn't have armor on, so it evened out the field.

Seven. Eight. Nine.

I ducked down, dodging a swing at my head. Kicking the man in the stomach, he fell to the ground. Hearing someone behind me, I flipped my sword around and drove it backward, connecting with the soldier.

Ten.

I pulled out my sword and spun away from another soldier. I dodged a few attempts and then slashed his side. The other man I had kicked down was back up, coming at me. I slashed the man near me again on his other side and then kicked him down.

The other man approached me, and we started swinging, my sword connecting with his over and over again. His thrusts slowed. I jumped to the side, throwing him off. Swinging my sword around, I cut off his hand holding his sword. He took hold of his arm, screaming out in pain. I drove my sword into his stomach and pushed him to the ground.

Eleven.

I went and stood above number twelve, the soldier who'd already taken two slashes. He looked up at me, his eyes pleading. I had to tell myself this was war. It wasn't personal against this man. But it was personal to New Haven. It was personal to those prisoners we'd just released. It was personal to me.

With one last roar, I drove my sword through his chest.

Twelve.

CHAPTER 28
Emmie

I pulled Mack's body off to the side, hiding him behind a tree. I took a moment to look up, analyzing our situation. We had a good number of New Haven residents alive, but some looked seriously injured and we were still outnumbered.

Forcing myself—and ignoring the pain in my arm—I went out to join Dante, Santiago, and Maya. The four of us stood back to back in a square, fighting off the enemy soldiers.

"What's the status of our weapons?" I asked, taking a swing at a soldier.

"Arrows are gone," Dante said. The sound of swords colliding could be heard all around.

"Ammunition on the towers is gone," President Brown said through my earpiece.

"The ammunition from Mack's side is out, too," Santiago said.

I immediately thought of my dad, Will, and Joshua and

wondered how they were doing.

"We still have some shells up here," Tina said. "But over half of my side has already jumped down, moving on to swords. It won't be too much longer until we're all out."

"Tina, what does it look like up there?" Bending forward, I barely escaped a sword chopping off my head. "Can you see how many enemy soldiers there still are?" With my eyes narrowed, I charged at the man, driving my sword through his side.

"At least seven to eight hundred," Tina said.

"How many of us?" Maya asked.

Tina sighed. "I don't know, maybe two hundred?"

We'd lost over half already. If we continued at that rate, they would surely finish us off.

"Ladies and gentlemen, may I have your attention please?" Derek.

"Who let him on this frequency?" Dante asked, making me laugh. Only for a second, though, and then another soldier dove at me and my laughter faded.

"No one," Derek said. "I can get on any frequency whenever I want. This is my specialty."

I took a swing at the enemy. "Would you like to enlighten me on why you're bothering us right now?" The enemy soldier stopped for a moment and looked at me confused. I smiled at him. "Oh, sorry, I'm not talking to you. I'm talking to my half-brother." I put my sword through his side. "We have nothing in common, trust me."

"First, Emmie, let me say I'm surprised you're still alive," Derek said. "Although, maybe you're just boring the enemy to death." He laughed, clearly amused at himself. "Second, I wanted to inform you that at least a thousand people are coming from the other side of the canyon right now."

My heart stopped. "What?"

"Did I stutter?" Derek asked. "A thousand people, coming at you. Well, in addition to the seven hundred and twenty-four still left of the soldiers already here."

"How do you know the exact number?" Santiago asked.

"My computer," Derek said. "Oh, seven hundred and twenty-three. Nice job, Maya."

I rolled my eyes. How could Derek still be interfering with our lives during the battle? I thought I would get a nice break from him for a while. "Are they more soldiers from Juniper?"

"They're still too far out to tell," Derek said. "I didn't have cameras installed all the way down the canyon. But there's a lot of them and from the way they're walking, they look like they're ready to fight."

"We need to check it out." Dante stepped next to me, stabbing a big soldier that I was fighting with.

"Thanks," I said. "That guy was huge."

"Why don't Emmie and I go check it out?" Santiago suggested. "It will give her arm a little break."

"Why you and not me?" Dante asked, his eyebrows raised.

Santiago shrugged. "Just because."

Dante glanced over at me and then turned his attention back to Santiago, smirking the whole time. "Why?"

"Don't make me say it," Santiago said. When Dante continued to smile at him, Santiago threw up his arm that wasn't holding a sword. "You're better with a sword than I am.

Okay? You happy?"

"Completely," Dante said, pushing me to the side and going at another soldier.

Santiago took me by my good arm and steered me toward the south side of the canyon, away from enemy soldiers. "Maybe we can make it down the side without being interrupted."

We stayed close to the side of the mountain, hiding behind trees when necessary. My arm and energy were thankful for the little break. It wasn't long until we had reached the end of the enemy line. Those guys hadn't even seen battle yet, which meant they were still full of energy.

"How's your arm?" Santiago asked, rubbing the cross tattoo behind his ear.

"It hurts like no other," I said.

Santiago took my arm and looked at it closer. "That looks pretty bad."

"Well, it feels pretty bad." I flinched when he touched it. "What are you doing? Trying to kill me?"

"Sorry, just wanted to see." He took off his shirt and wrapped it around my arm. "Maybe that will at least stop the bleeding for now."

I rolled my eyes. "You just wanted a reason to take off your shirt."

He couldn't hold back his usual smirk, which he referred to as a smolder. "You know it, baby."

I couldn't help but look. Of course, he was nicely built with the perfect abs. I sighed. I didn't want to be thinking about Santiago's abs at that moment.

He put his arm around my shoulder and squeezed. "I know it's hard to resist, but you're going to have to."

"Please," I said. "Eric looks better."

"I'm going to pretend like you didn't say that."

After about fifty yards, a group was coming toward us. There were a lot of them, tightly packed together, marching through the canyon. Santiago and I hid behind a tree and tried to get a better look.

The rain had lightened, making it easier to see. I went to another tree in front of us so I could look closer. I immediately noticed they weren't wearing armor like the soldiers from Juniper had. And they didn't have swords. They had guns.

I gasped. They looked like they were from …

"Yeah, baby!" Santiago said, running out into the open.

"What are you doing?" I hissed at him. "Are you crazy?"

Santiago looked at me. "You know I am, Emmie. But they're from Scorpion City. They're with us!"

"How do you know they're on our side?" I asked. "What if they were sent here to fight us?"

Santiago smiled. "Because I see my cousin and her family." He jumped into the air, pumping his fist and screaming.

The crowd did the same thing.

I stepped out from behind the tree to get a better look. The members of Scorpion looked ready to fight. They all had shotguns and tons of shells on belts and straps, like what Dee had made me.

Santiago ran at the group, screaming in excitement. A girl broke off from the bunch and ran to Santiago. Picking her up, he twirled her around a few times, laughing the whole time. I assumed that was his cousin. When he set her down, he hugged others in the group.

"Is everyone listening?" I asked, using my earpiece.

"Yes." A lot of voices came through, but I couldn't distinguish all of them.

"What's going on?" Dante asked. "Who is it?"

I couldn't contain my smile. "They're residents of Scorpion. They want to be part of the revolution and they're definitely ready to fight."

"Are you serious?" Maya asked.

"Yes," I said. "A thousand more people on our side."

"We're going to win!" Dante yelled. "We're going to freaking win this thing!"

"Emmie, tell them to hurry," President Brown said. "We're still losing lots of people over here. They need to attack from the other side."

"On it," I said. The entire group was now right in front of me. They all stopped when they saw me staring. "First, let me say I'm glad you're here. But we're getting our butts kicked and losing lots of good people. There are still at least seven hundred left of the enemy. They're all wearing silver armor and helmets with ridiculous feathers sticking out of them. You can't miss them."

"Now go kill them!" Santiago yelled, coming up next to me. The people ran, yelling out in excitement. Santiago pulled me off to the side so we wouldn't get trampled to death.

He continued to jump up and down, shouting words of encouragement at everyone. When the last of them passed by, we stepped out behind them, following them back to New Haven.

I looked at Santiago, who was still pumped. He punched the air, just like he did during a boxing match. "We're going to win this, baby. I just know it. We're going to take down that Juniper trash!"

He yelled out, balled his hands into fists and beat them against his bare chest. I started laughing, his excitement seeping into me and everyone in front of us.

The next thing I knew, Santiago turned to me, took me by my arms, and pulled me toward him, planting a big kiss on my lips.

When he pulled back, I punched him in the face, shaking my hand out afterward.

Santiago smiled, putting his hand over his eye where I hit him. "Totally worth it."

CHAPTER 29
Luke
∞

The air below Headquarters was stale and putrid. Dean had said I could find my father down here, but I wasn't sure what he'd be doing in the basement. I didn't even know the place existed.

As I walked down the hallway, I peered in the windows on the doors. Every room I passed had the lights off, so I couldn't see in.

I came to a T in the hall and looked each way, wondering which route to take. I had decided to continue forward until I heard a small cough from the other hallway, so I turned and went down that hall instead.

The first door on the right was open, so I stepped in. The room was empty. There was a door on the left wall and a big window next to it, so I walked over to it and peered in.

It revealed another room, empty except for someone lying on the floor. I took a few steps to the right, hoping to get a better look at the face. It took me a moment to realize who it was. Their face was so swollen, bruised and cut up, making it hard to see all their features.

I took a few steps back, running my hand over my head. It couldn't be. But it looked like him. Stepping forward again, I pressed my hands on the glass. It was him. I turned around, walked to the middle of the room and squatted down. Why would they do that?

"Luke." The voice startled me. I stood to see President Randall standing in the doorway. He stepped into the room, went to the window and leaned up against it. He looked inside, a small smile coming to his face. How could he be smiling? "I know what you're thinking, Luke."

"I'm not too sure about that."

President Randall turned to me, his eyes filled with satisfaction. "You're probably wondering why we hadn't caught one of them sooner."

"I …" His words surprised me. "Wait, what?"

"Those traitors have been gone for months, and we just now get our hands on one." He shook his head. "It's embarrassing, really. With all the technology we have, all the resources, it's pathetic. I'm not sure who to blame."

He should blame himself. But the fact that they hadn't caught anyone was *not* what I was thinking about. Tina came to mind. "So, you only caught Eric?"

He sighed. "Yes, unfortunately. He's not even the one I wanted. I gave Dean and Pierce one simple task of bringing me Emmie. But Eric will do for now. And Pierce was killed, so I guess that settles it." He came up next to me, putting his hand on my arm. "Trust me, son, this is not how I like to operate. I like results. And I like when my orders are followed. To my dismay, Dean has continued to let me down. And so has your father. But you, Luke, you have potential. I can see it in you. You have the drive and determination it takes."

I scratched the back of my head, trying to fully comprehend everything he said. "Really, sir? You think I have potential?"

President Randall went back to the window and stared down at Eric's body. For the first time, I realized Eric wasn't moving. "Yes, Luke, I do. You're going to do great things for this city. You're a natural-born leader. And you don't stop until everything's perfect." He looked at me. "I've been watching you during your training. I'm quite impressed. The amount of precision and thought put into every action you do is amazing."

"Sir," I said. "Is Eric still alive?"

"Barely. We checked on him right before you came in and he was still breathing. I do want to keep him alive for now until I get Emmie." He clapped his hands together. "Luke, I have an assignment for you."

I raised my eyebrows, excited at the prospect of working for the president. "What is it?"

President Randall laughed. "I love your enthusiasm. Dean and your father haven't been able to get anything out of Eric. I want you to try."

My face almost fell, but I quickly composed myself, not letting the president see my disappointment. That wasn't what I expected.

"I think he'll open up to you since you have already formed a bond. Let's use that to our advantage."

I shook my head. "Eric and I have never really gotten along. We don't see eye to eye on a lot of things."

"That's a good thing, Luke. You've made better choices in your life. Look at you standing here, in great shape, gaining muscle and knowledge every day, and on your way to marvelous things. Now, look at Eric, lying there on the cold ground, his life hanging in the balance."

My eyes went to Eric. He had never obeyed an order in his life. He was delusional and arrogant. His father was a traitor, and now he was too. But did he deserve to have this happen to him?

"You could've left with those delinquents," President Randall said, "but you stayed. You used your brain. Thought logically. There even was a pretty redhead that I'm sure could've satisfied many of your needs as a man, but you said no. You took the high road."

I was taken aback by his comment. He shouldn't have talked about Tina like that. No one should. "Sir, I'm not sure Eric will tell me more than he's already said."

He put his hand on my shoulder. "Son, I need you to do this for River Springs. That pathetic boy in there has tried to bring us down over and over again. We can't let that happen. We need to keep our city intact. Think of all the lives Emmie and her misfits have ruined. They've corrupted people. Fed them garbage. We need to fix it and make things right. We need to end this rebellion."

I nodded. The whole thing needed to come to an end. It wasn't doing anyone any good.

"I'm glad you understand, but before we get started, I

think we should go find your father."

"What for?"

President Randall gave me a smile that made me shiver. "You'll see."

I followed him out of the room and down the hall. We found my father sitting in a room with Dean.

"Carl," President Randall said. "I've brought your son down here." He looked at Dean. "I need to speak with you for a minute. Let's leave these two alone to talk."

President Randall and Dean both left the room, leaving me alone with my father. I shut the door and went and sat down in the chair Dean had been sitting in.

"Luke," my father said. "What brings you down here?"

"Uh, mom sent me to find you to see when you'd be home for dinner," I said. "You haven't been answering when she's tries to contact you."

My father had his hands clasped together in his lap, twirling his thumbs, something he only did when he was nervous or lying. "I've lost my communication device. I think old age has finally settled in." He laughed, but I wasn't buying it.

"Dad, President Randall gave me an assignment."

He sat forward, his eyes eager. "That's wonderful, Luke. It's about time. You're the best in your group. I've always told the president how smart and capable you are. And now you can prove it."

I looked down at my feet, not daring to look at my father. "I don't think I can do it."

"You can and you will," my father said, his tone telling me

it wasn't open for debate.

"Dad ..."

"No." He stood and walked over to me. "You'll do whatever he asks you to do."

"Even if it's something I think is wrong?"

He backhanded me across the face, the sting making my eyes water. "Nothing the president asks you to do is wrong. He's always right. Do you understand me?"

"I, uh ..."

He grabbed my shirt with both hands, pulling me up so my face was inches from his. "Do not question me, boy. Do not question the president of this city!"

I couldn't take it anymore. I shoved my father away from me. "He wants me to beat information out of Eric!"

"I don't care!" His face was red, his breaths coming out fast and loud. "You'll do it!"

"Why, dad?" I asked. "What's the point? Who cares if they left? Let them. They can go live their separate lives and we can continue without them."

My father moved so fast, I didn't have time to react. I was on the floor in no time, the force behind his blow to my nose that strong. Blood trickled out and onto my hand that I held over my nose.

He towered over me, making me feel small and insignificant. Just like he always had. "If you want to continue being a part of my family, you'll do this. That's final."

The door opened and President Randall and Dean stepped into the room. President Randall eyed me on the floor and then looked at my father and smiled. "I can't tell you how many times I've had to do that to Joshua. Sometimes the teenage boy in them is just too strong. We need to set them straight."

My father nodded, shaking his hand out from the hit. President Randall came over to me and held out his hand. I paused for a moment, not knowing what I wanted to do, but I reached out and took his hand, letting him help me up.

"Luke," President Randall said. "I need to know right now if you're dedicated to our city. I need to know if you're willing to do whatever it takes to stand for what you think is right."

I'd always thought that you needed to stand for what you thought was right. I slowly nodded.

"Do you think people should be punished if they rebel against us?" President Randall asked.

I nodded.

President Randall took a step closer to me. "Do you think people should be punished if they fail at a simple task?"

I looked at my father, who glared at me. Disappointment sat in his eyes. I always let him down. I never did anything right in his eyes. My father nodded at me, so I nodded back.

"Good," President Randall said. "Now that everything's settled, Dean, would you please?"

The noise from the gun was so loud, my hands flew over my ears. My heart raced so fast I thought it might explode. It took me a moment to realize that my father was on the floor. I ran to him and fell at his side. Blood poured out from his head.

"Dad!" I grabbed him and held him tight. "Dad."

President Randall's hand landed on my shoulder. "Get up,

son. There's no need to grieve. This was a necessity, just like you said. Your father failed at creating a drug to get Eric to talk and this was his punishment."

My whole mouth went dry. He'd shot my father in cold blood. Over what?

"Get up," President Randall said.

Letting go of my father, I stood with wobbly legs, completely stunned by the turn of events. I looked at President Randall who stared at me with admiration. Dean lowered his gun and put it back in its holster.

"Now," President Randall said, "let's go get some information out of Eric."

My legs were heavy as we walked down the hall back to where they were holding Eric hostage. My dad may have failed, but was that worth killing over? That wasn't the punishment I would have chosen. No one should have chosen that punishment.

I was so deep in thought I hadn't realized I'd stopped in the middle of the hallway. Dean had to grab my arm to get my attention. I looked up at him and he pointed to the room. Nodding, I slowly walked in. President Randall had opened the door that led to the room Eric was in.

"We just need to know where Emmie is," President Randall said. "Find that out and you'll feast with Dean and me at my home tonight." He gave me a mischievous smile. "Hell, if you find out where she is, I'll let you pick any girl you want to take home with you tonight." He winked at me.

A buzzer went off in his pocket and he pulled out a device. "Janice." President Randall looked at me. "I need to go to her now for an afternoon … meeting. But Dean will stay here and help." He patted me on the shoulder. "You can do this, Luke. Don't let me down." His smile twisted. "We both know what will happen if you fail."

He left the room without another word. I looked in at Eric, lying there helpless on the floor.

"Just put this under his nose," Dean said, handing me a small vial. "It'll wake him right up."

I took the vial from him and entered the room. The stench in the air hit me hard. There were so many smells, I couldn't pin them all down. Sweat, blood, urine, and vomit were some. I covered up my nose and mouth and went to Eric, bending down near his face.

My gasp came out louder than I meant it to. What had they done to him? Both eyes were swollen, his nose was broken, he had a long gash on his left cheek, a cut on his swollen lip, and he lay in his own vomit.

His arm was turned so unnaturally, it had been broken. His shirt had ridden up a little bit, showing off a bruised abdomen, which meant he had broken ribs. His chest barely moved, so at least I knew he was still alive.

I took my hand off my nose and mouth, the smell making me gag. I heard the door shut, leaving me alone with Eric. But Dean watched from the other side.

Taking the lid off the vial, I put it under Eric's nose. His eyes shot open and he rolled onto his back. His scream was so piercing, all the hair on my neck and arms stood on end.

"Eric," I said, reaching out to him. Eric looked at me, his eyes full of pain and hatred. He scooted his body away from me, only to scream out in pain again. "Eric, stay still. You're making it worse."

His mouth moved, but nothing came out. I put my ear next to his mouth so I could hear. "Get the hell away from me."

For the first time in my life, I respected Eric. He'd been right all along. Tina had been right all along. I should've listened to them and to Emmie. She tried to warn me, but I wouldn't listen.

And now my dad was dead, a person who should be my friend was lying in front of me very close to death, and I was given the order to continue hurting him.

I couldn't do it.

I glanced at the window, which was a mirror on this side. Looking back at Eric, I kept my voice low. "Eric, I'm sorry. I was wrong and I was stupid. I should've listened to all of you. I'm going to fix this. I'm going to get you out of here. I promise."

Eric just stared at me, his eyes full of confusion. I stood and looked in the mirror. "Dean, he told me."

Dean opened the door and walked in. "Already?"

I nodded. "Yes. It was a lot easier than I thought." I eyed his gun in his holster. He kept a knife on his ankle, too.

"Good," Dean said. "President Randall will be happy." He looked down at Eric and smiled. "Guess we won't need you anymore." He pulled his gun out and lifted it toward Eric.

I ran at Dean, tackling him to the ground. His gun went off as he fell. I slammed my foot down on his wrist, making him release his grip on the gun. As I kicked it away, Dean rammed into me. We fell onto the ground and Dean pounded me twice on the jaw. I pushed on his face until he moved back enough so I could knee him in the groin.

He fell back in pain and I reached for his leg, lifting the bottom of his pants. I grabbed his knife and pointed it at him. "Don't make a move."

"You're a fool, boy," Dean said. "I'm going to kill you."

I shook my head. "No, you're not."

Dean laughed. "Even if I don't, you won't get far. You won't make it out of here alive." He looked at Eric. "If you're thinking of taking him with you, you're insane. He'll just slow you down. Might as well just kill him and save yourself. You still have time to do the right thing."

"You're right." I went over and picked up his gun, shooting Dean once in each leg. "I do have time to do the right thing." I tucked his gun into my pants at my back then searched his pockets, pulling out his communicator and a set of keys. I didn't want him to be able to contact anyone quite yet.

It took a lot of effort, but I was finally able to get Eric up and put his arm around my shoulder. He didn't have much strength, so I had to bear most of his weight. But I didn't care. "I'm getting you out of here, Eric. You have my word."

When we walked out of the room Eric was being held in, I shut the door, making sure it locked so Dean couldn't crawl his way out. I leaned my head out into the hall to see if anyone was out there. There were no signs of life, so I carried Eric with me down the hall.

"We're going to need help," I said.

I wasn't expecting Eric to respond, so I was surprised

when he did. I couldn't hear what he said, so I leaned my ear in close to his mouth.

"Austin." Eric's voice was shallow. If I didn't get him help soon, he was going to die.

As we turned down another hallway, I took Dean's communicator, switching to a frequency the vice president used to use. Thankfully, my father had made me memorize each channel and what they were used for. I just hoped Austin was listening and no one else was.

"Austin?" After a couple of moments, I tried again. "Austin?" We were almost to the stairs leading up to Headquarters. This part was going to be the trickiest.

The sound of footsteps made me freeze. They were right above us. I looked around and saw a door to the right behind us. I tried the knob, but it was locked. The footsteps started coming down the stairs. I didn't have time to set Eric down, so I used the side he wasn't on and rammed my body into the door, breaking the lock. The door swung open and I dragged Eric inside and shut the door. The lights were out, so I couldn't see a thing. I gently placed Eric down and went back to the door, opening it just a crack.

A security guard was now in the hall, heading toward the room we were in. He must have heard me break open the door. He'd have to be deaf to have not heard it. When he was only a few steps away, I backed behind the door, waiting for him to come in.

The door slowly swung open and the guard stepped into the room, turning on the light. I jumped on his back, wrapping my arm around his neck and squeezing tight. I held on as he squirmed around, trying to peel my arm away from him. He slowly lost strength until he completely blacked out. I set him down on the floor and shut the door again.

"Hello?" A voice came from the communicator. "This is Austin."

"Austin," I said, looking up to see what was in the room. "This is Luke Nelson." I was in another hallway.

"Luke?" Austin sounded surprised, which he should've been. I was probably the last person he expected to contact him. "What are you doing with a communicator?"

"I don't have time to explain right now." I walked down the hall. Steel bars ran down both sides. "I need help getting out of River Springs."

"I haven't set up another group to leave yet," Austin said, "but I can start figuring it out. I just need to contact someone."

"No." I stopped in front of the first set of steel bars and my eyes widened. It was a cell. And people were in it. "I need to get out now. I have some people who are in danger."

"Who?" Austin asked.

The people in the cell in front of me were squinting their eyes and holding up their hands to block out the light. It made me wonder how long they'd been sitting there in the dark.

"Where are you?" I asked. "Can we talk in person?"

"I'm in Headquarters," Austin said.

"I'm down below," I said, "standing in front of some cells."

"I'm on my way," Austin said.

I put the communicator back in my pocket and continued to walk down the hall. There had to be around seventy to eighty people trapped down here. I ran my hand over my head, completely baffled. Why were they holding people? Some of them were just children. They couldn't be guilty of anything.

Someone at the end of the hall caught my eye. I walked up to the cell door, putting my hands around the bars. "Angela?"

She stood, reminding me just how skinny she really was. "Luke, what are you doing down here?"

"I should be asking you that." I looked around the cell. Tiredness and hunger sat in everyone's eyes.

"President Randall has been locking up any families he thinks don't support him." Angela pushed her glasses up on her nose. "The man's going crazy."

I looked down the hall at Eric lying on the ground, completely messed up. President Randall going crazy was an understatement. The door opened behind Eric and Austin walked in. He gasped when he saw Eric on the ground.

Austin looked at me at the other end of the hall. "What happened to him?"

"President Randall," I said.

Austin moved down the hallway, his eyes wide in shock at each cell he passed. When he got to me, he stopped. He looked at Angela. "How long have all of you been down here?"

Angela shrugged as she scratched the back of her head. Her already frizzy hair looked like a tangled mess. It definitely hadn't seen a shower or a brush in days. "I'm kind of losing track of time. Maybe a few days?"

"I had no idea," Austin said, shaking his head. "I know the president keeps a lot of stuff from me, but this is insane." He looked at me. "We have to get them out of here. Now."

I nodded. "I know. That's why I called you."

"I'll contact a guy I know," Austin said. "He can get us a bus so we can get out of here."

"We?" I asked, raising my eyebrows.

"I can't stay here anymore," Austin said. "I've stayed as long as I can, making President Randall think I'm supporting him, but I don't think he's buying it. It's only a matter of time before I end up in here. Or like ..." He turned around and looked at Eric. "I'll get a medical kit, too. Hopefully, it will keep him alive until we get to New Haven."

"New Haven?" Angela asked.

I was just about to ask the same thing.

"It's where the others live," Austin said.

I pulled out Dean's keys. "I'm sure one of these will open the cell doors."

"Good," Austin said. "Start getting them out and I'll get everything else ready. I'll be right back." He ran down the hall and out the door.

It only took me two keys until Angela's cell door unlocked. I hoped that was a sign that luck was going to be on our side. I hurried down the hall, opening each cell door. Everyone slowly made their way out, some weaker than others. When they were all out of their cells, I addressed them.

"We're getting you out of here," I said. "To a safer place. A place without President Randall."

There was a quiet collective cheer. Everyone seemed excited but too exhausted to show a lot of enthusiasm.

Only a few minutes later, Austin came back in the room, helping me get Eric off the floor. Austin looked at me as we walked out toward the stairs. "My friend's meeting us outside with a bus. Unfortunately, we don't have time to be secretive right now. We'll just have to go and hope for the best. Do you know how to shoot a gun?"

"Yes," I said.

Taking Eric up the stairs took a lot of effort, but we finally got him to the top. Everyone we passed in the halls of Headquarters looked confused but did nothing. That was the one nice thing about the city. No one made a move unless they were ordered to. With Austin telling everyone not to worry, they just nodded their heads and moved on.

I'd never realized how no one in River Springs had a backbone. We were all a bunch of pawns in President Randall's game. But as soon as President Randall got word of what we were doing, those pawns would be ordered to kill us. And kill us they would.

Austin's friend was waiting outside for us. He helped us get Eric onto the bus and then went to the driver's seat. Austin and I continued to get everyone else on as fast as we could. We were almost done when a noise came through Austin's communicator.

He looked up at me, alarmed. "He knows. President Randall knows. We need to hurry."

We pushed everyone in faster. There were only a few people left when the doors to Headquarters opened and security began firing at us. Austin and I shot back, keeping in front of those getting on the bus so they wouldn't get hurt.

We kept our backs to the door, stepping backward until we were at the steps of the bus. I took a step up, still shooting at security. I had just taken another step when Austin's body jerked. He fell to the ground, blood pooling out from under him. I went to grab him, but a bullet grazed my ear and hit the bus.

"Get in!" The bus driver yelled. He didn't wait for me to fully step on, he just put the bus into drive and took off. I fell back onto the steps as the door closed.

Standing, I ran over to a window, ducking as bullets shattered their way through. Everyone on the bus kept low, out of the line of fire. I looked out the window to see Austin's lifeless body lying on the ground.

I ducked back down, swearing at the loss of a great man. I sat on the aisle floor as we made our way through town and toward freedom. Eric lay on the bench near me. He was still alive for now. I could only hope he'd make it to New Haven.

When we got close to the gates leading us out of River Springs, the bullets started again.

"Hold on!" The bus driver yelled, and he slammed on the gas, breaking through the gates.

A lot of chatter went on around me as we drove farther away from the city. A lady had come up and taken the medical kit, trying to help Eric out as much as she could.

But all I could do was sit there, thinking how I'd been wrong all those years. I'd been manipulated by my father and the leaders of the city. How could all those horrible things have been going on without any of the general public knowing? Or did they know, and I was just too blind to see it?

Well, not anymore. I would no longer be a slave to River Springs or Infinity Corp. I would no longer be a pawn. I would be a fighter for New Haven.

I looked up at Eric, his eyes slightly opened, staring at me. I placed my hand on his shoulder. "Stay with me, Eric. Stay strong. We'll get you home. We'll get you fixed up. We'll get you back to Emmie."

I swore I saw a smile form on his lips, but he was too swollen to tell for sure. "I believe in you, my friend. I'm sorry for ever doubting you. But I'll fight with you until the end. I'll fight for our freedom. I'll fight for every loss, including Austin."

The image of Austin's body falling to the ground came into my head. I quickly pushed it out, trying to think of the positive. Austin may be dead, but he died for a cause.

He died a hero.

CHAPTER 30
Emmie

Santiago and I walked back to Dante and Maya. Both were still going strong, fighting with all their might. The residents of Scorpion attacking from the back threw off the soldiers from Juniper. It also gave our warriors, including me, a newfound strength. The end of the battle was now in view, just inches from our grasp.

I tried to give Santiago his shirt back, but he insisted on keeping it around the wound on my arm. Instead, Dante shrugged out of his jacket and tossed it at Santiago, who reluctantly put it on.

The four of us continued to defeat the enemy, taking down soldier after soldier, working together flawlessly. For the most part, there was little communication between us. We all kept each other in our peripheral vision, coming in to help when needed.

All the adrenaline lessened the pain from my gash, giving

me the strength and movement I needed. I knew it wouldn't last forever, though.

The one who surprised me was Maya. She was a soft-spoken person, but when put out in battle her entire demeanor changed before your eyes. She was a true warrior, determined, focused and full of drive. I never saw her once slow down, never hesitate, and never looked scared. She knew what she was doing and put all her might into it. I kept forgetting she was wounded.

Now and then, I'd see her stumble a little because of her leg, or see her face tighten up in pain, but she fought through it. I knew why she'd been chosen to be a revolutionary.

People from Scorpion made their way up front, relieving some of the New Haven warriors of their duty. I found Will near one of the towers, still alive and fighting. He looked tired and had a few gashes on his arms and legs. His glasses had been snapped in the middle, barely holding together.

I decided to have him and Dad start clearing the injured from the field and rushing them to the infirmary.

When Will finished with the soldier he was fighting with, I took him by the arm, dragging him off to the side. "Will, I need you to find my dad and start getting the injured out of here. Get them to Marie and Dr. Stacey."

Will kept his eyes on the ground and rubbed the back of his head. "Emmie, your dad …"

I stared at him, not wanting to hear what he was about to say. "What, Will? What happened?" Tears welled up in his eyes. I gently touched his arm. "Please tell me."

Will finally looked up, trying to straighten his glasses, but they broke apart. He held the two pieces in his shaking hands. "It wasn't long after we ran out of ammo. We went to help down here, but the first soldier who came at him killed him immediately. I'm sorry, Emmie. I'm so sorry. I tried to help, but the soldier was too fast."

I closed my eyes, trying to hold back the tears. I couldn't cry. The battle was still underway. There would be time for crying later.

I forced myself to open my eyes and looked at Will. His tears weren't helping. "Will, it's not your fault. What happened to the soldier?"

"I killed him." Will gave a weak laugh as he stuffed his glasses into a pants pocket. "The soldier was arrogant and gloating to his friend about how easy it was to kill your dad. It pissed me off."

I smiled and hugged Will. "Thank you, for getting vengeance for my father."

"Uh," Will said. "You're welcome?"

"Do you think you can get the wounded out of here?"

Will nodded. "Of course. I'll do anything to help out."

"Okay, let me find someone else to help you." My eyes scanned the area until I saw Joshua driving his sword into the side of an enemy soldier. "Joshua!"

Joshua glanced at me and then headed my way, stopping once to kill a soldier that came at him. He smiled when he came up to me and Will. He flipped the handle of the sword back and forth between his hands. "I must say, these swords are pretty sweet."

"I'm glad you approve," I said. "Joshua, do you mind

helping Will get all of the injured out of here?"

Joshua sighed, looking over his shoulder at the fighting. "If that's what you need me to do, I'll do it."

I shook my head. "I can't believe you'd rather fight."

"It's a good way to take out all of my anger from my childhood," Joshua said with a shrug. "But the thought of helping the wounded is very appealing, too."

I saw Vivica out of the corner of my eye, beating an enemy soldier. They had both dropped their swords and were in hand to hand combat. She ripped off his helmet and threw it away.

I went close enough so she could hear me. "Vivica, finish him off. I need you to help me with something."

Vivica turned to me and nodded. The soldier looked at me, confused. Vivica grabbed the soldier's neck and snapped it, letting him fall to the ground as she walked to me. "What do you need?"

"Joshua and Will are going to get the wounded out of here," I said. "Can you be their guard? Make sure no one tries to attack them."

Vivica glanced over at the guys. "No problem."

Movement to my right caught my attention. Tina limped toward us. I went to her, helping her walk the rest of the way. When we stopped, I looked down at her leg and saw a long gash on her thigh.

"We need to get you to the infirmary," I said.

Tina shook her head. "I'm fine. There are others worse off. Javier, for one. I left him near a tree on the north side, but I'm not sure if he has much time."

I nodded, letting the wheels turn in my head. "Okay,

Joshua and Will, start with the warriors in the worst condition. You can use a couple of jeeps. Put as many as you can in there and then drive them to the infirmary. I'll let Marie know you'll be coming soon so she'll be ready. Vivica will be your guard while you're getting injured from the field."

"Sounds good," Joshua said. He looked at Tina. "Where's Javier?"

"I'll show you," Tina said.

As they took off, I pulled out my communication device so I could contact Marie. "Marie, are you there?"

After a few seconds, I heard her voice. "Yes. What's going on?"

"We've been joined by more people from Scorpion," I said. "We're going to start sending the injured New Haven residents to you. Will and Joshua are bringing them. Don't let anyone else in without my permission."

"Okay," Marie said. "I'll start getting the equipment ready and let Naomi know to be on the lookout for Will and Joshua."

"Thanks, Marie," I said.

As I was walking back to Dante, Maya, and Santiago, I saw Thunder Thighs going at it with an enemy soldier. She kept up with his thrusts and yelled out with every connection. She did a spin and drove her sword through the soldier's side. "Twenty-four." She ran at another soldier, still roaring loudly. After a few swings, she connected with his side, sending him down. "Twenty-five."

I shook my head, realizing she was counting her kills.

A moment later, I got shoved from the side making me stumble and fall to the ground. I landed on a dead warrior, so

I got off them as quickly as I could and looked to see who it was.

My heart sank. Vice President Mendes. For the first time, I glanced around. James and Fernando were nearby, both dead.

I put my hand on my head and forced myself to look away, not wanting to see anyone else I knew. A hand rested on my shoulder, making me jump.

"Easy there," President Brown said. "It's just me."

I let out a deep breath. "President Brown, we should probably get you to safety now. The vice president's already dead. We can't lose both of you."

"I'm not leaving here until this is over," President Brown said.

"Fine," I said. "Terrance, are you listening right now?"

"Yes," Terrance said.

"Good," I said. "As our military leader, will you please instruct President Brown that he must get back to Headquarters, so we still have a president when this is over?"

The smile in Terrance's voice came through the speaker. "President Brown, I'm ordering you to get to Headquarters. You can help out with getting the injured into the infirmary so Will and Joshua can get back here faster."

President Brown sighed, looking at the battle in front of us. "You just won't give up, will you, Emmie?"

"Never," I said. "Besides, this is almost over."

"Well then, I best get going." He patted me on the shoulder. "See you when this is over."

I had only rejoined Dante, Santiago, and Maya for five minutes before I had another interruption.

"Emmie?" It was Derek. "We have a slight problem over here."

"Has Headquarters been breached?" I asked.

"No," Derek said. "No enemy has come into Headquarters."

"What's going on?"

Derek sighed. "Listen, I don't know how this happened. Nothing like this has happened to me, ever. I'm not sure how he did it." He let out a few swear words.

"What are you talking about?" I asked as I was fighting off an enemy. The soldier was smaller than most I'd dealt with, but he was the fastest.

"Steven," Derek said. "He escaped."

My heart stopped, making me pause. "What?" As I was distracted, the soldier came at me but fell when he was just a couple steps away. I walked away, heading out of the line of battle.

"You're welcome!" Santiago shouted from behind.

I just waved my hand behind me.

"How is that possible?" I asked Derek.

Derek swore again. "I don't know! One minute his door was locked and the next my screen flashed, saying that it had been unlocked. I ran over there as fast as I could, but the room we were holding him in was empty."

"I'm on my way," I said, running toward a jeep.

"I'm almost there now," President Brown said through the communication device. "I'll check the west canyon to see if he's on his way out."

Jumping into the nearest jeep, I started it, threw it into

gear and slammed on the gas. I went as fast as I could toward Headquarters, not slowing down for anything.

When I was nearing the homes, President Brown spoke. "He's not out here. I've searched all around. He couldn't have gotten that far so soon."

"I'm near his home," I said. "I'll check there."

I parked the jeep right in front of the door and ran inside. Steven's room was empty, but I could tell someone had been there recently.

"He was just here, President Brown," I said. "He's probably headed toward you. Stay at the entrance to the canyon."

"Will do," President Brown said. "I'll just ..." The communication went dead.

"President Brown?" I asked. When he didn't respond, I ran out of Steven's house and jumped into the jeep.

It took me only a few minutes to get to the entrance to the west canyon. Steven stood in the middle of the road, President Brown on the ground next to him, not moving. I couldn't tell if he was still alive or not.

I turned off the jeep and jumped out, cautiously walking toward Steven.

"Stop!" Steven yelled. "Not one more step." He wore some sort of black vest, one I'd never seen before. He grasped onto something tightly in his hand. "You make one more move, I'm releasing my grip."

"What are you holding?" I asked.

"A trigger," Steven said. "You take another step, I release my thumb, and this goes boom." He pointed to his vest. "It's full of explosives."

Instinctively, I wanted to take a step back, but I forced myself to stay still. "Okay, I'll stay where I am. Steven, where did you get that?"

Putting my hand in my pocket, I turned on my communicator so others besides those with earpieces could hear just in case I needed help.

"Where do you think?" Steven rubbed his head with his free hand. "It was a backup plan, Emmie, and you forced me to use it."

"You don't need to use it, Steven," I said, trying to keep my voice calm. "Let's just talk about this."

Steven clenched his jaw. "There's nothing to talk about. I had a simple mission, Emmie, and that was to give Amber information. We worked this out together."

"When?" I asked.

"It all started before we left River Springs." Steven paused, looking like he was deciding how much he wanted to tell me. I kept my mouth shut and hoped he would continue his own. After a moment, he did. "Amber found out from her dad that you were all being held under Headquarters and were going to be executed. Mack had come to me asking if I'd be willing to help you escape."

"Why you?" I asked.

I never really knew why Mack had chosen Steven of all people.

Steven choked back some tears. "President Randall killed my family. Mack knew about it. He figured I'd be upset about it to the point I'd want to leave."

I tried to read Steven's face, but it was hard to tell what he was thinking. "And you were."

He shrugged. "I guess. I never really got along with my dad." He opened his mouth to continue, but then stopped himself.

"So, you and Amber worked up a plan?" I asked, trying to prod him along.

"Yes. We wanted a backup plan in case the executions didn't go through. We decided I would come along with you and be a spy."

"Why?" I didn't like that fact that he was telling me so much. My stomach felt uneasy about the whole thing.

Steven looked down at President Brown and then back at me. "She wanted to prove she was capable of running security for River Springs. Make her dad proud."

"So how does your bomb vest fit into this equation?" I desperately wanted to shift my stance, but I didn't dare move.

"You should've let me go." He scratched the back of his head. "You should've let me go and this wouldn't be happening. You forced my hand, Emmie!"

I shook my head. "You put this on yourself, Steven. No one made you do anything. It was all a choice."

"No!" He pointed his finger at me. "This is your fault, Emmie! And now you're going to pay for your choices."

"Steven," I said, trying to keep my voice from quivering, "please don't do this. Think this through. No one else needs to get hurt." Steven looked up at the sky and mumbled to himself. "Steven, just let President Brown go. He hasn't done anything wrong."

Steven snapped his head back down, glaring at me. "He's just as guilty as you. He could've let me go, too, but he held me captive. He's the one leading New Haven!"

"Take me." Inhaling deeply, I stepped forward. "Take me, Steven."

"Emmie!" Dante's voice came through my earpiece. "What the hell are you doing?"

I ignored Dante. "Steven, please, I'm begging you." I got down on my knees. Tears fell down my cheeks, my chin shaking. Clasping my hands together, I pleaded with him. "Steven, take me back to Amber."

Steven's eyes widened. "You'd do that?"

"Yes," I said.

"Emmie, don't!" Dante yelled. "We're on our way."

Steven rubbed his head, his eyebrows furrowed together. "Why?"

I looked at President Brown lying on the ground and thought of all the good he'd done for New Haven. We'd already lost our vice president. We still needed someone to run New Haven and President Brown was the best person to do it. They didn't need me.

I looked up at Steven. "Because he doesn't deserve to die. I do. I'm the one you want. I'm the one who started the revolution in River Springs."

"Seriously, Emmie," Santiago said. "Stop it. We need you. Just hold on. Dante, Maya, and I are almost there."

"Steven, you have to take me now before anyone gets here. This is your chance to prove yourself to Amber and Whit." I shook my head. "President Randall." Scooting on my knees, I moved a little closer to Steven. "Take me."

The jeep rumbled in the distance. They'd be there soon. Steven looked behind me, probably hearing them coming. He glanced down at President Brown and closed his eyes. A moment later he opened them, looking straight at me. "You're too late." In a matter of mere seconds, Steven dropped to his knees and keeping his eyes on mine, released his thumb.

The shock wave from the blast sent me flying backward. I landed yards away, the impact stealing my breath. Heat flared on my face as I gasped for air. All I could hear was the ringing in my ears.

A minute later, someone grabbed my arms and pulled me back, away from the crater formed from the explosion.

A hand landed on my cheek, turning my face. I looked up to see Dante, holding me in his arms. His mouth moved, but I couldn't hear what he was saying. His tears fell onto my face and he pulled me closer to him.

I was in too much shock to move. When I closed my eyes, the image of Steven staring at me appeared. My body trembled all over, despite the heat.

What had I done?

CHAPTER 31

I had no idea how long we sat on the ground with Dante holding me tight. My ears were ringing, and I was stunned by what had happened.

At one point, Dante finally stood and carried me to the jeep. He got in the back and put me in his lap, keeping his strong arms around me. I curled into him as the tears finally came. He lay his head on mine, his tears falling onto my head.

When we came to a stop outside of Headquarters, Santiago took me from Dante so he could get out of the jeep, but Dante took me back the second he stepped out. He carried me through headquarters and into the infirmary. I have no idea how he had that much strength to carry me so long, seeing as we were just in a battle.

The infirmary was packed with people, all bustling around. All the movement made me dizzy, so I closed my eyes. Even with all the chatter, one voice stood out among the others. I focused my ears on the voice. The ringing in my ears had become lighter but was still noticeable.

"Why didn't you just let him go?" It was Eric's dad, Alexander. His tone held so much rage. I opened my eyes and looked around for him. He stood a few feet away, staring directly at me, his eyes filled with tears. For some reason, Santiago held him back.

Alexander trembled, his face red from anger. "Why didn't you just let Steven go?"

I shook my head in confusion, only to cause my head to spin. Spots appeared in my vision and I tried to blink them away, but they remained.

"Calm down!" Santiago said. He wrapped his arms around Alexander, keeping him from charging at me and Dante. Maya went and stood between us, keeping her stance steady in case Alexander got away from Santiago.

"They were going to let him go!" Alexander screamed. "They were going to release Eric!"

"What are you talking about?" Dante asked. I tried to wriggle my way out of Dante's arms so I could stand, but Dante kept a firm grip around me.

"They were going to do a trade!" Alexander stopped pressing forward and slumped his shoulders in defeat. "They were going to release Eric if I let Steven go."

"How do you know that?" Maya asked.

Alexander sobbed. His words were hard to understand. "I made an arrangement with them."

I tried again to get out of Dante's arms so I could go to Alexander, but the spots in my vision multiplied until I blacked out.

When I woke, someone held my hand. I turned my head slowly, looking to see who the hand belonged to. Dee. Tears streamed down her cheeks, her eyes red and puffy. I was sitting on a bed in the infirmary, Dee in a chair next to me.

"Dee." My voice was raspy, dry from the heat and smoke of the explosion.

"Oh, Emmie," Dee said. "I'm so sorry for what happened. For what you had to witness." She shook her head. "It's so wrong. But I'm glad you're okay."

Someone swore in the corner of the room. Looking over, I saw Dante leaning his head against the wall. I expected him to be sad, with the loss of his dad, but instead, anger danced in his eyes.

Santiago, Maya, Tina, Joshua, and Will were all in the room. Everyone had been bandaged and cleaned up from any injuries but were in desperate need of showers.

I placed a hand on my wrapped arm.

"Twenty-three stitches," Dee said, looking at my arm. "You might've lucked out not being aware of what was going on. I couldn't even stay in the room to watch, despite how much I love you."

I smiled at her. "You've always had a weak stomach."

"That stuff is supposed to stay on the inside of you." She scrunched her face. "We don't need to see what's beneath the skin."

Dante fumed in the corner, so I turned to Santiago. "Is it over?"

"Yes," Santiago said. "Thanks to my city showing up. I didn't know there were that many left that were part of the revolution." He grinned. "In fact, everyone left in Scorpion is part of it. The rioting is over. The president's dead. Only the good are left. It's the best news we've had all day."

"How many did we lose?" I asked.

Maya's voice came out in a whisper. "Two hundred and eighty-six." Well over half.

"Any one I need to know about?" I asked, not looking up. That was the part I wasn't looking forward to.

"Some of them you probably already know," Tina said.

"Let's see." Santiago sat down on the edge of my bed. "For starters, both of our dads." He gave me a half-smile. Santiago wasn't one to cry, but sadness sat in his eyes. "Javier didn't make it. Fernando, Mack, James, Denise, Charles, Will's dad." Santiago looked at me and paused. He opened his mouth but closed it again.

Dee squeezed my hand. "Richie didn't make it."

I shook my head. Richie was Eric's cousin and a brand-new dad. Now his wife and child were without a husband or father. A lot of people in our city were now in that position. I coughed, so Maya handed me some water. I smiled at her and took it, the water cool on my throat.

"Where did they put everyone who ..." I paused, hating to ask the question. "Who didn't make it?"

"We moved them over near the cemetery," Will said. White tape was wrapped around the middle of his glasses, holding the broken pieces together.

"Lined them up one by one," Tina said. "We'll start digging graves tomorrow morning."

Santiago squeezed my foot. "I think we could all use a

good night's sleep before we start."

"Try ten nights," Tina said. "I'm worn out." Everyone let out a strained laugh, except for Dante.

"What about the injured?" I asked.

Dee tucked a curl behind her ear. "Marie and Dr. Stacey are still working on some, but it looks like they'll all make it through."

"Archie lost his freaking hand," Santiago said. "Luckily it was his left hand since he's right-handed, but still. That has to suck."

"A lot of the women that were here in the infirmary during the battle have been helping out," Maya said. "Including Rosie. That girl was born to be a nurse. Nothing fazes her and she loves to help out."

I nodded. "Sounds about right."

"They've sent all the others back home." Tina stood near me, her arms folded across her chest. "They cleared the less injured so they could free up room. This place was insane just a little while ago."

"How long was I out?" I asked.

Santiago smiled at me. "A few hours. You blacked out for most of it."

"How long have all of you been standing here staring at me?" I asked, my eyebrows raised.

"We had nowhere else to go." Dee squeezed my hand. "Besides, I wanted you to be able to see my beautiful face when you woke up."

"And mine." Santiago winked at me followed by his smolder. I rolled my eyes.

Maya rolled her eyes, too, and then smiled. "You'll be happy to know that Bruce and Gideon got the virus into the water supply. We'll send some people out there in a week or so to see what the effect was on the city."

"They also rescued some prisoners," Dee said, her smile huge. "They contacted Terrance to let him know and once the battle ended, he immediately sent a bus to go get them."

"How many did they rescue?" I asked.

"It was two-hundred and sixty-eight," Maya said. "Bruce contacted me a little while ago to say they've lost three since. It could be more by the time they get here, but hopefully not much."

Laying my head back against the pillow, I took a deep breath. The weight of everything started to sink in. My whole body felt tired and weak. A pounding headache resonated through my skull causing my sight to go a little blurry. I closed my eyes and sighed.

Dee squeezed my hand. "We'll get out of here and give you some space." She kissed my forehead and released my hand as I opened my eyes back up. Maya and Will both smiled at me as they left the room.

Tina kissed my cheek. "Let me know when you're ready to go and I'll take you home. Marie cleared Dee to leave the infirmary since they needed her bed. She's moving in with us and we were thinking you could, too, if you wanted."

I smiled, looking over at Joshua. "Thanks, but I don't think it'd be a good idea to leave Derek and Joshua living alone together."

Laughter escaped Tina's lips. "Good point. See you later."

"Bye, Tina," I said.

Joshua came closer to me and I could see a few cuts and scrapes on his face and arms. He looked tired and dirty, but happy. "I'm glad you're okay. I don't know what I'd do if you left me here alone. You're my only ally right now."

Smiling, I reached my hand out to him. "True. I'm glad you're still here, too. I finally got a brother I can stand, and it would suck to lose you so soon."

Joshua ignored my hand, bending down to hug me. "I know I've said this a million times but thank you."

"You're welcome," I said. "Normally, families get along and stand up for each other, so I thought we could try that out."

Joshua laughed lightly as he released me. "I'll see you back at home."

Once he left, Santiago and Dante were the only ones left in the room. Santiago looked at Dante, but he was still staring into the corner.

Shrugging, Santiago looked at me, obviously just as confused as I was about Dante. He gave me a wicked smile. "Still mad at me for what I did?"

I rolled my eyes. "Of course. I won't be forgiving you any time soon. And if Eric ever finds out ..."

"I'll be watching my back." His expression became serious, something that didn't happen very often. "But, hey, now that this is all over, we can go get him. I'm still keeping my promise about that."

"Thanks," I said. "We can talk about it tomorrow."

"Sounds good." Santiago stood and walked over to me.

"Can I kiss you on the forehead?"

I narrowed my eyes. "As long as it's just the forehead."

Santiago nodded and bent down, kissing me gently on the forehead. He pulled away, smiled at me, and left the room. He shut the door when he left.

"You want to tell me why you're pouting over there in the corner?" I asked Dante.

He stepped away and looked at me. "Because I'm pissed at you, that's why." He took a few steps closer to the bed. "But first, what was that all about? What did Santiago do to you?"

I ran my hand through my hair, noticing that someone had taken out my ponytail. My hair felt dry and dirty. "You really want to know?"

"Yes." He took a seat in the chair Dee had been in.

I stared at him for a minute, debating whether I should tell him. He wouldn't be happy about it, but he wouldn't stop pestering me until I told him. "He kissed me."

He stood so fast his chair slid backward. "He did what?"

"He was just so excited the residents of Scorpion showing up," I said, waving my hand. Maybe if I played it down, Dante wouldn't be so mad. Maybe. "I just happened to be the closest female to him. Well, the closest person. I think if it was a guy, he still would have kissed them."

Dante swore. "That doesn't excuse it. I told him to keep his hands off you."

My hands tensed around the blanket draped over me. "What?"

"You know how he is. He says exactly what's on his mind and sometimes the things he thinks about you aren't so ..." He looked at me, mulling it over in his head. "Appropriate. But I told him to keep it friendly and if he tried anything both Eric and I would kick his butt." He grabbed his chair and moved it back next to the bed. "When we get Eric back, I'm keeping my promise."

"Dante," I said, taking his hand, "beating him up won't do any good." Looking down at my fist, I smiled. "Besides, I already punched him for it."

His eyes went wide, a smile creeping onto his face. "The black eye was from you?"

I nodded. "Yup."

"Nice job, Em. But I can't have him thinking he can get away with stuff like that. But he insists you're free game until you're married."

My jaw dropped. "Free game? He said that?"

"Yes. Like you're an object. Listen, I like the guy and all. He's a hard worker and an amazing fighter, but he has no tact. He needs to learn how to treat women."

"Well, you can teach him," I said, squeezing his hand. "Now, are you going to tell me why you're mad at me?"

Dante took his hand away from me. "Are you kidding me? You were about to turn yourself over to Steven. I can't believe you'd do that."

"He had your father. Our president. Your dad's dead because of me. If he'd just taken me, your dad would still be alive."

Dante had said Steven would get his reckoning, but it felt more like I got mine.

Standing, Dante paced the room. It reminded me of his

father. "No, Em. This isn't your fault. It's Steven's. He's the crazy psycho who strapped a freaking bomb to his chest and committed murder and suicide." He sat down on the bed next to my side and took my hand. "Don't ever do that again. I don't think you realize how important you are to this city and everyone in it." He looked at me, his eyes soft and kind. "How important you are to me. You're my best friend, Emmie. I've already lost so many people in my life. If I lose you, too, I'll be forced to have Santiago as my best friend. That could cause a lot of damage to me."

I smiled, the motion causing me to flinch. If Marie had given me any pain medication, it had started to wear off. "I'm sorry, Dante. It was a heat of the moment decision."

"Like Santiago's kiss." Running his hand over his fro, he shook his head. "I can't believe he did that." He paused and raised his eyebrows. "How was it?"

"Wet." I stuck my tongue out, gagging a little. "Kind of like what I'd imagine kissing a fish would be like."

He laughed. "I'll spread the word around the city and make sure all the ladies know." He leaned forward and kissed me on the forehead. "I'm glad you're okay, Em."

"Me, too," I said. "Thinking about it now, the thought of being handed over to Amber is making me nauseous."

"I'll never let that happen. You have my word."

"How are you doing, by the way?"

His face fell. "I don't know. I haven't been able to wrap my head around the whole thing. I keep thinking I'm going to see my dad walk through the door and that this was all just some crazy dream." He squeezed my hand. "What about you?"

"Same. It all seems surreal. I just want everything to go back to normal, but I know it won't." A big yawn escaped my mouth.

"You should probably get some rest." Dante let go of my hand and stood.

I shook my head. "I can't sleep here. I need my own bed. Will you just take me home?"

"Sure." He pulled out an IV in my arm, which I hadn't even noticed was there. "Don't let Marie know I'm the one who let you loose."

"I'll blame it on Santiago."

Dante smiled. "I like that idea. Do you want me to tell Tina I've taken you home?"

"Yes," I said as he helped me stand. I craned my neck to look up at him. "Seriously, how tall have you grown?"

"A lot." He stood up straight. "I'm over six feet now."

I slapped him on the arm. "Well, it's about time. You look good."

"Thanks. Now I just need to outgrow Santiago."

"Good luck with that," I said. "You know, on second thought, can you have Tina meet me at my house? I need to take a shower and will probably need some help. I can barely stand on my own."

Dante gave me a playful smile. "I'd make some inappropriate comment right now, but I think you've had enough of that kind of stuff for today."

"Thank you for that," I said as I rolled my eyes.

CHAPTER 32

Gideon and Bruce showed up later that night. They lost no others on the rest of the trip, which we were all glad to hear. Marie and Dr. Stacey checked everyone out to make sure there was no serious damage. Mostly, everyone was just dehydrated and underfed.

Everyone wanted to let me rest, so no one woke me at the time. I heard they were scrambling to find places for everyone to sleep. We had new residents from both Juniper and Scorpion. The ground outside was still damp from the storm, so we had to squeeze everyone into people's homes, Headquarters, and the infirmary. I'm not sure how, but they made it work.

The next morning, we all went to work digging the graves. We had a lot to dig and we wanted to do it right. We made sure to map it all out, marking where we wanted to put our fallen warriors. We let any surviving family members pick out the location they wanted for their loved ones. We also made sure to put James right next to Lou.

We let our residents take as many breaks as they needed. It was hard on everyone and we were already tired from the day before. It wasn't until dusk that we were starting to dig the final graves. The following day we'd put the warriors in and fill the graves back up with dirt. We couldn't make caskets since there were so many that we lost. Some of our women residents that could stomach it spent the day cleaning up the fallen heroes, so they were more presentable before we buried them.

Halfway during my final dig, a jeep pulled up behind me. I didn't think anything of it until I noticed Tina had stopped digging in the grave right next to me. Resting my hands on the handle of my shovel, I glanced over at her. Tina covered her mouth with her hands, tears falling down her cheeks.

In one swift movement, Tina had hopped out of her hole and ran at someone, throwing her arms and legs around them. I watched them for a moment, trying to figure out who would cause such a rise out of her. Her long red hair covered the person's face, so I climbed out of my hole and walked toward them.

My heart stopped for just a beat when Tina pulled back to kiss the person she was hugging. It was Luke. Part of me wanted to look away since it was such a passionate kiss, but I stared in disbelief. Why was Luke here?

Someone touched my arm, making me jump. I put my hand on my chest and looked to see who it was. Dee's mom stood there.

"Mrs. Jennings," I said when I finally composed myself.

"Hi Emmie," Mrs. Jennings said. She pulled me into a hug and held me tight. I had forgotten how much Dee and her mom were alike. Not only did she have the same brown eyes and curly hair, but she also hugged with sincerity just like Dee did. Mrs. Jennings always gave me a big hug every time I saw her.

As we were hugging, I looked behind her to see Dee's dad and little brother. They both smiled and waved at me. I pulled away from Mrs. Jennings, wiping some tears from my eyes. "Dee is going to be so happy to see you."

"Do you know where she is?" Mr. Jennings asked.

I looked over at him and nodded. "She's at her house watching some children while we work."

"Emmie," Luke said, walking up next to me. Tina had finally let go but held his hand tightly. She looked at me and laughed, wiping her tears as best as she could. They were still flowing with no sign of slowing down.

I wrapped my arms around Luke, and he wrapped his free arm around me. "I'm so glad to see you, Luke."

"You, too, Emmie," Luke said. We pulled away and he looked at me, the sadness deep in his brown eyes. "Emmie, I'm so sorry. For everything. I should've listened to you."

"Why the sudden change of heart?" I asked. He had been so against our revolution just a few months before.

Luke closed his eyes, a look of pain, or maybe regret, crossing his face. After a moment he sighed and looked at me. "Let's just say I finally saw the side of President Randall that you saw all along." His eyes told me he didn't want to continue the subject. I couldn't imagine what Whit did to make him completely change his mind and turn his back on River Springs.

I nodded in understanding. "Well, I'm glad you're here so don't worry about it. Besides, I threw so much at you in a matter of minutes. I'm sure it was a lot to process."

The side of Luke's mouth turned up into a smile. "That's an understatement." He looked at Tina and then back at me. "We have a lot of catching up to do, but we need to go back to Headquarters."

I glanced over at the Jennings' who were patiently standing there. "I need to show the Jennings' where Dee is."

"I can do that," Maya said. I turned around to find her, Santiago, and Dante all watching.

"Thanks, Maya," I said.

As Maya and the Jennings family walked away, Dante came up to Luke, sticking out his hand. "You must be Luke. I'm Dante."

Luke shook his hand. "Nice to meet you. So, I guess these two have been talking about me."

"More than we wanted them to," Santiago said, walking up and sticking out his hand. "Santiago."

"Nice to meet you," Luke said, shaking his hand. He looked at me. "Emmie, we really should get back to Headquarters."

"Is everything okay?" Dante asked.

Luke scratched his head and looked at me. "Uh, yeah, it's just … Emmie, I have some bad news about Austin."

My momentary elation at seeing Luke and the Jennings family quickly vanished. "What is it?"

"Austin helped all of us escape." Luke rocked back and forth where he stood, his face telling me he didn't want to go on. But he did. "When we were getting on the bus, the security came out and started shooting."

I put my hand over my mouth and closed my eyes, not wanting to hear any more. Dante put his arm around me.

"He didn't make it?" Santiago asked.

Luke stared at the ground and shook his head. "I'm sorry. I wanted to get his body, but they were still shooting, and the bus driver was already closing the doors so we could leave."

Tears formed in my eyes, so Dante pulled me into a hug. I couldn't believe we'd lost another Oliver. How were we going to tell his sister and mother?

"He died a hero, Emmie," Luke said. "He risked his life so we could get away."

Dante rubbed my back. "He risked his life so everyone who's wanted to escape River Springs could get out."

"Emmie, there's something else," Luke said. "I brought Eric back with me."

My world stopped. For a moment I heard nothing around me, not even my own heart beating. I forced myself to look at Luke. "Is he okay?"

"He's alive." Luke looked like he was debating what to tell me. "Emmie, they really hurt him. I'm sure he'll recover from most of it, but you should know he doesn't look good."

"What did they do to him?" Dante asked. His arms had stiffened around me.

Luke hesitated for a minute before he spoke. "He has a broken nose, lost a couple of teeth, broken arm, four broken ribs, and two broken fingers. His face is completely swollen, he has scratches on his face and arms. There's a long gash on his left cheek that will probably leave a scar. He's dehydrated and famished ..."

Dante cut him off. "Let's go. I'm driving." He helped me to the jeep, lifting me into the passenger seat and closing the door. Luke, Tina, and Santiago jumped into the back.

The whole ride to the infirmary passed in a blur. I was so excited to finally have Eric back, but I wasn't sure if I could stomach seeing him like that. Listening to everything they did to him made me want to throw up.

Dante had to snap me back to reality when he pulled up in front of Headquarters. He held onto me as we walked through Headquarters and back into the infirmary. Marie walked out of a room and stopped when she saw me.

"Oh, Emmie," Marie said. Her eyes were watery. "You should know ..."

I held up my hand. "I know. Luke told me. I just want to see him."

Her eyes sympathetic, Marie nodded slowly and moved to the side so I could walk in. She gently touched my arm as I passed her. I took a deep breath and stepped into the room.

CHAPTER 33

No matter what Luke and Marie could've told me, nothing could've prepared me for what I saw.

I stopped only a few feet after I walked in and gasped. I barely recognized him. His whole body was covered in bandages, scrapes, and bruises. When I walked up to the bed, I could see how swollen his face was. His nose was bandaged up and he had some stitches on his lip, cheek, and forehead. He had two black eyes and a bandage above his right eyebrow.

Alexander stood at the foot of the bed, his eyes red and puffy from crying. He looked at me and the tears started again. "Emmie, I must apologize. Everything I said earlier, I ..." He looked at Eric. "I just wanted my son back."

I pulled him into a hug. "It's okay. I understand. But we have him back now and that's all that matters."

"Yes, it is." Alexander pulled away and kissed me on the forehead. "I'm going to go get some sleep. I've hardly slept since they took him." He glanced at Eric and smiled. "But now I'll be able to sleep tight knowing I have my boy back.

Goodnight, Emmie."

"Goodnight." I watched Alexander walk out and then turned back to Eric.

I wanted to kiss him or take his hand or something, but everything sounded like it would hurt him. Instead, I pulled a chair up and sat down. I put my hand over my mouth, the tears flowing down my cheeks.

His left arm was bandaged and in a sling. After a few minutes of crying, I took my finger and gently ran it down his arm to his hand. When I touched his hand, I noticed he was holding onto something. As softly as I could, I opened his hand.

A small laugh escaped my mouth. My butterfly necklace. I took it from his grip and placed it around my neck, the feel of the butterfly against my chest filling me with warmth.

"You can't just take things from people." His voice was quiet and raspy, but I could hear the smile.

I looked at his blue eyes that were staring at me, not able to hold back my smile. "I believe it's mine."

"Oh, Emmie," Eric said, tears coming to his eyes, "you have no idea how much I missed you."

I laughed through my tears. "I'm pretty sure I do. I've thought about you every day. I wanted to come save you, but I couldn't."

"What happened?" He coughed, a little bit of blood forming at the corner of his lips. I grabbed a tissue from the stand near the bed and wiped his mouth.

"We can talk about that later," I said, "when you've had some time to recover. It's a long story."

Eric closed his eyes, grunting a little in pain.

"Did Marie give you anything for the pain?"

He nodded. "She did, but there's too much broken and bruised to really help."

"I'm so sorry, Eric. I'm so sorry this happened to you."

"I'm just glad to be back with you." He glanced over my face and then looked at my arm. "What happened to you?"

"I had a battle of my own," I said. He tried to sit up, alarm in his eyes. Gently placing my hand on his shoulder, I pushed him back down. "I'm fine, Eric. New Haven's fine. We had a small battle and lost some good people, but we won."

"We won?"

I nodded, smiling. "Yes, we actually won. Now I just have some sweet battle wounds that I can show off."

Eric tried to laugh but started coughing. Once he stopped, his eyes drooped. "I'm so tired."

"Get some sleep. I'll be here when you wake up."

"Come lie next to me."

"Eric," I said, shaking my head, "I'll hurt you."

"I don't care." His eyes pleaded with me. "I need you by my side. I need my Emmie."

"Marie will kill me."

"No, she won't. She'll understand. Now come here."

I stood and went to the door, looking outside. When I was positive no one was looking, I shut the door and snuck back to the bed. Eric scooted closer to the edge of the bed, cringing in pain as he did.

"You'll have to hop on the other side because of my arm," Eric said.

Going over to the end of the bed on the left side, I crawled my way up, being very careful of what I touched. I lay my head on the pillow next to him, resting the top of my head against his. I put my hand on his chest, right above his heart. Feeling the beat gave me comfort knowing he really was there with me, alive.

His whole body sighed. "I love you so much, Emmie."

I smiled and looked into his eyes. "I love you more than words can ever say."

"Emmie, I need you to listen to me for a minute," he said, his tone worrying me, "and you can't say anything until I'm done."

"But ..."

"Seriously, Emmie, no interruptions. Promise me."

I sighed. "I promise."

"Good." He cleared his throat. "These pasts few months have taught me a lot. I've grown more in just that little amount of time than I have my whole life. These past couple of weeks have taught me even more. It made me realize how much this city means to me. It made me realize how much you mean to me. It also made me see that life can be taken away from you in a blink of any eye." He coughed a few times, trying to get some breath. I'm sure he hadn't talked that much in a while.

I opened my mouth to say something.

"No, Emmie," Eric said. "I'm not done. This is not the way I thought it would go, and I know we're young, but Emmie Woodard, I need you to promise me right here and right now that you'll marry me one day."

I sat up, looking at him, stunned. "I, uh ..." I ran my

fingers through my hair. "Are you being serious right now?"

"Yes." His eyes searched mine, desperate and hopeful. "I want to spend the rest of my life with you."

My smile got so big, I thought my face might break. "Yes, of course, Eric. I'll marry you whenever you want."

He released a deep breath. "Good."

I lay back down and rested my head against his. "I love you."

"I love you. I promise I'll do it right one day, I just wanted a confirmation now so I can sleep better at night."

It didn't take long until Eric fell asleep. I just lay there, smiling, so glad to have him there next to me. Despite everything that had taken place, I was the happiest girl in the world. I kept my hand on his chest, feeling his heartbeat until I finally fell asleep.

I ended up sleeping through the evening and into the early night. My body was exhausted from the battle. When I woke, Eric was still asleep. I looked at my wristwatch to see that it was three in the morning. I brushed my lips against Eric's forehead and did my best to get out of the bed without rattling him.

Being as quiet as I could, I opened the door and stepped out, shutting the door behind me. The halls were empty, except for someone lying down outside of Eric's room. They were lying on their stomach, wearing a jacket with the hood up.

I bent down and pulled the hood back. "Derek?"

Derek let out a snore and turned his head toward the wall. Putting my hands on his head, I turned it back to me. He swatted one of my hands, his voice coming out in a groan. "Leave me alone."

"Derek." I shook him gently. When that didn't work, I shook him until he opened his eyes.

"Stop. Oh, Emmie." He sat up. "I've been waiting here forever. While I should be scolding you for sleeping with your boyfriend, I have a very important matter to discuss with you."

I sat down next to him. "What's so important that you'd sit out here and wait for me?"

"And not scold you," he said, his finger pointed at me.

"Yes, thank you for that."

Derek's eyes lit up. "You'll never guess what happened."

"I'm too tired to think of a sarcastic remark, so you're going to just have to tell me." I pulled my legs into my chest, resting my chin on my knee.

He turned his body so he faced me. "You're not fun anymore, you know that?"

"That happens when you're faced with serious issues."

"This is a serious issue."

I lifted my chin and looked at him. "Then please tell me, Captain Awesome."

Derek beamed. "Get ready, because this is huge. I mean, brace yourself."

"I'm braced." The giddy look on his face made me smile. I placed my hand on his arm. "You're killing me! What happened?"

"I need to set the mood here." Derek sat up straight, using his hands and face for animation. "The battle had been raging for hours. So many people were dying, so many lives ruined.

Then the Scorpion residents arrived and saved us. A couple of hours later, we were declared the winner. We were victorious." He pumped his fists into the air, quietly shouting victory so he wouldn't wake anyone.

Derek put down his hands, looking me right in the eye. "We were alone in the room, just Naomi and me. I turned to her and held my hand up for a high five, but she surprised me by throwing her arms around me and she ..."

"She what?" As much as I hated to admit it, sometimes I loved the way Derek told stories. He always had fun doing it.

"She kissed me, Emmie. Naomi kissed me." I don't think his smile could have gotten any wider. "Like on the lips. And. It. Was. Awesome!"

My jaw dropped. "Are you serious? She kissed you?"

Derek nodded, his smile still breaking records. "It was the best moment of my life. It outshines every second of my life before you were born."

I threw my good arm around his neck and hugged him tightly. "I'm happy for you, even though you just took a jab at me."

He squeezed me back. "I'll never stop making jabs at you, Emmie. I hope you know that. You've always been my favorite person to tease."

"Why is that?" I asked, pulling back.

Derek shrugged. "You're the only one who will humor me and get me back. It's just not fun with anyone else." He rubbed his eyes. "Now, I'm going home and going to bed. I'm freaking tired." He stood and held his hand out to me. "Are you coming home now?"

I shook my head as he pulled me up. "I don't think I can sleep right now."

"Alright," he said. We walked in silence down the hall. Once we entered Headquarters, Derek looked over at me. "You're lucky dad isn't here to find out you spent the night with your boyfriend."

I rolled my eyes. "You know nothing happened."

"How would I know that?" He raised his eyebrows at me. "You were alone with him in a room with the door closed."

"Seriously, Derek? You really think seeing my boyfriend like that would turn me on?"

Derek scratched the back of his head. "Yeah, probably not."

"Not so much," I said, shaking my head. I linked my arm through his. "I'm going to miss him. Dad, I mean."

"Me too, Emmie. Me too." He looked like he was fighting back tears. "How are you holding up?"

I sighed. "I don't know, really. Too much has happened. I haven't had a moment to process everything."

"That's understandable," he said, nodding.

"What about you?" I asked.

He shook his head. "It just doesn't seem real. I'm sure it'll take a few days for it to really sink in."

"Well, as much as we tease each other, I'll always be here for you if you need to talk."

"Thanks, sis. I'll be here for you, too."

I stopped and hugged him. "I love you, my awesome big brother."

"I love you, too, my crazy, yet fun, little sister," Derek

said, squeezing me tight. He patted me on the head, making me roll my eyes.

We parted ways once we left Headquarters. I went to the ladder that led up to the alcove, looked up, and sighed. It took me a while to get to the top because of my bad arm, not to mention I was sore all over from the battle. I'd never used my muscles that much in my life.

As I sat down on a rock, I looked up at the sky. The storm had cleared out, leaving behind a beautiful, clear atmosphere. Stars lit up the sky, the sight taking away some of the stress in my life. The view from up there, plus the cool air on my skin, calmed my nerves. It was my little safe haven inside of New Haven.

A noise behind me instantly took away my peace. A figure stepped out from the dark. I was about to jump up, but then I saw the spiked hair. I placed my hand on my chest. "You scared me to death, Maya."

Maya came over and sat down next to me on the rock. "Sorry, I didn't mean to." She glanced over at me. "Couldn't sleep?"

"I fell asleep early," I said, pulling my legs into my chest. "Did I miss anything?"

"Not too much," Maya said. "We finished digging the graves and then went to work filling them. We were able to get all the corpses in, but we'll have to cover them back up tomorrow."

Talking like that made me shiver. Less than a year ago, I would never have imagined having that kind of conversation. "How are we going to handle the funeral? Just have one big one?"

"I think that's the only plausible answer." She crossed her ankles and leaned into me. I linked my arm through hers, glad to have someone out there with me.

"We shouldn't plan anything specific," I said. "Just have an open forum where anyone can get up and talk about any of the fallen."

"I agree," Maya said. "Do you think you'll be up for talking about anyone?"

I sighed, thinking of Dad and Mack. There was no way I could just stand there and not acknowledge the impact they'd had on my life. "I have to." I reached over and ran a finger over one of her bracelets. "The charm for your next birthday is going to have to be a warrior. You were great out there in battle."

She stared at the bracelets. "I was hoping to master something less dangerous, like a set of drums."

"You want to learn to play the drums?"

"It sounded fun," she said with a shrug.

I leaned my head against hers. "Then let's get you a set of drums."

CHAPTER 34

I stayed up on the alcove the rest of the night, my mind unable to stop buzzing. Maya had left me a few hours before so she could get some rest. I played with my butterfly necklace as the sun came up over the mountains. Pink and orange hues painted the sky, the clear air starting to warm up a bit.

"I thought I'd find you up here." I looked over at the top of the ladder to see Vivica stepping out onto the alcove. She came up next to me and sat down on the rock, her posture straight.

Even though she was exhausted with dark circles under eyes and had some cuts and bruises on her face, Vivica was still stunning. She looked at the sun, a mixture of sorrow and hope in her eyes.

After a moment, she turned to me. "I'm sorry."

"What for?" I asked.

Vivica sighed, turning back to look at the sun. "I've been somewhat of a brat to you since we first met."

I thought of Amber and let out a little laugh. "I seem to have that effect on some people."

"Has Dante ever talked to you about our mom?" She had her long legs stretched out, her ankles crossed.

"No." I'd tried a few times to ask him about it, but he never seemed to want to talk about it and I didn't want to push the subject.

"She was killed right before we escaped." Tears formed in her eyes as she slightly shook. "I was supposed to be watching over and protecting her. I got distracted for just a moment. When I looked back at her, an arrow was right through her heart." She put her hand over her mouth, her tears falling down her cheeks.

I placed my hand on her arm. "Vivica, you know her death's not your fault, right? You couldn't have stopped what happened."

She shook her head. "I could've stopped it. If I was paying attention, I could've pushed her out of harm's way or taken the arrow for her."

"You don't know that. You can't blame yourself. It'll just eat you alive. Trust me, I'd be completely insane by now if I blamed myself for every bad thing that's happened to those around me. Those I love."

Vivica looked at me, not masking the shame or regret she felt. "I got distracted by a boy. A stupid boy that I had a crush on. I lost my mom because of a little girl crush."

I put my arm around her shoulder. "You lost your mom because of a battle going on in your city. You lost your mom because a bad person killed her. It's that person's fault. They were the one holding the bow. They were the one who released the arrow."

"I try to tell myself that over and over again." She leaned into me, resting her head against mine. "It's why I've been so rude. I thought shutting myself out from the world would help in some way. I thought if I just pushed everyone out, I'd never feel that hurt again." Her smiled reached her eyes. "But then you come along and throw all of that out the window."

I pulled away and looked at her, startled. "What?"

Vivica laughed. "I like you, Emmie, and I have no idea why. You're so strong and determined. You fight for what you want." She looked at me. "You're just how I was before I closed myself off."

"Uh, thank you?" My face scrunched in confusion.

"I was jealous at first. Mostly because you and Dante were getting all the attention. And then seeing how happy you were with Eric drove me nuts. I thought hating you would be a good idea, but obviously, it wasn't."

I smiled. "I always wondered why you hated me so much."

"But I don't. Dante told me about that Amber girl. I know exactly why she hates you."

"Why?"

"Jealousy."

I shook my head. "Amber's not jealous of me. She can get whatever she wants."

Vivica eyed me. "She's jealous, Emmie, completely jealous. You're tougher, smarter, hotter, and from what I hear, people tend to like you much more than they like her."

"If she wasn't such a brat, people might like her. But she

treats people like dirt."

"It's a defense mechanism. I would know. I'm just like her."

I held up my hand. "Trust me when I say you're nothing like her. She's a psychopath. You're a good person, Vivica, and you're a tough woman. I watched you fight in that battle. You were absolutely amazing and completely selfless."

She looked down at the ground. "I don't know about all of that."

"You saved a lot of lives. You made sure not one hair was harmed on Joshua and Will while they were rescuing the wounded." I looked at her. "You're a protector. It's who you are. Which is why you blame yourself for your mom's loss. It's why you tried to protect your heart by closing yourself down."

Vivica raised her eyebrows, rubbing the tears away from her eyes. "How did you become so wise? You sound like this little old lady from Kingsland. We called her The Wisdom. People would always go to her when they needed advice or guidance in their lives."

I let out a laugh. "Please, I'm far from wise. I've done nothing but make rash and stupid decisions since I've come here."

"Yet, they've all turned out to be right." She crossed her arms over her chest as she stared at the horizon.

"It's luck."

"It's wisdom."

This wasn't an argument I'd win. I glanced over at her while I twirled my butterfly. "How are you doing, by the way? I mean, about your dad."

Vivica shrugged. "I've been trying my hardest to keep myself together."

"It's okay to break down and cry about it. He was an amazing man and an amazing leader. In his short amount of time here, look at what he's done for New Haven."

"I know." She smiled at me. "Don't tell anyone, but I was sobbing like a little girl last night. I cried myself to sleep."

I thought about my breakdown earlier. "It's good to get it all out of your system. It's part of the grieving process. Now you can pull yourself back together and start all over again. Make your mom and dad proud of you. Show them the fighter and protector you are."

We were cut off by someone coming up onto the alcove. Dante paused when he saw the two of us sitting right next to each other, both smiling. "I'm going to be honest; this is the last thing I expected to see."

Vivica and I both laughed. I looked at Dante. "What brings you up here?"

"For starters," Dante said, walking over to us, "I wanted to make sure you were okay."

"I'm doing as fine as I can be," I said.

Dante nodded. "Good. I also came to say that you need to get your butt off that rock and get down to the cemetery. We have a lot of dirt to shovel today."

I held out my hand to him and he helped me up. "When should we have the funeral?"

"I was thinking tonight or tomorrow morning," Dante said, helping Vivica up. "It depends on how the day goes."

"Oh, that reminds me," Vivica said. "I was thinking I

could take all the children and we could use my paint to draw pictures or sayings on some rocks. That way we can place a rock on each grave to have something to remember each hero by."

"I love that idea," I said, smiling. "I think the children will love it, too."

Dante nodded. "It will be a good way to make them feel a part of our community."

"I think Dee and Marie would love to help with that, too," I said.

"Maybe I can grab all the kids," Vivica said, "and go pick out rocks. We can take them back to the infirmary where we can paint them. That way the injured can help, too."

"Sounds good," I said. "I'll have Naomi give you a list of everyone we lost."

Right after Vivica started making her way down the ladder, Dante looked at me. "We need to talk. All of us revolutionaries."

I nodded. "We have a lot to talk about."

"Let's plan on talking after the funeral," Dante said. "We've lost our president and our vice president. And one of our military leaders."

"We're going to need to find someone else to take over. Someone who can run New Haven and handle the four of us."

Dante laughed. "That's a mighty big job for a person. They're going to need a lot of will power to put up with us."

We finished filling in all the holes in the late afternoon. Eric woke up a few times during the day, so I went to him every time. He didn't last very long, usually less than thirty minutes, but I treasured every second.

We had Vivica, Dee, and Marie bring all the children out and as a city, we placed a rock on each grave. Tears came to my eyes when I saw the one painted for my dad. Rosie had insisted that she be the one to color his rock. On the top she had printed, Philip Woodard. Below that she wrote, loving father of Emmie and Derek. My favorite was the drawing. My dad was in the center, with Derek on his left, me on his right, both hugging him tightly.

When I saw the one for Mack, I couldn't stop laughing. A little boy from River Springs had done the rock. On the top he wrote, Mack: The Meanest Warrior. Then he drew a picture of a guy with huge muscles and a very stern face. He even had a vein popping out of his forehead. I'm sure that was how all the children saw Mack since he was such a serious and tough guy. But the man I saw had a big heart and not a selfish bone in his body.

By the time we were done, everyone was exhausted. The thought of having a funeral right now was too heavy. Santiago's mom, Carmen Mendes, suggested that instead, we should use the night to celebrate the lives of those we lost and remember the good times.

We turned on some lights outside of Headquarters, right where we wanted to build the school. Residents of Scorpion had brought drums and guitars with them, so they played music while the children danced around, entertaining us all.

Dinner was brought out that night, so we all ate out on blankets, watching the sun go down and the stars come out.

We all shared uplifting stories of our fallen warriors, trying to focus on the fun memories we had of them.

Derek stole the spotlight, telling grand tales of our dad, most of them exaggerated, but it didn't matter. Everyone was enjoying them. Watching Naomi stare at him, a smile on her face, made me happy. I never thought he'd find someone who could put up with him, but I was so glad he did. Although, I still thought Naomi was too good for him.

My heart swelled watching Dee dance around with the kids and Will. The medicine had been working just as Marie, Alexander, and Dr. Stacey had hoped. They were optimistic that this meant it was the cure, but it was still too soon to tell. Before we'd really know, we'd have to see how Dee did over time and see how it worked on any others that got sick.

We also had the problem of limited medical supplies and the only place that had what we needed was River Springs. With Austin gone, we had no more contacts there, so we weren't sure how we were going to get our hands on more. If another resident came down with the disease, the cure wouldn't mean anything if we didn't have the ingredients for it.

Eric woke up right before the festivities started and insisted on coming. He was still in horrible shape, but Marie cleared it for just a few hours. We took him out in a wheelchair and set him close to the entrance of the cave that led to Headquarters, but still in a place where he could see.

I sat next to him most of the night, watching our residents have fun for the first time since we'd all come to New Haven. Everything we'd gone through had bonded all of us together, making our city strong. We had so much work ahead of us, but at the moment, it didn't matter.

Dante asked Eric if he could steal me for a little while so I could join in on the dancing. Tina and Luke kept Eric company while I danced around with Dante, Santiago, Maya, Vivica, Rosie, Dee, and Will. After a couple of songs, I snuck my way back to Eric, Tina, and Luke.

I took Eric's good hand and held it in mine. "Did any of you think we'd ever be sitting here together, watching people dance around to music?"

Luke laughed. "If you'd told me six months ago that this was going to happen, I'd say you were completely crazy." Luke had his arm around Tina, holding her close.

"Well, I'm glad it did," Tina said. She kissed Luke's cheek. "I wouldn't want it any other way."

"Did Emmie tell you the good news?" Eric asked Tina and Luke.

I brushed some hair out of his eyes. "Not yet. In fact, I haven't told anyone yet."

"Don't want people to know?" Eric asked, a small smile on his face.

"Know what?" Tina asked.

I looked at Eric. "The time just hasn't come up. But if I could, I'd shout it from my rooftop."

"How about an alcove?" Luke asked, pointing up to it.

"I would if Eric could get up there with me," I said. "This is news that we both need to share."

Tina stood. "I'll be right back." She ran over to the musicians and the next thing I knew, the music completely stopped. Tina ran back over to where Eric and I were sitting and stood behind us. "Can I have everyone's attention?"

"Uh, Tina," I said, looking up at her. "What are you doing?"

Tina smiled at me. "Giving you your moment to shout your good news."

"Unless you're too embarrassed," Eric said.

I kissed him on the cheek. "Of course, I'm not." Keeping his hand in mine, I stood. Everyone in New Haven was completely quiet, all eyes on us. I was glad it was dark so they couldn't see how red my cheeks were. "Citizens of New Haven, I have an announcement to make." Eric squeezed my hand, giving me the courage I needed. Those with drums started to do a drum roll, making me laugh a little. "Last night Eric asked me to marry him one day and I said yes."

A loud cheer erupted through the night, making me laugh even more. I bent down and kissed Eric lightly on the lips, trying to avoid his stitches. "I love you."

"And I love you," Eric said.

I heard a squeal coming toward me and I looked up to see a blur of brown curls crash down on me.

Dee threw her arms around my neck. "I'm so happy for you."

"Thank, Dee," I said.

Dee pulled back and clasped her hands together. "We have so much work to do! Oh, I can't wait to design your dress! We're going to have to come up with color schemes and a menu."

I held up my hand. "Whoa, Dee, I think you're getting too

excited. I said one day, not next week."

"I know that," Dee said. "Can't I be prepared? I have to make sure everything goes smooth. This will take months and months of planning."

"Maybe you should try years and years." I tucked my hair behind my ear. "We're only eighteen."

Rolling her eyes, Dee folded her arms across her chest. "Fine. But since you're making me wait so long, you can't complain every time I come to you with questions or measurements."

"Deal," I said.

After that, there was a long line of people wanting to congratulate us. I had never received so many hugs in my life. Rosie even asked me if she could be the flower girl. I had no idea what that was, but I still agreed since her eyes were so pleading.

Dante squeezed his way to the front, pulling me into a big hug. "Congratulations."

"Thank you," I said.

Dante released me and patted Eric on the shoulder. "You're a lucky guy."

"I know," Eric said, smiling at me.

When Eric was distracted, Dante leaned into my ear. "Even though it won't be for a long time, make sure you get a ring. It'll keep Santiago away and I'll sleep easier at night knowing he won't be trying anything on you."

"I don't think you'll be sleeping well very long." I pointed near the band where Santiago was dancing with Vivica. There wasn't much distance between them, if any, and she laughed at everything he said. "It looks like he has found someone else."

Dante looked over to where I pointed, and he swore loudly. "My sister?" He stomped away, mumbling to himself.

When the line finished, I sat down next to Eric, intertwining our fingers. The residents went back to dancing, while I soaked in every second of it, grateful to have come that far.

CHAPTER 35

We started the funeral the next morning after breakfast.
It was another beautiful day, the weather perfect for
being outdoors. The residents who wanted to speak sat next to
the grave of the one they wanted to talk about. Everyone stood
up one by one, sharing their words, row after row until there
were no more. The rest of the residents surrounded the entire
cemetery, watching on as we spoke.

I had placed Dad and Mack right next to each other in the
cemetery. I sat between the two graves, patiently awaiting my
turn. Derek and Joshua both sat next to me, giving me their
support. Derek had decided it would be best if I spoke about
Dad. It wasn't until that moment that I realized how hard it
really was for him. He'd never lost someone this close to him
before and I think it was finally starting to sink in as he sat
there, staring at Dad's rock.

Dante and Vivica sat nearby, next to their dad's grave.
Santiago, Rosie, and Carmen sat between Javier and Vice
President Mendes' graves, Rosie clinging to Santiago as her

tears flowed.

When it was my turn to go, I took a deep breath and stood, straightening out my green dress—Dad's favorite color on me. I had spent countless hours trying to come up with the right words to say, but nothing seemed to give justice to these two extraordinary men. So, I just had to follow my heart.

I reached my hand down to Derek and he held on tightly. "As most of you know, I have an interesting family dynamic." There were a few chuckles from the crowd, calming my nerves. "My true dad, Philip Woodard, was the kind of father anyone could hope for. He worked long hours throughout our childhood, but he always made sure Derek and I received the attention and love we needed. He always stood by our side, giving the perfect advice, or stepping back and letting us make our own decisions."

Derek shook a little from laughter. I squeezed his hand before I continued. "I think both Derek and I can tell you that whenever he let us make our decisions, they were definitely the wrong ones. But they were growing experiences and made us stronger individuals."

Closing my eyes for a moment, I thought back to Recruitment. "Our father took his job at Infinity Corp very seriously. He was dedicated and loyal, always giving every piece of him to every task. But when my life changed in a blink of an eye, when my life was almost taken away, my dad dropped everything and was there at my side. He never doubted me for a second and he left our city, our life, behind us and trusted that I knew what I was doing."

A slight breeze came by, the crisp scent of pine in the air.

I looked down at Dad's grave, still holding onto Derek's hand. "Our father was a brave man. He fought for New Haven with everything he had, never once giving up."

I glanced at Joshua sitting on the other side of me. He looked up at me and smiled as he rolled the end of his tie wrapped loosely around his neck. "And when my other brother showed up, my dad welcomed him with open arms and let him into our home, no questions asked. My dad always saw the good in people and trusted his instincts. I love him with all my heart and will miss his kind demeanor for the rest of my life."

Letting go of Derek's hand, I went and stood next to Mack's grave. I couldn't help but let out a small laugh. "I'm not going to lie. When I first met Mack Clark, I was intimidated."

Derek laughed. "I think that's an understatement. I was freaking terrified." A lot of people chuckled, agreeing with us.

"Mack can come off a little rough around the edges," I said. "He's very strong-willed and determined. He doesn't back down for anything and he took his job as military leader seriously. But I think that's one of the first things I admired most about him. He always took full responsibility for anything that happened under his watch. He never tried to pass the blame onto someone else like some people I know." Whit came to mind.

"Mack taught me how to be a fighter." Clearing my throat, I shifted where I stood, blinking back tears. "He showed me what it really meant to be brave. He taught me to be strong and independent." I looked out at everyone, my voice now steady and sure, my sorrow replaced by resolve. "He taught me to fight for what I want. For that, I will be forever grateful for this man. He's been such an important part of my life, and he'll continue to be. Every obstacle I face from here on out, I will conquer it for Mack. I will fight for New Haven and I will never back down."

I wasn't expecting any reaction from the crowd. Most had been silent throughout the memorial, with just a few murmurs and quiet laughs here and there. So, I was surprised when everyone started cheering.

Santiago got into it, jumping up and getting the residents involved. Every time he shouted, "What are we fighting for?", the crowd would yell back, "New Haven!"

Joshua and Derek both stood next to me, each holding one of my hands and pumping their other fist into the air. I looked out at our residents, feeling their excitement. We were now a tight community and we weren't going to back down. We were going to continue to fight for New Haven, no matter what.

Two weeks later, Dante, Santiago, Maya, and I stood on our alcove, looking out over New Haven. The construction of the school was already underway, along with more homes for all our new residents.

Hiro and Gideon had taken a trip back to Juniper to find out the effect of the virus. When they searched the city, they didn't find a single soul alive. With that city down and Scorpion now completely with us, we were only left with Kingsland and River Springs to contend with.

We had sent some of our residents down to Scorpion City to manufacture more weapons and ammo. They already had a factory set up; we just had to make some adjustments to add different weapons to the product line.

We decided to have the four revolutionaries be the main leaders over the military unit. We still had a lot of planning and training to do to prepare for the war with the other cities. We divided the unit into sections, with officers appointed over each style of weapon.

Terrance was over archery, Gideon was over guns, and Hiro was over swords. They worked closely with us revolutionaries with all training and decisions made, helping the four of us gain knowledge that we could use in the future.

A mandatory self-defense course was set up for every resident, children included. We wanted everyone to learn basic skills, but also build character and confidence. Tina and Vivica ran the class, with Luke, Joshua, and Bruce as their assistants. Once Eric was all mended, he would help, too.

With the president and vice president gone, we had to vote in new ones. Santiago had suggested that we just step up and lead, but the other three of us thought we needed to focus on the revolution. We'd let a new president and vice president watch over the residents of New Haven so we could turn all our attention to making sure there still was a city of New Haven down the road.

The four of us had come up with our nominees and we addressed New Haven, asking if they agreed or had anyone else they'd like to nominate. A few more nominees were added in and the voting began.

In the end, Carmen Mendes was elected President, and Dee's father, Harold Jennings, was elected Vice President. I was excited to have Carmen as President. I had nominated her myself. She had all the characteristics of her family wrapped into one. She was passionate and opinionated, spunky, loved to joke around, serious when the job called for it, and had a huge heart. She considered everyone's thoughts but was able to make a final decision that would best suit our city. And boy, could she cook.

President Mendes was the opposite of her boys when it came to her height and weight. She was short and had, what she liked to call, more cushion for the pushing. She kept her dark black hair short, which made her round hazel eyes stand out. Every resident of New Haven adored her as I did.

Vice President Jennings was soft-spoken and gentle with his tone. But he was a smart man, capable of making the right decisions and he was thorough in all his work. I swear the man never ran out of energy. He woke up early and went to bed late, making sure that everyone was taken care of and all our needs were being met. He was a little shorter than me and much skinnier. Being petite ran in the Jennings' family. He had thick brown hair and light brown eyes, and every feature on his face was small and thin.

Our first order of business once everyone was settled in was to get Joshua's last name changed. Derek was reluctant at first because he didn't want to share his last name with someone with "full Randall blood" as he called it.

But over the weeks, Derek had grown to like Joshua. They found a topic they had in common, which was security. They shared stories and I caught them a few times in the house just talking and laughing with each other. It helped ease the tension in our household.

Overall, things in New Haven were going well. We were still dealing with our losses, but it was nice having so many people who knew exactly what you were going through. President Mendes had made it her personal mission to make sure her door was always open for those who needed to talk.

I had gone to her office to talk with her alone a few times. It was helpful to talk to someone who understood everything I'd been through but wasn't a close friend or family.

I replayed Steven and President Brown's death in my head over and over again. No matter how many times I had someone tell me it wasn't my fault, I knew it was in some way.

President Brown was right; I should've let Steven run the first time. If I hadn't stopped him, he would have gone back to River Springs without hurting anyone. Yes, he knew where we were, but I'd always figured that they would find out where we were someday. If I'd let him run, Steven wouldn't have found the need to do something extreme. President Brown would still be alive.

The whole experience had made me grow up faster than I thought possible. I still had a lot to work on, but I was ready for the challenge. I was ready to face everything that came my way and no matter how hard it was, my emotions needed to be put aside when making decisions. There were too many lives at stake and we'd already lost so many good people.

As I stood out on the alcove, I felt pride for our city. Watching everyone working together and working hard to build up our city made my heart warm. There were a lot of good people down there, and I didn't want to let anyone else down.

"Is it just me," Dante said, standing to the right of me, "or does it feel like it was a lifetime ago when we first stepped into this place?"

I smiled, twisting the ring on my finger. "It doesn't seem right that it's only been a few months." Eric had made me a simple ring, just two pieces of twine braided together. It was perfect.

"Where do we go from here?" Maya asked. She stood to the left of me, Santiago on the other side of her.

"Wherever life takes us." Santiago whistled. "No matter how prepared I think I am, every twist and turn that's been thrown at us has never ceased to amaze me."

Dante let out a small laugh and folded his arms. "Well, I'm ready for a break. I'm worn out."

"Let's hope it's a while until we hear anything from River Springs or Kingsland." I glanced over at Dante. "Are you still in contact with someone from Kingsland?"

"Yes," Dante said. "I'm not too worried about any threat from there right now. We should be fine for a while."

Santiago reached behind Maya and swatted my arm. "It's your city I'm worried about. With Austin gone, we have no contact."

I rocked back and forth on my heels, the whole thing making me wary. "We desperately need eyes and ears in there, but I don't know how that's possible. I think Eric and Luke's group were the last rescue attempt."

Smirking, Dante nudged me. "You can always become friends with Amber."

"I'd rather go swimming with sharks." Goosebumps

The president stood and patted me on my shoulder. I hated how he treated me like a child. I was more of a man than he'd ever be.

He walked over to his wall covered in plaques. President Randall had one made for every important person he'd killed. He stopped in front of my father's.

"I'm proud of you, Austin," President Randall said. "You've turned out to be twice the man your father was."

"My father was weak, sir," I said. "He didn't have the backbone to run a city."

President Randall looked at me. "And you think you do?"

"I think I've proved that to you countless times." I walked over and stood next to him, standing up straight so he had to look up at me. "I've done everything you've asked of me."

"That you have. We're missing a plaque on here, though."

I nodded. "I know. Don't worry, sir. Emmie's plaque will be on here in no time."

"There's still something that's bothering me, Austin."

"What's that?" I clasped my hands behind my back.

"You claim your father never told you where the secret location was. I still don't believe you."

"I wish you'd trust me, sir," I said, walking back to the window.

President Randall laughed. "I've never trusted an Oliver. You must know that."

I clenched my jaw. I had to refrain myself from getting too worked up. I needed to stay calm. "I'm not like my father or any other Oliver before him. I'm better than them."

"So you say." President Randall stepped up next to me.

He puffed out his chest, making me laugh on the inside. He was so arrogant.

"Where do we go from here?" I asked, even though I already knew the answer. It was going to go where I wanted it to.

"We need to make a move."

I shook my head. "It's still too early."

"What are you waiting for, Austin? You claim to want to help Infinity Corp, to help me, yet you're hesitant to take action."

"I want to do it right. We don't have room for mistakes. We need to make sure we're truly prepared."

I could feel President Randall staring at me. "Austin, they're extremely outnumbered. We have everything we need to wipe them off the face of the earth."

"I don't think so." Looking over at him, I tried to keep my expression calm and my voice even. "They have lots of weapons now and the skills from the other cities. We know Dr. Stacey took the virus from us. And you killed Carl."

"His services were no longer needed," President Randall said flatly.

I closed my eyes, keeping my temper at bay. "He was the only one here who could replicate the virus."

"We don't need the virus!" President Randall did not hide his anger.

But I couldn't afford to act out. "We need more ammo, whether it's ammo for guns or secret weapons like the virus. When we strike, it needs to be big. It needs to be final, not giving us room to lose."

"I'm sending a few security members out tomorrow. They're leaving first thing in the morning. If you won't tell me where Emmie is, I'll go and find her."

"You've already sent people out. You've been looking for months and haven't found them. What makes you think you'll find them now?"

"I never give up, Austin. I'll keep looking until I find her."

I sighed and turned away, walking toward the door. "That's your problem, sir. You're only focused on Emmie. You're not looking at the big picture."

President Randall slammed his hand down on his desk. "I am looking at the big picture! And I'm thinking that you're not going to be in it."

I stopped walking, still facing the door. "I'll be in it, sir."

"I don't think so. You have a lot of thinking to do, Austin. If you want to be a part of this city, you need to tell me where they're located."

Keeping my mouth closed, I forced myself to be quiet.

He gave a small laugh. "Well, I've given you the chance to do something right and prove yourself, and you've failed."

"What do you mean, sir?" I asked, turning around to look at him.

"You really think I just let Luke and the others leave without following them?"

"If you had them followed, why do you keep asking me where they are?" I couldn't believe how pretentious he was.

His face turned red. "I just told you! I was giving you a chance, Austin, to show you were willing to fight for our cause. But it doesn't matter now. I will know where they are soon and

then we can end this all. We'll be in total control of the world."
He gave me a twisted smile. "Unfortunately, you won't be in a
leadership position anymore. Your services are no longer
needed here at Infinity Corp."

I turned around again and faced the door. It was hard for
me to keep my temper down and I didn't want him to see it in
my eyes. "What are you going to do with me?"

"You'll know soon enough," President Randall said. I
could hear the smile in his voice. "You can leave my office
now."

I smiled, reaching my hand down to my side. "This won't
be your office much longer."

"Excuse me?" President Randall asked.

I turned around, smirking at Whit. "I'm afraid your
services are no longer needed."

Pointing my gun at his head, I pulled the trigger.

Other Books by Sara Jo Cluff

YA Dystopian:
NEW HAVEN SERIES:
RECRUITS
RECKONING
RISE

YA Contemporary:

Filler Friend

The Kiss List

Middle Grade:

THE IMMORTAL LIFE OF COTTON WYLEY

ACKNOWLEDGMENTS

I'm going to keep this one short and simple.

Chad, thanks for your continued support, and for being so hot. You make everyday fun. I'd be lost without you. You're great with every type of navigation imaginable. Love you!!

Princess Buttercup, I'm not sure how much time you have left on this earth, but you, my dear kitty, are the light of my life. No writing companion will ever compare to you. I'm one lucky cat mama!

Mom, you're the best mama ever and I'm so lucky to have you in my corner! I love you so much!!

As always, Dr Pepper, thanks for fueling my writing. I'd be lost without you. #PepperPack #Ambassador #DrPepperislife

Oh, I haven't forgotten about you, Watermelon Sour Patch Kids. I love you with all my heart.